Summer Breezes

Summer Breezes

JANE ORCUTT

Guideposts
New York, New York

Summer Breezes

ISBN-13: 978-0-8249-4804-7

Published by Guideposts
16 East 34th Street
New York, New York 10016
www.guideposts.com

Distributed by Ideals Publications, a division of Guideposts
2636 Elm Hill Pike, Suite 120
Nashville, Tennessee 37214

Library of Congress Cataloging-in-Publication Data

Orcutt, Jane.
  Summer breezes / Jane Orcutt.
    p. cm.—(Tales from Grace Chapel Inn)
  ISBN 978-0-8249-4804-7
  1. Sisters—Fiction. 2. Bed and breakfast accommodations—Fiction.
  3. Pennsylvania—Fiction. I. Title.
  PS3565.R37S86 2010
  813´.54—dc22

                                          2009049480

Cover by Deborah Chabrian
Design by Marisa Jackson
Typeset by Nancy Tardi

Printed and bound in the United States of America
10 9 8 7 6 5 4 3 2 1

GRACE CHAPEL INN

A place where one can be
refreshed and encouraged,
a place of hope and healing,
a place where God is at home.

Chapter One

Summer in a small town never fails to enchant. Children play sports in vacant lots, students cheer for freedom from school and citizens have greater opportunity for greeting each other as warm weather inspires them to spend more time outdoors. The pastel colors of spring give way to deeper greens and blues, and birds twitter and chirp as they nest in thick, leafy trees.

Acorn Hill, Pennsylvania, was no exception. One hour west of Philadelphia, the town was proud of its values and of its exemplary citizens, not the least of whom were the three Howard sisters, Louise, Alice and Jane, who ran the Grace Chapel Inn bed-and-breakfast in their family home.

A gentle breeze wafted up the impatiens-lined walkway to the three-storied, cocoa-colored Victorian and swirled a white paper napkin from the wicker table to the porch.

"There goes another one!" Alice Howard, the middle sister at age sixty-two, rose from her wicker rocker and bent past the flower-filled terra-cotta pots to retrieve the errant napkin. She brushed a stray bit of dirt from the leg of her jeans and straightened her cotton shirt. Smiling, she tucked a strand of her reddish-brown bobbed hair behind her ear. "I think that's the third napkin that's tried to escape the porch."

"I appreciate all the trouble you've gone to to serve our dessert outdoors, Jane, but are you sure we shouldn't retreat to the kitchen before we're blown away?" Louise Howard Smith, the oldest sister at age sixty-five, tried her best to hide a smile. Every strand of her short silver hair was in place, her beige cotton skirt and light-blue sweater and pearls making her appear as though she'd stepped out of a catalog.

Jane, the youngest Howard sister at age fifty, flipped back a strand of long dark hair. She poured a cup of tea for Alice. "Don't you like eating outdoors, Louise? It's just a lit-tle breeze."

"I think it feels nice," Alice ventured, smiling as she accepted the filled china teacup. She took a sip, then set it alongside the china dessert bowl on the wicker coffee table, which was placed strategically within reach of her rocker. "It's good to be outdoors during this lovely weather, espe-cially on this first day of summer."

"I thought that was a good reason to celebrate." Jane seated herself in the swing alongside Louise, her casual gauze skirt and blouse a contrast to Louise's more conservative attire. Jane lifted her bowl from the table. She had trained and worked as a professional chef before moving home to open the bed-and-breakfast with her sisters. With a critical eye, she studied the dessert in her oldest sister's bowl. "How's the spiced-plum shortcake?"

"It's delicious," Louise said.

Alice nodded her agreement, taking another bite.

Jane leaned back satisfied, then sampled her own serving. "Not bad," she murmured, then ate another bite. "Not bad at all."

Alice finished and sighed with satisfaction. "One of the things I like best about summer is all the new foods you cook, Jane."

"And I always seem to gain five pounds by September," Louise said good-naturedly, smiling at Jane. "But don't think I'm complaining. I look forward to the new dishes as much as Alice does."

"Good. I have several new recipes—summer supper dishes—that I plan to try." She took a sip of tea and sighed. "I guess we'd better head toward town. The mayor might make his mysterious announcement without us."

"He *has* been vague," Alice murmured. "It's supposed to be something important, but not even Aunt Ethel knows what he has up his sleeve."

Mayor Lloyd Tynan was a special friend of the sisters' aunt, Ethel Buckley. The seventyish woman lived in the carriage house behind their home and was famous for popping in unexpectedly. A bit flighty and self-centered, she was nonetheless a favorite relative of the sisters, and more than once they had smiled over her sweet relationship with Mayor Tynan.

"Perhaps Aunt Ethel would like to go to town with us," Alice said. "Should I go see?"

"No need." The screen opened, and a plump woman with bottle-red hair stood on the porch. She put her hands on her hips. "So *this* is where you three are. I thought you had left for the meeting without me. I came in through the back door. Imagine my surprise when I didn't find my three nieces, only a sink full of dirty dishes."

"Jane thought it would be nice to have dessert on the front porch since it's the first day of summer," Alice said.

"Won't you have a seat, Auntie?" Louise asked. "I'm sure Jane wouldn't mind getting you some of this wonderful shortcake if you'd like."

"Thank you, but there's no time for that," Ethel said,

waving her hands. "If we're going to walk to town, we'd better get going."

Jane glanced at her watch. "Aunt Ethel's right. Let's put our plates in the sink. I'll clean up when we get back."

Ethel stared at the bits of plums and spices swirling in the whipped cream at the bottom of Jane's bowl. "I'd be glad to help you tidy up when we get back, in exchange for some of that dessert."

Jane grinned. "That sounds like a fair exchange to me."

The sisters and Aunt Ethel headed toward town, passing Grace Chapel, for which their bed-and-breakfast was named. Their father, Rev. Daniel Howard, had been pastor of the small church until his recent death. His replacement was the middle-aged Rev. Kenneth Thompson, a friend of the sisters, who waved to them as he exited the chapel's side door.

"I was tending to a squeaky pew and nearly forgot about the meeting. I imagine you four ladies are headed for Town Hall." His hazel eyes twinkled. "May I join you?"

"Of course," Alice said. She had to smile up at Rev. Thompson, who was slightly over six feet tall. Only Jane, the tallest of the sisters at five foot nine, came close to being able to talk eye to eye, and she fell into step beside him as they headed down Chapel Road. They began to talk about a theologically based novel they'd both recently read.

"Summer always seems to bring out the romance in folks," Ethel observed quietly to Alice and Louise.

"What? Jane and Rev. Thompson?" Louise laughed. "You know they're just friends, Aunt Ethel."

The older woman glanced at them covertly. "You never know when Cupid will let fly with one of his arrows," Ethel said.

"Cupid had better check his calendar," Louise said. "It's closer to the Fourth of July than it is to the fourteenth of February."

"Hi, ladies!"

"Hi, Fred. Hi, Vera." Alice waved at the middle-aged couple who joined them as they turned onto Hill Street. Fred Humbert ran the local hardware store, and Vera taught fifth grade at Acorn Hill Elementary School.

Smiling broadly, Vera joined Alice while Fred chatted with Ethel and Louise. Alice grinned at her friend. "I know why you're in such good humor. School's out for the summer."

Vera nodded. "I love my students, but I love my free time as well. Neither of the girls is coming home this summer, so Fred and I are thinking about taking a vacation."

"That would be lovely, Vera. Where are you thinking about going?"

"That's the problem," she said in a low voice so that Fred couldn't hear. "I want to take a long, extended trip. Fred's afraid to leave his store for too long. Since ours is the only hardware store in town, he's in great demand, particularly during the summer when a lot of people tackle home-improvement projects. So I'll be lucky if I get a weekend in Potterston," she said, referring to Acorn Hill's nearest larger town.

"I was lucky to get him to attend this meeting the mayor's called." She sighed. "Fred's so preoccupied with the store right now. He agreed to take some time off, but getting him to follow through is another matter."

"I'm sure it will work itself out," Alice said.

They walked through the parking lot on Hill Street to the front of Town Hall on Berry Street. It was crowded with citizens streaming through the door.

Sticking close to Jane, Louise and Rev. Thompson, Alice and Vera took their seats on folding chairs. A podium stood at the front of the meeting area, and Mayor Tynan tested the microphone. Under the lights, his bald spot gleamed and his gray hair shone. His administrative assistant, Bella Paoli, set a glass of water on the stand. Alice hoped that didn't indicate a long evening.

Craig Tracy, a short, slender man with light-brown hair, sat down next to Alice. The owner of Wild Things, Acorn Hill's florist shop, he was a friend of the sisters. "Hi, Alice."

"Hello, Craig. It's nice to see you. How's the flower shop?"

"Doing well," he said. "How's the hospital?"

Alice worked part-time as a nurse in Potterston. "Doing well." She smiled. "I hope we have a great season too."

Craig grinned and greeted the others in Alice's group, then turned to greet those around them. Alice and Vera did likewise. Sylvia Songer, owner of Sylvia's Buttons, sat in front of them next to Nia Komonos, the librarian. In the row behind sat Viola Reed, the owner of Nine Lives Bookstore, and Carlene Moss, the fiftyish editor of the weekly *Acorn Nutshell*, the town newspaper. She carried a small tape recorder and leaned forward to chat with Alice.

"I can't imagine what Mayor Tynan will announce," she said, pushing her glasses to the bridge of her nose. "I brought my tape recorder so that I wouldn't miss a single word."

Alice glanced around the crowded room. "I'm glad you'll have an accurate record of the speech. I think that a great many of your newspaper readers are here tonight, Carlene."

"It certainly looks like it," she agreed.

"Ladies and gentlemen," Lloyd said, tapping on the microphone. "Ladies and gentlemen, if I may have your attention, please."

The crowd quieted, and the last few stragglers hustled into the room. The seats were all taken, so they had to stand against the wall.

Lloyd waited until they had settled, then cleared his throat and adjusted his customary bow tie. Carlene clicked on her tape recorder and held it up.

"Thank you all for coming," Lloyd said. "I'll keep this brief so that everyone can return home before it gets too late. I'm sure that you, like me, are enjoying our summer weather."

Murmurs of agreement rippled through the crowd. Many nodded.

"As I look out at the faces of Acorn Hill, I see many friends. People I've known for many years. Good citizens of this town." Lloyd's smile faded, and he gripped the podium. "But I'm aware that there are people not here tonight, citizens as well, who are perhaps not as well known. Folks who live on the outskirts, perhaps, who don't—or can't— make it into town to become acquainted."

"Amen." Someone near the podium obviously agreed with the mayor.

Lloyd squinted against the lights. "My point is that I believe we should take a town census. We should have a record of everyone who lives within the Acorn Hill limits, and we need to find out if their needs are being served. We all got here under our own steam tonight, but what about those who live too far out to walk and perhaps don't have a car? What about health services and food? Are all our citizens getting enough to eat?"

Audience members turned to each other, murmuring. Alice thought about some of her patients at the hospital and knew that there were always needs. How many of them were not being met in Acorn Hill?

Jane raised her hand. "How can we proceed, Mayor?"

Lloyd beamed. "I'm glad you asked that, Jane. What I propose is that we begin plans to take a town census. I know it will take some of you from your summer fun, but it seems like a good time to accomplish the task. The weather's nice for traveling door to door, and some of you have a little more time on your hands now that summer is here. When we take the census, we need to find out about our citizens and whether they require any care from this town's government. I pledge all our available resources to help those in need."

The crowd applauded. Jane remained standing, and

when the noise died down, she said, "If you're looking for volunteers, I'd be glad to help."

Craig Tracy rose. "Me too."

The crowd applauded again, but Lloyd gestured for them to stop. "You two read my mind. Since you've shortened this meeting considerably by volunteering your services, all I have left to say is that Jane and Craig should meet in my office tomorrow at ten o'clock. Anyone else who's interested in working with us on the census can contact them later. I hereby put Jane and Craig in charge of this project—with my guidance, of course—unless there are any objections."

No one said a word. Lloyd drank from the glass of water, then smiled. "In that case, let's get to the other business of Acorn Hill."

After the minor business had been discussed and attended to, the crowd got to its feet. Everyone was still eager to discuss Lloyd's idea about the census. Alice rose beside Craig. "That was good of you to volunteer. I know you and Jane will do a wonderful job."

"Thanks," he said. "I probably should have thought about it a little more. I mean, I'm not sure how much time it will take, or what we'll be able to accomplish or who will watch my shop. But it just seemed like the right thing to do."

Alice smiled. "I've learned that whenever God nudges us to do something, it's always best to make ourselves available right then."

"I have an idea that Lloyd's right," Craig said. "There are probably lots of people in our area who need assistance of one kind or another."

"I agree. And don't forget that God always blesses those who answer his call. Not necessarily in money or prosperity but in ways we often can't imagine. I'll be eager to hear what He does for you."

Craig smiled. "I'd better huddle with Jane and get some kind of preliminary game plan going before tomorrow."

On the walk back to Grace Chapel Inn, Alice could scarcely pay attention to Vera. Her mind was on Lloyd's census plan. Should she volunteer to help? Jane had been the first one to stand up, and while Alice was proud of her sister, she wondered if perhaps she should have been equally eager.

After they said good-bye to Vera and Fred, Alice and Louise walked back up the hill alone. Ethel had stayed behind to talk to Lloyd, who promised to give her a ride home. Jane was meeting with Craig at the Coffee Shop to discuss some ideas before they met with Lloyd the next day.

"You're rather quiet, Alice," Louise said. "Is anything wrong?"

Alice shook her head. "I suppose it's nothing, but I've been wondering if perhaps I should have volunteered along with Jane and Craig."

"Is census-taking something you're interested in doing?"

Alice thought for a moment. "Not really. Does that make me a bad person?"

Louise laughed gently. "Not at all. You employ your gift of service in so many ways, primarily in your work as a nurse. I do not believe that God expects us to volunteer for every project."

"Then you don't feel guilty for not signing up yourself?"

"Not at all. I have my music students to keep me busy, even now. Don't forget the inn, either. We're booked through the summer, and our guests require our attention."

"But Jane will somehow manage to cook for guests."

"Exactly," Louise said. "We know she would never shirk her cooking duties, but she will be away from home for who knows how long each day, for whatever amount of time it takes to conduct the census. You and I will, of course, cheerfully pick up any slack in her absence."

Alice let out a relieved sigh. "I suppose you're right." She paused. "The truth is, Louise, I had rather looked forward to a quiet summer. Oh, I'll still have my job and we'll have our guests, but something about the season makes me want to kick off my shoes and curl up on a chaise lounge with a good mystery novel. Or even go somewhere as a tourist."

Louise laughed, and Alice blushed. "That sounds childish, doesn't it?"

"Oh, Alice." Louise linked arms with her younger sister. "On the contrary. It sounds perfectly normal. Most of us wish for our childhood summer vacations, don't we? I certainly do."

"Really?"

Louise nodded. "I heard some of Vera's plans for a vacation, and I must admit that I was a bit envious. Wouldn't it be fun to go to the beach for a few days? We never seem to get any time away, what with our jobs and the inn."

"It would be fun. Or swimming lessons…white-water rafting…softball games."

Louise smiled. "I was thinking more along the lines of that chaise lounge you were talking about."

"That would be fun too."

Louise sobered. "Sometimes when I feel that way, Alice, I realize that I need a break of sorts. I love music and my students, but doing the same thing all the time can lead to burnout. Is that how you're feeling?"

"Perhaps," Alice said tentatively. "Or maybe I just need a change of pace."

"I've been feeling a bit like that, too, lately." Louise patted Alice's arm. "I'm sure you'll find some time to read a mystery novel or two during the coming months. Maybe that will make you feel better."

"How about you? What sort of diversion would you like?"

Louise smiled. "I'm not sure, but I'll know it when I see it."

"Then let's both concentrate on keeping our eyes open."

Chapter Two

Over sodas at the Coffee Shop, Jane and Craig discussed several ideas for the census-taking. In the end, however, they decided to wait to hear Lloyd's plans and ideas when they met with him in the morning. Jane was so excited about the project that she could hardly sleep. She loved a new adventure, but more than that, she loved talking to people.

She and Craig met at Lloyd's office promptly at ten o'clock. Without design, they both walked through the door to his reception area at the same time.

"Well!" Bella Paoli smiled at them. "Are you going to elbow each other to be the first to the mayor's office?"

"I hadn't planned to." Craig laughed.

"Please have a seat then." Bella indicated the chairs across from her desk. The blonde woman in her fifties held out a candy dish while they sat. "Caramel? Peppermint?"

Craig declined with a shake of his head. "No thank you," Jane said, smoothing her royal blue skirt.

Bella popped a caramel in her mouth, smiling. "I love these things even if no one else seems to."

Jane laughed. "Everyone else has to watch their weight, but not you, Bella."

The assistant leaned forward confidentially. "I think I burn it all off in working for Lloyd. He's a great boss, but he keeps me busy." She smiled.

The door to Lloyd's office opened, and he stepped into the reception area. "Craig! Jane! I should have known you'd be right on time. Step into my office and let's get right to work."

With a wink at Bella, Jane obeyed. Lloyd settled into his leather chair, while Craig and Jane perched on chairs in front of the desk. "Now then," Lloyd said, shuffling through a stack of papers. "Oh, where did I put that information?" He punched an intercom button. "Bella? Do you have the folder on that census project?"

"It's on top of the stack of papers," she said through the intercom.

Lloyd rifled through some papers. "I don't see it."

"Try the stack on the right side."

Lloyd reached to the edge of the desk. "Do you mean my 'in pile'?"

"That's the one."

Lloyd waved a red folder. "Found it! Bella, what would I do without you?"

Jane heard the assistant laugh. "I'm not sure, Mr. Mayor."

Lloyd clicked off the intercom and opened the folder. "Let's see what we have here." He picked up a piece of paper and turned it around to lay it on the desk so that Craig and Jane could see. "This is a map showing the town limits of Acorn Hill. I've broken it into what should be manageable areas for canvassing. Some of it is obviously in the town proper and some of it is in the outlying areas. Since you two volunteered first, I thought I'd let you choose which area you'd like."

"*Hmm.*" Jane studied the map. "It would be easier to tackle the town, of course, but it might be more fun to hit the rural areas."

"All I ask is that people work in pairs," Lloyd said. "Particularly in the rural areas."

Craig let out a breath. "That would be a little more difficult for me, since I have a store to run." He glanced at Jane. "I do want to work with you though."

"Good, good," Lloyd said, bobbing his head. "I don't envision this taking more than a couple hours a day. I'll have you two meet later with a few other people who have volunteered, but I wanted to talk with you two first to get you started. Most folks in Acorn Hill work or are busy with their families. Jane, I know you have an inn to help run. I don't want to intrude on personal time, but I do want to find out if all our citizens' needs are being met."

"I can spare a few hours a day if you can," Jane said to Craig. "Perhaps if we went early in the morning, say from eight to ten, you could be back in your shop at a decent hour."

"I can always open the shop a little later than normal," Craig said. "My customers would understand."

"Splendid!" Lloyd said. "Now that that's settled, let's discuss the questionnaire you'll be filling out." He thumbed through the folder until he located another piece of paper, which he likewise turned around to Craig and Jane. "I've made up a checklist of questions to be filled out, much like the federal census every ten years. Name of occupants, ages, address … Beyond that, it's going to take a little sleuthing on your parts."

"What do you mean?" Jane asked.

"We want to allocate the resources of our town to its members, but some of them might be reluctant to express their needs."

"I'm sure we don't want to sound too nosy either," Jane said.

"Exactly." Lloyd beamed. "That's why I'm glad you two volunteered for this job. I think most folks living near the center of town are well known, and we know each other's concerns. When someone needs something, we pitch in to help. That may not be true with the citizens who live farther out."

Lloyd leaned forward. "Let's see if we can come up with some more questions to ascertain whether all our citizens are in good shape. Beyond that, you two will have to use your intuition to find out if more help is needed. Think you can handle that?"

Craig and Jane looked at each other. They both broke into grins at the same time. "Maybe we can give you a progress report this afternoon," Jane said.

"Fine, I'll be in my office until five thirty."

After they had talked for half an hour, Craig and Jane agreed to head out for a short trial run. Jane phoned the inn to let Louise know her plans and that she would be back in time for lunch. Craig agreed to open his store at noon that day but said that he needed to hang a sign on the door that said when he would return. "We can also pick up my truck and get started on the canvassing," he said.

"Great. I'm rarin' to go," Jane said.

After Craig made sure the shop was in good shape for him to leave—no orders waiting to be immediately filled—he hung a sign on the door that had a clock face on it. It said *Will Be Back At*, and Craig pointed the hands on the face of the clock to noon. He and Jane got into his pickup truck and consulted the map.

"Why don't we start here?" Jane asked, pointing to a corner. "It's south of town, yet not into Riverton."

"That's still in Acorn Hill?" Craig asked, squinting at the tiny area.

"Evidently. Lloyd said there are some homes there still within the town limits."

Craig shrugged and put the truck into gear. They drove for a while, then turned off onto a tree-lined gravel road. "I think this is it," he said.

Jane looked at the map. "There aren't any street names here."

"There's a house," Craig said.

"I think it's a mobile home," Jane said. "I see another one beyond that. We should be able to knock the two of them off our list before we need to be back at noon."

Craig pulled the truck off the gravel road onto a dirt driveway. The double-wide mobile home looked to be several decades old with faded green paint on the lower half. To the side was a plastic playground set for tots, complete with slide and swings. Beyond that sat a vegetable garden, carefully enclosed with stakes and wire. A multitude of variously colored geraniums sat in terra-cotta pots by the front door, giving the home a splash of color.

Craig and Jane got out of the truck and approached the home. Craig knocked on the door, and a young woman with long brown hair and a baby on her hip answered. "Yes?"

"Hi. I'm Craig Tracy and this is Jane Howard. We're citizens of Acorn Hill, like you, and we're conducting a census at Mayor Tynan's request."

"I'm Bonnie Ethedridge," she said. "What do you need to know?"

"It's nice to meet you, Bonnie," Jane said. "Mostly we're trying to find out if our citizens' needs are being met. Mayor Tynan wants to know if city government can help out in any way."

Bonnie thought for a moment. "We're doing pretty well, I 'spect. My husband, Darryl, has a job working with Gerald Morton in construction. Until he gets home, it's just me and the three kids."

Craig copied down information about names and ages on his clipboard.

"Is there anything the town can help you with?" Jane asked. "Any social services?"

"I'm not real sure I know what you mean by social services, but we're getting by just fine. With me not working, there's not enough money left over for dinners out, but we're managing."

"How about health care?" Craig asked.

Bonnie smiled. "We're all pretty healthy, thank the good Lord. Just a case of the sniffles occasionally. And Darryl has some insurance if anything bad should happen. I hate to be rude"—she shifted the baby on her hip—"but if you folks have all the information you need, I've got beans on the stove that need tending to."

"I think that's it," Jane said. "Thank you for your time."

"Thank *you*," Bonnie said, shutting the door.

Jane and Craig looked at each other. "They don't seem to need any help," Craig said. "It sounds like they're managing all right. Shall we try the next home?"

Jane shrugged. "Why not?"

They could see the next mobile home in the distance. As a regular jogger, Jane wouldn't have minded the exercise a walk to it would provide, but Craig pointed out that canvassing would go faster if they took the truck.

The next mobile home looked less tidy than the

Ethedridges'. There was no vegetable garden or any cheerful flowers. In fact, the grass was overgrown and dotted with weeds. The home listed to one side, and one window was cracked.

Jane knocked on the front door, and when no one answered, she cupped her hands and peered through the grimy window of the front door. "I'm not sure anyone lives here, Craig. Do you suppose we can check with Lloyd later? Maybe he or Bella can check the property records."

"Most likely Bonnie Ethedridge would know. Or maybe someone at that next home." Craig nodded up the gravel road. He glanced at his wristwatch. "Shall we give it a try before we call it a day?"

"I'm game," Jane said.

She and Craig piled back into the truck. Gravel crunched underneath the tires, but when they reached a bend in the road, gravel gave way to dirt. The path was filled with rocks and branches from oak trees lining the road.

"We're really off the beaten path here," Craig said. They bounced over several fallen limbs that he couldn't avoid. "Good thing we're in a truck and not a car. It'd be easy to break something."

Jane gripped the handle above the passenger door.

"Y-yes," she said, trying to keep from being jostled against the window or the front dash. "And I'm glad you're driving."

At last the house came into view. All alone in a small clearing, the mobile home was surrounded by shrubs and other plants that had probably been lovingly planted in years gone by but had not been tended to and were growing wild. The dead branches of a tree stood in stark contrast to the white-clouded, blue summer sky. A chipped and faded windmill, two of its blades missing, stood listless in the side yard of dead grass.

A chain-link fence surrounded the back side of the property, and a large trellis, no longer supporting flowers, pointed toward the sky. A black Labrador barked at Craig and Jane as they walked toward the front door. The animal stopped barking and put its paws on top of the fence and wagged its tail as they got closer.

"Easy, pup," Craig said. "We're friends."

"I think she just wants some attention," Jane said, moving closer to the fence, her hand outstretched.

"Uh, Jane, I hate to sound like someone's mom, but you don't know if the dog has had its shots or if it might be the kind to bite once you get closer."

Jane brought her hand closer to her body. "You're probably right," she said with a sigh.

They walked up the two steps to the porch, hardly more than a rickety wooden platform. Jane noted that the skirting of the mobile home was covered by rusted corrugated aluminum. She couldn't stop the negative reaction that she felt, or the critical thoughts of the lack of pride in ownership. Yet just as quickly, she felt shame creep up her neck in the form of a blush. No doubt her father would have had much to say to her about not judging a book by its cover or people by their habitats.

Craig knocked softly on the door.

"Just a minute," a voice called.

They heard the rattle of a door chain being unlatched before the door opened. A hunched elderly woman, stooped by a widow's hump, looked up at them. Jane wanted to tell her immediately to sit down because she was certain the effort of standing pained the woman. Yet the smile in her heavily wrinkled face seemed pleasant enough. "Can I help you?"

Craig cleared his throat. "We're here on behalf of Acorn Hill."

The woman's smile fell. "You're not from the utility company, are you? I thought they had gotten the payment straightened out. I hope you're not going to shut off my—"

"We're not here about your utilities, ma'am," Jane cut

in. "We're census takers, here on behalf of Lloyd Tynan, Acorn Hill's mayor."

"Tynan…Tynan," she said. "I went to school with a Tynan. I believe his name was Lawrence, though. Is he the mayor?"

Jane and Craig glanced at one another. Lloyd was in his seventies. This woman looked much older than the current mayor. "I believe Larry—or Lawrence—Tynan was Lloyd's father," she said gently. "Perhaps it was he you went to school with. But he's been dead for many years."

"That doesn't surprise me. It seems like just about everyone I know has passed on. Would you two like to come in?" She stepped aside. "I don't want to leave you standing on the porch."

Jane and Craig glanced at each other.

The woman's faded blue eyes twinkled. "I made some fresh-squeezed lemonade."

Craig held up the clipboard. "We're just here to ask a few—"

"We'd love some lemonade," Jane said, shooting Craig a glance. Shrugging, he held open the door, and Jane followed the woman into her home.

It took a moment for Jane's eyes to adjust to the dimness. How in the world could the woman see? The only available light shone through a small window over the sink. Jane had to feel her way through the home, squinting in the darkness. Evidently the lack of light was not a problem for the woman, though, as she deftly poured three jelly jar glasses of lemonade out of a plastic pitcher she had retrieved from an ancient refrigerator. She handed a glass each to Craig and Jane. "I hope it's not too tart for you," she said. "I like my lemonade with a little *zing*."

Jane took a sip. "It's delicious. And you squeezed it yourself?"

The woman laughed softly. "Wouldn't have it any other way. I refuse to buy that frozen nonsense. And forget that powdered stuff. Phooey! Anything worth drinking or eating is worth making from scratch, I always say."

Jane smiled. This woman was a kindred spirit.

"Now, what can I help you two young people with?"

Craig set his glass on an aging blue tile counter. "We're collecting data for Mayor Tynan. That is, Mayor *Lloyd* Tynan. He wants to make sure Town Hall has a record of everyone in Acorn Hill."

"I don't believe I've seen you around town," Jane said. "I'm Jane Howard, and I live at Grace Chapel Inn. This is Craig Tracy."

"Grace Chapel Inn? I don't believe I recollect that place. You don't mean Grace Chapel, do you?"

"The inn is close to the chapel, though we're not affili-
ated," Jane said. "My sisters and I opened up our family home
as a bed-and-breakfast after our father passed away."

"Daniel Howard?"

"Yes, ma'am. I'm his youngest daughter. My older sisters are Alice and Louise."

The woman smiled. "Your father was a lovely man. I
attended Grace Chapel when I was just a girl, but I switched
churches when I got married. When your father became the
pastor, he always teased my husband and me about coming
back to Grace Chapel. He didn't mind that we attended
another church, but I always knew we'd be welcome at his
place if we ever decided on something new." She held out
her hand. "And here I'm forgetting my manners. I'm Bernice
Sayers."

"How do you do?" Craig shook her hand.

Jane took the woman's wrinkled hand in her own. "How
do you—" She broke off. Her vision had adjusted, and she
noticed that the woman's eyes were filmy and vacant. "Do
you have trouble seeing?" she gently inquired.

Bernice laughed. "You guessed my secret. Oh, I'm not
totally blind, maybe not even legally blind. I don't rightly
know. I can make out things if I squint a bit, but the truth
is that I know my way around this old place so well that I
don't bump my shins very often. In fact, it keeps me from

noticing the worn-out things that I used to keep shipshape, and having the drapes drawn helps to keep the place cooler. But you two must be tired. Why don't we take our lemonades and sit on the divan?"

She gestured toward the front room where they'd entered. In between two overstuffed paisley club chairs sat a dark-green sofa. It had the Victorian touch of antimacassars on the back and arms and was pressed against a veneer-paneled wall. Jane would have marveled at the unusual furniture, but her eyes went to a more amazing sight. The wall and both walls abutting it were covered with buttons of all shapes and sizes. No two seemed alike.

Jane touched one, then others, reveling in the textured change from simple white plastic to gold-scrolled dome to red hearts. "What are all these?"

"You mean my button collection?" Bernice moved beside Jane and reached for a small table lamp. "Maybe this will help you see better. I forget that I don't need the light the way other people do."

Instantly the walls were illuminated, buttons shining. "Wow," Craig said. "That's some collection. Most folks would have just saved them in a big jar."

"Exactly," Bernice said. "I wanted my buttons where I could see them every day. If they were in a jar, these old arthritic hands of mine would have to fumble to look at them. Half the collection would just wind up under the divan. It's amazing what a little glue can do."

Jane stood on tiptoes, then bent low, examining all three walls. "Where did you get all of these?"

Bernice eased herself onto the sofa, waving off Craig's proffered assistance. "I have been a seamstress since I was five years old. Had a real knack for it, my mama said. Sometimes she'd give me a scrap of cloth and a needle and thread just to keep me busy. It didn't take me long to grad- uate to sewing buttonholes and hemming my sisters' skirts." She passed her hand in front of her eyes. "But that was a long, long time ago."

Jane sat beside her and took her hand, moved by the eld- erly woman's memories. "All these buttons must have been left over from sewing projects."

Bernice nodded. "That oblong wooden button was one left over from my granddaughter's jacket. Prettiest blue car coat. It had loops to hold the buttons. She loved that old thing. And that shiny silver button there? It was from my friend Marge's prom dress. My, we didn't have much money back then, and I can't say that my stitching was as good as what you can buy in a department store now, but she was pretty happy with that old dress. It had a silver tulle skirt and matching lace bodice. Oh, but you don't want to hear about my memories of old clothes."

"Why, yes I do," Jane said. "I think it's fascinating."

"Do you have any family, Mrs. Sayers?" Craig asked. "Any folks to look after you?"

Bernice shook her head. "Just Birdie, the dog out in the yard. I had just let her outside before you folks showed up. I hope she didn't frighten you. She's harmless as a lamb, but she does like to bark sometimes."

"We saw Birdie," Jane said. "But who else takes care of you? And who takes Birdie for her shots?"

Bernice laughed softly. "Like I said, it's just me and her. Once in a blue moon my grandkids will show up." Her face fell, and her lip quivered. "My own kids are all gone now. Funny, isn't it? A mother isn't supposed to outlive her children, but here I am still ticking along at ninety-five."

Jane and Craig exchanged a glance. Jane was deeply moved, and she felt shame over her earlier misjudgment. "How do you get your groceries?"

"That nice Bonnie Ethedridge up the road buys things for me when she can, but she has her hands full. I don't like to be a bother."

Warning bells went off in Jane's head. "Do you have enough food now?" she asked. "Craig and I would be glad to—"

"Now, now, don't you be worrying about me." Bernice waved her hand. "I've got some leftover macaroni and cheese for dinner."

"But you need more than that to eat," Jane said.

"Honey, I'm an old woman. I lost my appetite a long time ago. Part of the good Lord's provision in aging, I 'spect. I eat enough to get by."

Craig unobtrusively pointed at his watch, mouthing the word *noon*. Torn between wanting to stay and needing to leave, Jane rose. "Bernice—may I call you that?"

"Of course, dear. I wouldn't have it any other way."

"Craig and I could come back. Would that be all right?"

"I'd love it. I'll even make you some more lemonade," Bernice said, smiling.

"Is there anything we can do for you before we leave?" Craig asked.

"I'll be fine. Come and see me any time."

Craig scribbled on his clipboard, noting her address. "What's your phone number?"

"Oh pooh! I haven't bothered with a phone for years. If anybody needs me, they know where I am."

"Well we certainly do, and we'll be back. I promise." Jane rose. "No, don't see us out. We'll find our way."

Bernice followed them to the door anyway. "It was lovely to meet you young people. Thank you for stopping by."

"Thank you for the lemonade," Craig said as he and Jane left the home.

Bernice stood at the door and watched until Craig put his truck in reverse and backed onto the road. Jane knew that the elderly woman couldn't see them, but hospitality—even after all these years—no doubt dictated that she watch her guests leave. Jane and Craig were silent until they had traveled back up the dirt road to gravel, then finally back to a paved road. Jane stared out the window, not seeing the passing scenery.

"I believe we have someone in need," Craig said.

"Indeed." Jane turned toward Craig. "What are we going to do to help her?"

"I suppose that's up to Lloyd."

"Something tells me that Bernice's going to need more help than Town Hall can give. This is more than our local government can handle, I'm afraid."

"You're probably right. But if we put our heads together, I'm sure we can come up with something."

Chapter Three

Alice hung up the phone in the reception area under the staircase in the foyer. She made a notation to herself on a calendar.

Carrying a laundry basket, Louise descended the stairs and saw Alice scribbling. "More guests?" she asked.

Alice nodded, finishing her writing with a flourish. "Remember that cancellation we had next week? It's been filled."

The phone rang, and Alice grinned at her older sister. "It's really jumping around here, isn't it?"

Louise laughed and headed for the laundry room at the back of the house.

Alice smiled after her sister and lifted the receiver. "Grace Chapel Inn."

"Alice? Alice Howard?"

"Yes?"

"I hope you still remember me. This is Lilia Joly."

"Lilia! Of course I remember you." Alice cradled the phone closer. "You were one of my ANGELs...how long has it been?"

"Too long." Lilia laughed. "Do you still lead that middle school group at Grace Chapel?"

"Every Wednesday night."

"Some things never change, and I'm glad of that. Those were good times. Long ago, but good times."

"How are you, Lilia?"

"I'm fine. I went to college, got a degree in social work and am happily married. My husband and I live in Potterston, and we're expecting our first child this summer."

"How wonderful! Perhaps I'll see you at the hospital when your baby is born. I still work as a nurse there."

"Well... I'm hoping to see you before then. That's why I called—although I'm certainly glad to catch up with our news."

Alice leaned her elbows against the desk. "So, what's up, Lilia?"

Lilia drew a deep breath. "I work with a group of at-risk girls in Potterston, though we take girls from the surrounding area as well. Normally I supervise them during the summer, but since I'm having the baby, the doctor doesn't want me to get involved in any strenuous activity."

"What kind of activities do you usually have for the girls?" Alice envisioned helpers working on their study skills, improving their reading or maybe teaching home economics classes.

"Physical stuff, mostly. Swimming, canoeing, rock climbing..."

Alice felt as though her elbows would slide off the desk. "By any chance do you want to know if I can fill in for you?"

"I know it's asking a lot, and I'm sure you're busy with nursing. A member of your church recommended you, and of course, I know how wonderful you are with young people."

"I'm also running our family home as a bed-and-breakfast with my sisters."

"Oh, that is a lot." She sighed. "I need someone for two or three days a week, say, twenty hours a week, more or less, depending on the activity."

Lilia's voice sounded so downcast that Alice hastened to reassure her that she wasn't yet saying no. "What age group are these girls?"

"Older junior high and young high school girls. Maybe just a little older than your ANGELs. They're a little bit too young to take care of themselves—they certainly can't drive."

"I'm flattered that you thought of me, Lilia."

"No one understands girls like you, Alice. These girls may be a bit hard around the edges, but they're not so different from your ANGELs. They need somebody who's not afraid of physical activity, but, more importantly, is not afraid of discipline."

"Tough love?" Alice asked.

Lilia laughed. "That's exactly right. So have I interested you? I'm afraid I can't pay anything more than your expenses."

The mystery novels Alice had planned to indulge in suddenly didn't sound entertaining. How much more satisfying it would be to spend time with girls all summer long, perhaps making a difference in their young lives. "It sounds like a challenge and something I'd like to tackle, Lilia. I think I can adjust my nursing schedule so that I can give the time that's required."

Lilia smiled. "Perfect. Some activities might require a full day and others just a few hours. Would that work for you?"

Alice indicated that it would. "When do we begin?"

"Is there any chance you could come to my office in Potterston this afternoon so that we could go over particulars?"

Alice agreed to the idea, and after getting directions, she hung up the phone. Louise returned from the laundry room, her basket now empty. "More guests?"

Alice shook her head. "My summer won't be so slow or

boring after all. That was Lilia Joly, one of my ANGELs from at least ten years ago." She quickly explained Lilia's request and her agreement to help out.

"That sounds right up your alley," Louise said. "I'm sure Lilia appreciates your help."

"I just hope I can keep up with the girls. Apparently there's a lot of strenuous activity involved—rock climbing, canoeing, swimming."

"But you and Vera walk so often—not to mention all the physical activity that nursing requires—that you're in good shape," Louise pointed out. "Most likely you won't have to participate fully. I'm sure if you're just present when they're at their activities, that will be enough."

"Lilia and I are getting together late this afternoon to discuss what my role will entail, so I'll find out more then." She paused. "I hope it doesn't take away from my duties here, Louise. First Jane accepted a summer task, now me. Neither of us wants to leave you to handle everything."

"You won't," Louise said. "If I get too busy, I'll certainly let you know, but I have a feeling you and Jane won't be too far from the daily responsibilities."

"I wish something would come your way too, Louise. I think it makes a summer exciting to have something fun and different to accomplish."

"My summer will be exciting enough." Louise winked. "Besides, I'm at the age where I appreciate a bit of routine."

Craig pulled up to Wild Things and shut off the truck's engine. "Are you sure I can't take you home, Jane?"

She shook her head. "I want to walk around and think about what we can do to help Bernice. And who knows who else."

"Do you still want to meet with Lloyd at five o'clock?"

"If you can make it," Jane said. "I'd like to learn who else has volunteered to help us with the census. It would be good if we could toss around some ideas for helping people like Bernice."

"Okay, I'll see you at Town Hall at five then."

Jane strolled from Wild Things down Hill Street to the Coffee Shop. Maybe a cup of coffee or tea would help her think.

As usual, June Carter, the owner of the shop, had the day's menu hand-lettered and posted in the front window. Normally Jane perused the list, but she found she had little interest in food at the moment. Once inside the shop, she slid into a booth. Hope Collins, the waitress, showed up right away with an order pad in hand. Hope, whose hair was naturally dark but often gave evidence of experiments with color, was sporting blonde streaks.

Jane smiled. "Summer do?"

"You like it?" Hope primped her hair. "I thought the blonde was in keeping with the warmer months, but I didn't want to go *all* blonde. Sometimes when I do that it just turns out white."

"Your hair looks good no matter what you do. I admire your use of color."

"So does Betty Dunkle," Hope said, referring to Acorn Hill's hairstylist. "When she sees me coming, she knows she's got a high-dollar job to perform. Hair coloring is not an inexpensive indulgence, my friend."

"I'll keep it in mind."

Hope grinned. "What can I get for you today?"

"I hate to take up space, but just a glass of sparkling water. If you need the table, feel free to boot me out."

"I will, but I don't think that will be necessary. One water coming right up."

Hope departed for the kitchen, and Jane rested her head in her hands. She was deep in thought when someone slid into the booth on the opposite side of the table. "You look like you've lost your best friend," Nia Komonos said. "May I join you?"

"Hi, Nia. Please do." Jane straightened. "Are you on a break from the library?"

"Lunch hour, actually," she said, placing a napkin onto the lap of her stylish tan suit.

"I probably won't stay long anyway. I need to get home to join Louise and Alice for lunch."

"If you have just a minute before you go, I've wanted to tell you how much I admire you for volunteering to work on the census project." Nia leaned forward. "I don't have time for canvassing, but will you keep me in mind if there's something else I can do?"

"Sure, Nia."

"Hey there." Hope set down a glass of bubbling water in front of Jane. "Good to see you, Nia. Do you want the usual for lunch?"

"You know it. One Greek salad," she said, beaming. "Just like Mama used to make."

Hope tapped her pad, smiled and left.

"June's a good cook," Nia said, "but I had to help her a little bit in perfecting her salad."

Jane took a long drink, surprisingly thirsty despite the glass of lemonade she had at Bernice's. "I'd love to stay and chat while you eat your lunch, but I'd better get going."

"Go ahead, don't worry about me. Besides"—Nia held

up a book—"I always bring a friend. Don't forget what I said about calling on me if you and Craig need any help with Lloyd's project."

Over zucchini-tomato frittata served in pita pockets, Jane told Alice and Louise about her morning. They both shook their heads over Bernice's predicament. "Imagine not having any family nearby to help," Alice said.

"Perhaps there's something we can do," Louise said.

"Craig and I are scheduled to meet with Lloyd later today. What worries me is that there will be more people like Bernice."

"I'm sure you'll come up with a good plan to help. Of course you'll let us know what we can do," Alice said.

"Of course." Jane bit into her pita pocket, feeling comforted by the food. Then she thought of Bernice. Would she have enough to eat for the rest of the week?

"Alice got some exciting news of her own," Louise said.

"Oh?" Jane looked up from her plate. "What happened?"

Alice explained about her plan to help at-risk girls for the summer.

"That sounds interesting," Jane said. "I'm sure Lilia appreciates your helping out, especially on such short notice."

"Well, I appreciate this new sandwich you've made, Jane," Louise said. "Nice and light for warmer weather, but definitely tasty."

"Thanks. Hopefully I can surprise you two with more tempting dishes."

Louise laughed. "With you both involving yourselves in new projects, do you think our family can stand any more surprises?"

Later that afternoon, Jane headed back toward town to meet with Lloyd and Craig. Alice got her purse and keys to head for her visit with Lilia. Before she could open the front door to leave, however, Louise hurried down the stairs. "Alice, wait!"

She turned back. "What's wrong?"

Louise put a hand over her heart to catch her breath. "May I ride with you to Potterston? I just recalled that I need to pick up some sheet music for my students."

"I'd love the company, if you don't mind waiting for me. I don't know how long my meeting will last."

"I don't mind. I can always find a way to kill time. The music store is on Main Street. I can enjoy poking around in all the shops."

"Lilia's office is a few blocks off Main Street, so we shouldn't have any trouble finding each other," Alice said.

The sisters enjoyed the drive to Potterston. Because of recent rains, the grass alongside the road was green and dotted with wild honeysuckle and orange daylilies. They rolled down the windows just enough to keep their hair from getting mussed and sniffed the warm air appreciatively.

"I love this time of year," Alice said. "I'm no gardener like Jane, but I can just feel everything growing and blooming."

"I like that I only need one blanket at night. It's nice to be able to open a window and have fresh air."

"And to hear the birds chirping in the morning when we wake up. Who needs an alarm clock?"

"It's a good thing there isn't a rooster in the neighborhood," Louise said. "I wouldn't want to wake up *too* early."

Soon Alice turned onto Potterston's Main Street. They passed many early twentieth-century brick buildings set back from the street. A variety of businesses kept the street busy with cars and pedestrians—small eateries, antiques stores and law offices. Alice found a parking space in front of Scales and Arpeggios, the music store, and let Louise off. "Shall I pick you up back here? Would an hour be too long?"

"I wouldn't think so, but take your time with Lilia. If I find myself with nothing to do, I'll browse the shops and watch for you."

Alice smiled, then drove away. Louise walked across the broad sidewalk to the store's entrance. The glass was tinted so that no one could see inside. The name of the store was painted in gold lettering on the front window, and several musical instruments were painted in silver on the door. When she entered, she let her eyes adjust to the change in light, pausing to examine an electronic piano on display by the door. Beyond it sat a complex-looking drum set, a display of school band instruments, and an entire shelf of acoustic and electric guitars.

Louise played a note on the electronic piano. When a tone didn't sound, she sheepishly realized the switch was turned off.

Cyrus Uhlig, the store's owner, approached her. A balding, middle-aged man with a white shirt rolled up at the sleeves and a striped tie, he greeted Louise with a smile. "Are you interested in one of these babies, Louise?"

"Hello, Cyrus. No, I'm afraid I'm just browsing. I'm quite happy with my baby grand, thank you."

He laughed so hard that his cheeks puffed out pink. The sparse hairs that crisscrossed his bald spot wavered.

"The day I sell you an electronic piano is the day that I retire. What can I get for you?"

"I need some sheet music for some of my students. A new exercise book for my beginners, a book of duets for some of my older students and a copy of *Moonlight* Sonata."

"Everyone should learn how to play that one," he said. "Step right this way."

He led her into the store. Beyond the musical instruments were display cases of accessories—guitar picks, strings and straps, reeds for woodwinds, and sheet music holders. At the back of the store, sheet music was arranged by individual instruments, then books and single pieces.

The front door opened. "Excuse me, but I need to see to this customer," Cyrus said. "He's a high school band director, and I've been expecting him. Do you mind?"

"Not at all," Louise said. "I can find what I need. I'm also inclined to browse, so I'll be fine by myself."

She found the music she needed right away. She was grateful that she had to wait for Alice because it had been a while since she allowed herself time to flip through the store's sheet music. She loved the glossy exercise and theory books and the popular piano pieces with their illustrated covers. The sheet music was arranged in vertical order, and she checked to see what was new since her last visit.

"Louise! Louise Howard."

She turned to find a pleasant-looking, smiling man who held a sheaf of flyers in one hand. "Yes? Oh, Rabbi Cohen. It's good to see you."

He shifted the flyers so he and Louise could shake hands. "How are you?" she asked. "And your wife?"

"I am well, thank you. So is Gail. She'll be pleased you asked about her. And how are you and your lovely sisters? It must be the busy season for you."

"We do have a lot of guests lined up, and it seems that Alice and Jane are involved in summer projects as well."

"Speaking of busy, I'm hoping to persuade my good friend Cyrus to allow me to hang up one of these announcements in his window."

"What is it?"

The rabbi held up the paper so that she could read it. "Gail and I are members of the Potterston Dance Club, and our group is holding a friendly competition this summer."

"Competition?"

"Did you see that TV show *Dancing with the Stars*?"

Louise shook her head. "I'm afraid my sisters and I don't watch much television."

"The show paired experienced dancers with celebrities. Then they had a competition at the end of the training to see which team could score the most points with the judges. We're not getting celebrities, but we're also pairing beginners with more seasoned dancers. We'll hold the competition in a few weeks and give the winning beginner a plaque." He smiled. "It's all in fun. For Gail and me, it's good exercise. Of course, we're getting to the age where even getting up in the morning is good exercise. But what can we do about it?" He shrugged good-naturedly.

"You're not that old," she said, smiling. Rabbi Cohen acted as though he and his wife had one foot already in the grave, when in truth they were probably only in their early forties at most. "You have a few years to go just to catch up with me."

"What about you? Maybe you would be interested in our competition?"

"Me?" Louise laughed. "Oh no, Rabbi. Thank you for the offer, but no."

"You said you're not doing anything extra this summer. What if you're supposed to have fun, perhaps?"

"I haven't done serious dancing in years," she said.

"Ah ha!" He waggled his fingers in pretend exasperation. "But you *have* danced before? Maybe you should be one of our experienced dancers?"

"Oh no, not at all."

He shrugged again. "I tried. You want you should take this flyer, in case you change your mind?"

"Of course." She accepted the paper as a courtesy. "When you and Gail are not busy with your dance club, you should come out to Grace Chapel Inn. We'd love to have you join us for dinner."

"Food is something about which I never change my mind." He winked. "Just say the word and we'll be there. Meanwhile, I see our friend Cyrus is finished with his discussion. I'd better talk to him before he gets involved with something else. It was nice to see you, Louise."

"You, too, Rabbi. Give our regards to Gail."

He nodded and moved to speak with Cyrus. Louise had had enough of browsing; she paid for her purchases and stepped outdoors. The idea of shopping was no longer as enticing as it had been, so she found a café with a small patio facing the street. She ordered an iced tea and sat at a wrought-iron table with an Italian umbrella overhead for shade and watched for Alice.

While sipping the cool beverage, she studied the flyer Rabbi Cohen had given her. She and her late husband Eliot had been fond of dancing and had, in fact, been members of a Philadelphia dance club that no doubt was similar to the one in Potterston. They had learned all manner of dance styles, participating for years and eventually competing on a local level simply for fun. They had loved the physical exercise and the sheer artistic beauty of the art form—and yes, the romance.

She missed many things about Eliot, but oddly enough she hadn't thought of dancing in a long time. She had pledged her heart to Eliot Smith many years ago, and no one could ever take his place. Particularly on the dance floor. And what would Cynthia, her thirty-four-year-old daughter, think?

Louise laughed softly as she thought of Rabbi Cohen's invitation. *Imagine, a dancing competition! I'm afraid my dancing days are well behind me.*

Alice found the social services building where Lilia worked. The lot was nearly full, but she pulled her Toyota into the last available visitors' spot. The red brick building seemed to have been built about the same time as the ones on Main Street, but whereas those were maintained to appeal to tourists and shoppers, the social services building was off the beaten track and had fallen into disrepair. Broad-leafed weeds and dandelions grew in the cracks of the walkway. The concrete steps were chipped, and the wooden handrail needed replacing—or at least a fresh coat of paint. Thank goodness the street address was painted over the front door, or Alice might have imagined herself lost. She had the impression that not many people concerned themselves with the building. She hoped the same could not be said for the workers within, or the clients they served.

Inside the building, she found a directory posted next to an ancient-looking elevator with scarred metal doors. Finding Lilia's name and office number listed, she pressed the up button and waited. At last the elevator creaked down the shaft. When it opened, an old-fashioned cross-hatched metal gate slowly moved to one side, admitting Alice into the car. She half expected to see an elevator man in a pillbox hat, asking for her floor. The elevator didn't offer sophistication so much as nostalgia. She hoped that the mechanics of the conveyance had kept pace with changing technology.

She tapped her foot as she ascended to the third floor and was relieved to be deposited at her destination with no mishap. Outside the elevator, scuffed linoleum led down a plain hallway to Lilia's office. Alice took a deep breath and entered.

She expected to find a waiting room with a reception-ist, but surprisingly, she found herself in a small, cramped but colorful office filled with stuffed bookcases and an assortment of ivies and ferns. A circular rag rug covered the floor from doorway to desk, its circumference ringed with beanbags and director's chairs. Just the sort of furniture teens would love.

Behind the desk sat Lilia Joly, bent over an enormous book at her left hand and a pad of paper at her right. She looked up. "Hi! I didn't hear you come in. I get so absorbed in my work that I sometimes lose track of where I am. It's so good to see you."

"Hello, Lilia," Alice said warmly. "It's good to see you too."

Lilia pushed back her tattered vinyl office chair, its casters squeaking against linoleum. Her extended stomach barely cleared the desk, and she laughed. "I bet I look a lot different from how you remember me last."

"You look just fine." Alice smiled. "You're the picture of health."

Lilia laid a hand on her stomach. "I don't feel quite like that, unfortunately. The pregnancy is going fine, but I've been feeling a bit ungainly the past month. Like an obese duck."

"That's normal for someone at your stage. You won't be waddling forever."

"Have a seat, Alice. Um, you might want to grab one

of those director's chairs. The beanbags sit pretty low to the ground."

Alice pulled up a chair by the desk, glancing for any side doors to the office. "Do you work by yourself?"

Lilia shuffled her book and paper out of the way, nodding. "It's just me. Our organization doesn't have much money, certainly not enough for another employee. My girls and I make do, however, but it's poor timing for me to have the baby this summer. It's our busiest time, with the girls being out of school."

She sighed, resting her chin in her hands. "I am *so* glad that you agreed to help me out. You were the first person I thought of to help, but honestly, I don't know who else I would have—or could have—called on."

"What exactly will I be doing?"

"The girls are helping out three days a week in a free day care. That way they keep busy and offer a service to the community. The day care runs on grants, so obviously we can't afford to pay them. However, we provide fun activities for their days off. You'll meet with them two days a week. I've already lined up lots of activities for a reduced rate at several places in the area. The rec center offers a climbing wall, as well as volleyball, basketball, weights and a swimming pool. Crazy Jack's Racetrack offers go-cart racing—"

"Go-carts?" Alice said, her stomach flipping at the thought.

"The girls love it. You will too."

Alice swallowed and reserved comment.

"Then there's white-water rafting. I think I'd save that for one of the final weeks. It can be a bit of a workout, and it's good to build up to it. For one thing, it gives the girls a chance to become acquainted before they have to face that challenge. Some of them have been with me for a while, but others are new. I'm sure alliances will shift until they realize that they're all part of a team."

"It's a bit different from the ANGELs," Alice said. "We don't normally have such physical activities."

"These girls are a little bit older than your junior high girls. I've found that plenty of physical activity keeps their minds and bodies occupied. It's when they're bored that they're more likely to get into trouble—boys, drugs, you name it."

"So sometimes I'll be spending all day with them?"

Lilia nodded. "We provide them a sack lunch. Do you have a car?"

"I have a small Toyota."

"Does it have enough space and seat belts for four girls?"

Alice nodded, then breathed an inward sigh of relief. "They're only four? I thought there might be a large number."

"Nope, only four," Lilia said cheerfully. "Do you mind driving them to the various locations?"

Alice shook her head. "But surely they won't spend eight hours climbing walls or swimming, will they?"

"Not at all. What I've found works best is to spend at least half the day on some sort of physical activity and the rest on something quieter. A character-building activity or something like a simple sewing lesson. Maybe a movie with a good, wholesome story. Some sort of fun like we used to have in the ANGELs."

"Perhaps they'd like to go to Acorn Hill occasionally," Alice said. "Most of them are from Potterston, aren't they?"

"I'm sure they'd love to see Acorn Hill. Carlene Moss could show them all the old typesetting equipment at the *Acorn Nutshell*, or they could tour Town Hall. Whatever you think might be interesting. In fact, I wanted to meet with you in person to make sure this was something you really wanted to pursue, and if so, to get you brainstorming. If you're sure about participating, perhaps you can suggest activities." She pushed a paper across the desk. "I've made a list of the physical activities, but feel free to add more. And of course any quiet-time activities you want to add."

Alice smiled. "I don't think these girls would be content to make biblical stick figures out of Popsicle sticks, but I'm sure I can come up with something. I'll be glad to help, Lilia."

The younger woman sighed. "Thank you, Alice. I'm so glad I can leave my girls in capable hands. And just because I can't actively participate doesn't mean I won't be in touch. You can call me any time—every day, in fact—and ask for advice or suggestions."

"Thank you." Alice rose.

Lilia stood, too, and held out her hand. "What am I doing?" She smiled at the formality of the professional gesture and pulled Alice into an embrace instead, made awkward by her advanced pregnancy. They shared a laugh. "Maybe the handshake was a better idea after all," Lilia said.

Chapter Four

*I*nside Lloyd Tynan's office, Jane and Craig took their chairs, while Lloyd sat at his desk. Bella poked her head through the doorway. "If you don't need me, I think I'll head home."

"Go right ahead. I'll see you tomorrow," Lloyd said. He clasped his hands on his desk and faced Jane and Craig. "Now, tell me what you discovered today."

Craig showed him the clipboard with the filled-in pages. "We only went to three houses. One of them seems to be doing well. The second was vacant."

"In the last house on the road was an elderly lady— I think she said she was ninety-five," Jane said. "Bernice Sayers. She thought your father was still mayor."

Lloyd smiled. "It must have been quite a while since she's been in town."

"I think so," Jane said. "At any rate, she needs help, Lloyd. She doesn't have any way to get groceries other than to rely on the kindness of her neighbor."

"And she's partially blind," Craig added. "Actually, *mostly* blind."

"I don't know what she does all day," Jane said. "I didn't see a radio or a TV. Not that she could see the television, anyway. Obviously reading is out."

"She does have a dog for a companion, but that's about it. She doesn't even have any family in the area."

Lloyd leaned back in his chair and put his hands behind his head. "This is exactly the kind of person we need to reach. Do you have any suggestions?"

Jane felt somewhat useless at the moment. Where would they even begin to get Bernice Sayers the aid that she needed?

"We should survey some other people and get a better idea of what our broad needs are," Craig said.

"Wisdom if I've ever heard it," Lloyd said.

"But what about Bernice?" Jane asked.

"I don't feel that Acorn Hill can help her until we have a bigger picture of what our citizens need," Lloyd said. "We can't start a food drive for just one person."

"Why not?" Jane knew she sounded stubborn, but she couldn't see waiting for all the red tape to be cut.

"I have to agree with Lloyd," Craig said. "It wouldn't be practical to direct our energies to individual cases. We can meet more needs if we plan to be efficient."

"So if no one else we survey needs help with food, are you saying we still won't help Bernice?"

"Jane...," Lloyd said.

Realizing how she must have sounded, Jane shook her head. "I'm sorry, Lloyd. I know what you and Craig say makes sense. I'm just eager to help, that's all."

Lloyd smiled. "I know your heart, and I'm glad you're concerned. You and Craig do some more canvassing. We'll pool your results with those that we get from other volunteers. We should have some solid answers in a week or two. Keep up the good work. We'll get help for your new friend. Don't worry."

When Louise and Alice returned home, they headed to their rooms. The guests' rooms were on the second floor and the sisters' on the third. When they redecorated and remodeled their family home as an inn, they took great pains to make sure that their own rooms reflected their individuality. The youngest and most modern of the sisters, Jane had painted her walls in a reddish purple eggplant color and filled the room with blond Danish furniture. She decorated the walls with her own artwork, paintings representing the seasons of her life. Alice's room reflected her homespun nature with its buttery yellow walls, antique patchwork quilt of pastel yellow, green and violet, and a hand-braided rug in matching colors.

Louise's room had a more Victorian feel with its floral wallpaper and green woodwork. She always felt right at home when she retired to her room, as she did now, to freshen up for the evening. Gathering a light sweater in anticipation of a cool evening in the parlor, she decided to try out some of the new sheet music she had purchased for her piano pupils.

As she reached the bottom of the stairs, however, the phone rang at the reception desk. She made her way to it. "Grace Chapel Inn," she said automatically.

"Louise Howard, please."

"Speaking."

"Oh, hi. This is Gail Cohen. I'm Ben Cohen's wife."

"Hello, Mrs. Cohen. I just saw your husband today in the music store."

"That's why I'm calling. I know we've never met, but he told me that you two spoke about our dance club's competition."

"Yes, we did," Louise said, bewildered.

"I understand that you and your late husband used to be quite the dancers."

Louise was shocked into silence. She couldn't recall having said anything about Eliot to Rabbi Cohen.

Gail laughed. "I'm confusing you, I'm sure. You see, after you left Scales and Arpeggios, Ben ran into one of our dance club members, Erik Shams. Your name came up in conversation, and it seems that Erik knew you and your husband from a dance club in Philadelphia."

Louise remembered the young man—probably no longer a *young* man—from the days when Eliot taught at the music conservatory. Erik had been a student at a local college and an avid club member. "I haven't seen him in years. How is he?"

"He's quite well. When he told Ben that you and your husband had been one of the more talented couples in the dance club, Ben knew that we had to appeal to your love of dancing."

Louise blinked. "For what?"

"Why, to participate in our competition this summer, of course. Since you're an experienced dancer, we'd like to pair you with a beginner."

"You mean…you want me to show the way?"

Gail laughed. "Naturally. What do you say?"

Louise was stunned. "I can't believe that Erik remembers Eliot and me that way. It seems like a lifetime ago. I don't know, Gail. It would seem like a rather forward thing to do. I haven't dated any men since my husband died."

"Date, schmate. This is dancing, that's all. If I can be bold, Louise, I think it would do you good to have some fun. Ben told me how busy you are teaching piano and running the inn. Besides…it's summertime. Don't you ever get the urge to do something different, to try something new, especially during the summer months?"

"Well…"

"And listen. Ben and I are dancers too. I know that once it's in your blood, you don't want to give it up forever."

Louise thought for a moment. "Would you pair me with someone close to my age?"

"I have the perfect person in mind for you. He's eager to learn the different dance styles, and I think you'll find him an apt student. He's the athletic type."

Louise pictured a golfer or perhaps a tennis player. "If you really need my help…"

"I would consider it a good deed to help out fellow dancers in a pinch."

"All right." Louise let out a breath, wondering what she was getting herself into. "Where do we meet and when?"

"Thank you, Louise. We're meeting tomorrow at the dance studio in the Potterston Rec Center at seven o'clock. Don't forget to wear comfortable shoes."

Because of the sisters' activities, dinner was somewhat late that night. They would have no guests until the next day, so they followed no timetable for meals. None of them was particularly hungry either, so Jane prepared a summer vegetable salad made with zucchinis, summer squash, mushrooms and cherry tomatoes. After they had all helped to clean the dishes and stack them in the dishwasher, they retired to the living room.

The room had been faux painted in gold and had a creamy white wainscoting. The fireplace certainly wasn't needed tonight, but during the winter it was a welcome center around which they gathered. Their mother Madeleine's antique rocker sat in a corner, more as a tribute than as a piece they used with any regularity. Jane ensconced herself on the burgundy-colored sofa while Alice took the matching overstuffed chair. Louise sat straight at the other end of the sofa, smiling as she gently pushed Jane's feet aside to make room.

"Sorry," Jane said sheepishly. "I've been on the go all day, but that doesn't excuse me from invading your territory."

"You're perfectly welcome to encroach on my side as long as you leave me enough room to sit," Louise said good-naturedly.

"Thanks, Louie," Jane said, using the term of endearment

for Louise that normally she only employed when she wanted to tease her eldest sister. She propped a throw pillow under her head and stretched out her legs as far as possible without touching Louise.

Alice picked up a mystery novel she had left on a nearby table, while Louise reached into a knitting bag beside the couch and withdrew her latest project.

With one eye open, Jane studied her. "Are you knitting anything in particular?"

"I thought I'd make another baby blanket. They're fast and fun to do. Even though it's warm now, I thought it would be nice to make some before fall arrives."

"That's nice," Jane murmured, burrowing into the pillow, both eyes closed. Alice continued her reading, gaze focused intently as she turned the pages.

Louise knitted a few stitches, then said calmly, "I've agreed to participate in a dance competition."

Jane opened first one eye, then the other. "What did you say, Louise?"

Alice looked up from her book.

Louise continued her knitting. "I said that I'd agreed to participate in a dance competition."

Jane sat upright. "Who with?"

"I don't know *with whom* I'll be dancing, but I was invited by Rabbi Cohen and his wife, Gail. They're in a dance club at Potterston, and they're doing some sort of *Dancing with the Stars*—type competition, where they match beginners with more experienced dancers."

"So you're the beginner half of the couple?"

"*Humph!*" Louise set down her knitting.

Alice smiled at Jane. "You were in San Francisco when Louise and Eliot lived in Philadelphia, Jane. They were members of a dance club there. I never saw them dance myself, but I understand they were a pretty good pair."

"We could hold our own on the dance floor," Louise said.

"Wow, Louie! I'm impressed." Jane set the throw pillow aside. "I didn't know that about you. What sort of dance steps did you do?"

"All types." Louise shrugged.

"Come on, Louise. Out with it." Jane's eyes glowed. "Did you do the fox-trot?"

"Yes."

"The tango?"

"Yes."

Jane grinned. "This is getting more and more interesting. What was your favorite dance step?"

Louise thought for a moment. "Eliot and I were rather partial to the Lindy Hop."

"Get *out!* I thought you'd say something like the waltz. I can't believe this is my big sister Louise talking."

"It's not as though I were Isadora Duncan, Jane."

"You're sure you don't know who your partner will be?"

Louise shook her head. "I'm supposed to find out tomorrow when we meet for our first lesson."

"Do you know anything about him?"

"*Now* you sound like you're a teenager, checking your big sister's date."

Alice smiled. "Some things never change, Louise. Just humor her and eventually her curiosity will be satisfied. Right, Jane?"

"Maybe," she said, hugging her knees to her chest. "Now, come on. Tell. What do you know about him?"

Louise sighed. "The only thing Gail said about him was that he was eager to learn, an apt pupil and the athletic type."

"Maybe he's a Little Leaguer," Jane teased. "Or a pee-wee football player."

"Now, Jane. That's enough," Alice said.

"Did Gail say how *old* your partner would be?"

Louise thought back. "Actually, no. I asked her if he would be near my age, but she didn't answer. Oh dear."

"I'm sure he will be," Alice said, shooting Jane a quieting look.

The message evidently was received. "I'm sure he will be too." Jane smiled gently at Louise. "I know you still miss Eliot. I just want you to have some happiness doing something you love. You work hard with your piano students, too hard sometimes, I think. I want you to have fun for fun's sake. Promise me you will, okay?"

Louise smiled. "I'll try, Jane. I do know that you were only teasing."

"Maybe if you think of your dance partner as just another student, it won't feel quite so daunting," Alice said.

"That's right," Jane said. "You love to teach. This will be something new. There's no reason you can't teach *and* have fun, right?"

Louise drew a deep breath. She had committed to helping the Cohens, so there was no backing out now. She might as well make the best of it. "Right."

The next morning, Jane and Craig headed out in his pickup. Again he displayed the sign saying that he would be back at noon. Once they were headed to a new location, they discussed their canvassing hours. "I think by now most people in Acorn Hill know what we're doing, so if they need me, they won't show up until the afternoon. If they know in advance they need me, they can always phone. You and I have a flexible schedule."

"We certainly do. We have guests arriving today. But unless there's anything special I need to do, once I get breakfast cooked, served and cleaned up, I'm free until twelve." Jane rolled down the window and sniffed the air. "It smells great outside. All warm, clean and bright. I'm glad Lloyd didn't decide to do this during winter."

"That reminds me. We should ask the people we meet about their ability to heat their homes during the colder months. It might be that we can help out during that period."

"Good idea." Jane scribbled a note on the clipboard.

Craig turned down a gravel road not too far from Bonnie Ethedridge's. Instead of mobile homes, however, the rural acreage was dotted with small, older homes that looked as though they had been built during the first half of the last century.

"I think this was a new development during the 1930s and 1940s," Jane said. Craig was not a native of Acorn Hill, so she doubted he was familiar with the town's history from that period.

"Isn't it a little far out of town to be a development?"

"I believe they thought the town would grow out this

way, but it never did." She paused. "My father grew up in a rural area."

"Near Acorn Hill?"

"No, Englishtown. Right off a country road like this one." She glanced out the window thoughtfully. "Englishtown doesn't exist anymore. I wonder if this area will go the same way."

Craig pulled up at the first house, a weathered gray home. Shutters that had lost their paint and been removed sat stacked next to the front door. Jane rang the doorbell and waited a respectable amount of time. When no one appeared, however, she knocked loudly on the door. The door, peeling and chipped, looked as though it might cave in under her knuckles.

Again, they waited a respectable time with no response. Jane turned to leave. "I guess no one's—"

"Who is it and what do you want?" a quivering female voice asked behind the door.

"Ma'am, we're Craig Tracy and Jane Howard," he said. "We're here as representatives from Acorn Hill on behalf of Lloyd Ty—"

"I'm not interested in whatever you're peddling."

"We're not selling anything," Jane said, using her best cajoling voice. "We only want to ask you a few questions so that we can determine—"

"Go away, I'm not interested, I said."

Craig tried one more time. "But we—"

"I've got a baseball bat in my hands and I'm not afraid to use it!"

Jane and Craig shared a glance. "Time to cut our losses," Jane murmured. Craig nodded his agreement.

"We'll leave, then," he said. "Please contact Mayor Tynan if you have any concerns or need any assistance from the town."

"I don't want the government poking into my business, and I don't need charity."

"All right, ma'am. Sorry to bother you." Jane felt as if she couldn't get back to the pickup fast enough. "Whew!" she said, once they were safe in the truck and backing out of the driveway. "Do you think she meant what she said?"

"I doubt it. She's probably just old and suspicious of strangers."

Jane laughed. "I've heard of people being afraid of revenuers. Did you get the feeling we were back in the 1930s, and she thought we were government officials looking for moonshine?"

Craig laughed too. "That *was* a bit ridiculous. Maybe one of her neighbors can tell us something about her though. I'd hate for her to be the type that really needs help but is too proud to accept it."

The next house was a faded yellow two-story with white shutters and a rickety detached garage around back. They headed up the crumbling stoop to the wooden planked porch. Half off its hinges, a wooden screen door creaked when Jane knocked. "I'll be there in a minute," a voice said from the home's interior.

Eventually a corpulent woman with gray-flecked dark hair appeared at the door. She wore polyester pants and blouse, covered by a folksy floral apron. "Sorry about making you wait," she said, wiping her hands on the apron. "Dad's puttering in his workshop and I was cleaning up the kitchen."

Craig explained why they were there, and the woman listened intently. When he finished, she smiled. "What a nice idea. We don't get into town much, but I know Mayor Tynan by sight. It's good of him to worry about us who live out this way."

"So you don't mind answering a few questions?" Jane asked.

"Not at all." She pushed open the screen door. "Come on in."

The woman had a hodgepodge of worn but clean furniture from different time periods—a 1940s vintage sofa with a high back and rolled arms, a 1960s Eames-type chair, a Papasan loveseat and 1970s swag lamps. A lava lamp sat on a pair of tall, bulky speakers attached to what would have been called a hi-fi in the 1950s. Though she felt as though she had walked into a collectibles store, Jane noticed that the room was immaculate.

"Pick your favorite chair," the woman said, waving vaguely at the furniture assortment. Jane chose the Papasan, while Craig gravitated toward the Eames. The woman perched on the edge of the sofa. "Now tell me what kind of questions I can answer for you."

Craig cleared his throat and started reading off his list. By now, the questions were rote, so he rattled them off with scarcely a pause. The woman listened carefully, then held up a hand. "First of all, my name is Inge Starr. If you need my age, I'm thirty. I live here, where I was born and raised, with my parents. I was married for five years, but that didn't work out, so I moved back home. My parents' names are Thomas and Dotty Gilpin."

"Are they in good health?" Jane asked. She wondered if Inge was too, given that she likely weighed close to three hundred pounds.

Inge nodded. "They're fine. They're only in their sixties. Would you like to meet them?"

"Of course," Craig said.

Inge led them to the kitchen. Like the living room, the kitchen decor was a mixture of different time periods— a chrome table with a Formica top, yellow vinyl chairs, a braided rag rug underfoot and a cat-with-a-swinging-tail clock. The cabinets and appliances, however, looked as though they had been installed straight from the latest home trends magazine: a stylish ceramic-tile floor, stainless-steel refrigerator, stove and double oven, and marble countertops with coordinated white glass-front cabinets.

"Your kitchen is…different," Jane said.

Inge laughed. "All of our house is. We like so many different styles that we can't pick just one. We throw it all together, sort of like a tossed salad." She shrugged. "It's not for everybody. Mom!" She pushed open a door to the backyard. "There are some people here to see us."

"I'm out here," a woman's voice responded.

Inge shut the door. "She likes to garden. Dad must have gone out to the garage, but we can track him down."

"We don't want to interrupt," Jane said, thinking that perhaps the man was tinkering with a car.

"It's no bother. I'm sure he'd love for you to see his trains."

"Model trains?" Craig asked. "I've love to see them."

"Then you're in for a rare treat. Right this way." Inge led

them through the door and along a flagstone path toward the garage.

"Hi there!" A woman whom Jane assumed to be Inge's mother waved at them from the yard. Wearing a huge straw hat with a red grosgrain ribbon, Dotty Gilpin knelt in the dirt on a foam gardening pad to protect her knees. She held a small spade and scooped potting soil from a voluminous bag into several terra-cotta pots. An assortment of summer plants—marigolds, petunias and zinnias—sat in their nursery flats.

"Mom, these folks are from town. They're doing a census."

"Nice to meet you, ma'am," Craig said. "This is Jane Howard, and I'm Craig Tracy."

Jane nodded her acknowledgment as well.

Dotty rose a bit stiffly. "Welcome, both. You're the florist, aren't you, Mr. Tracy?"

"Yes, ma'am."

"I'd love to chat with you sometime about gardening."

"Come visit the store. I'd be glad to chat. Seeds and plants will cost you, but the advice is free."

Dotty's face fell. "I don't get into town much. I don't drive."

"Maybe your husband or your daughter could take you," Craig said.

Dotty knelt on the foam pad again as though ending the conversation. "It was nice to meet you both," she said, turning back to her pots.

Inge blushed. "Are you ready to see the model trains?"

Jane and Craig nodded, speechless. What had upset Dotty Gilpin?

Chapter Five

*A*lice took a deep breath as she pulled up outside the building where Lilia Joly worked. They had agreed that the first meeting with the girls should be in a familiar location. After that, if Alice wanted to arrange a different place for them to get together, she could feel free to do so. Alice's primary interest was in making sure the girls were comfortable with her and that the transition would go smoothly.

"Thanks for coming early," Lilia said when Alice entered her office. She gestured around the room. "You can have your pick of the seats."

Alice glanced at the assortment and laughed. "I don't think I can manage a beanbag."

Lilia pulled up a director's chair, one with sky blue panels. "Then have a real seat."

Alice barely had time to settle herself before the door burst open. A teenage girl with long brown hair and mocha-colored skin entered, tugging a denim skirt down as far as it would go—which was well above her knees. Lilia gave her a hug, then a mock frown. "What have I told you about wearing skirts that are too short?"

"I forgot," the girl said, giggling.

Another girl pushed in behind the first one, a large girl in a too-tight tank top with a rose tattoo on her upper left arm. Like her friend's skirt, her shorts were shorter than decorum required. In Alice's estimation, they did nothing to enhance her chubby figure either. The girl seemed glad to see Lilia—her eyes twinkling and mouth smiling—but wary at the same time, stepping neatly away from a hug. "So what's up for today?"

Lilia gently persisted in putting her arm around her, and Alice noticed that the girl flinched. "First I want you to meet a friend. This is Alice Howard. Alice, this is Esmeralda Vale and her friend with the short skirt here is Isidra Kreisman."

Isidra giggled and nodded. "It's nice to meet you, Mrs. Howard."

"Just Miss," Alice said, smiling warmly. "I never married." She held out her hand and Isidra shook it, though she looked slightly perplexed by the adult greeting. "It's nice to meet you girls." Alice turned to shake Esmeralda's hand, but the girl had already moved past her into the room, disdaining any salutation or even small talk. She plopped down in a beanbag and glanced around the room as though surveying her kingdom.

"Like I said, what's up today?"

"Esmeralda," Lilia said softly. "What have we mentioned about manners?"

The girl rolled her eyes and extracted herself from the chair. "Sorry," she said less than sincerely, extending her right hand.

Alice shook it. "It's nice to meet you. *Esmeralda* is a lovely name."

"Yeah, thanks." The girl sank back into the chair. Isidra took another beanbag beside her, and they launched into a private conversation.

Lilia smiled apologetically at Alice, then turned to greet another guest. "Ah, Julie!"

A tall, thin, freckle-faced girl with strawberry blonde hair pulled back in a ponytail stepped hesitantly into the room. She barely glanced up from the floor, where all her attention seemed focused. "Hi, Lilia," she mumbled in return.

A fourth—and presumably the final—girl in the group rushed around the doorjamb, panting. "I hurried," she said, her face dewy with light perspiration under a terry cloth headband. Her deep brown eyes looked concerned. "Am I late?"

Lilia put her arms around both of the latest arrivals, ushering them into the room. "You're both right on time. Running again, Sabrina?"

The last girl nodded, and Alice noticed that she wore runner's shorts, shoes and a light athletic T-shirt. "I've got to stay in shape if I want to be on the track team this fall."

"Yeah, yeah, big deal," Esmeralda said, picking at a ragged cuticle. "The track team."

"I think it's pretty cool," the blonde—Julie—said.

"Yeah?" Esmeralda looked up. "Who asked you, Stick?"

"Girls!" Lilia said. "Julie Pepperell, Sabrina Ordonez, meet Alice Howard."

"Hi!" Sabrina said. "I'd shake your hand, but it's a little sweaty."

"Grab a towel out of that cabinet there," Lilia said.

"Hello, Julie," Alice said, extending her hand. The girl shook it listlessly, mumbling a reply.

"Have a seat." Lilia and Alice returned to their chairs. Sabrina, the towel retrieved and put to use wiping her hands and face, sat next to Alice. Julie sat on the floor, slightly apart from the rest of the group.

Lilia smiled. "You all know I'm going on maternity leave soon, right?"

"You're kidding!" Isidra pretended mock exaggeration, eyeing Lilia's extended stomach, then smiled.

Lilia laughed. "I've been ordered to take my leave a little sooner than I'd thought, so I've asked an old friend of mine, Alice here, to help us out."

"*Old* friend is right," Esmeralda murmured.

"As I was saying," Lilia continued, shooting a glance at the girl, "Alice is a dear friend. She mentored me when I was about your age. I was in her ANGELs group at Grace Chapel in Acorn Hill, where she lives. She and her two sisters run Grace Chapel Inn, which is a bed-and-breakfast. Yes, Isidra?"

The girl lowered her hand. "What is your ANGELs group?"

Alice launched into an explanation about her middle school group for girls. Sabrina raised her hand, then without waiting to be called on, asked, "Why is your group called ANGELs?"

Alice and Lilia shared a smile. "The group's name is an acronym—A-N-G-E-L—but each letter's meaning is a secret that only members know," Lilia said.

"Hey! Maybe we should have a secret name for our group," Isidra said.

Esmeralda poked her. "We already have a name, but it's no secret. We're the at-risk girls."

Sabrina wrinkled her nose. "I like that. A-R-G."

"Yeah!" Esmeralda put her hands around her throat and pretended to choke herself. "Arrrggh!"

Alice was the first to laugh. "I'm glad to see you have a sense of humor."

The others continued to laugh, but Esmeralda put her hands down and frowned.

"So," Lilia said to break the tension. "Why don't we discuss what you girls will be doing this summer?"

"Sports, I hope." Sabrina popped her headband for emphasis.

Lilia nodded. "Besides introducing you to Alice today, I thought that we could talk about what activities you all wanted to try. Alice and I have a few suggestions, so see what you think."

As Lilia went down the list of suggestions, Alice studied the girls. Sabrina and Isidra looked enthusiastic. Julie, who hadn't said a word since she'd sat down, played with the zipper on her light jacket, casting occasional nervous glances at the others. Her gaze met Alice's, and the girl quickly looked down.

Esmeralda appeared to listen to Lilia's suggestions, but she merely shrugged when asked her opinion. Her attitude signaled that she would go along with whatever was decided, but Alice wondered if she was already bored. Perhaps she didn't want to be here, or perhaps she didn't want anyone to replace Lilia.

Alice smiled to herself. Over the years, some of her ANGELs had been reluctant participants, attending the meetings only because their parents insisted. Somehow they had always found something at the group to keep them returning. Alice often had to dig deep to find out what made the more recalcitrant girls tick, but all had eventually enjoyed becoming a part of the group.

What would the enticement be for Esmeralda Vale?

Alice thought about the girls during the drive back to Acorn Hill. She hadn't cut short their meeting, but she hadn't lingered either. She had promised Louise that she would be home in time to help her with their arriving guests. Jane would join them as well after she and Craig finished surveying, but the two weren't certain exactly when they would be back.

When she arrived, she saw an unfamiliar car parked at Grace Chapel Inn and knew that at least one of their guests had arrived. Louise greeted her as she entered, meeting her at the door.

"How did your meeting with the girls go?" she asked.

"A little rocky," Alice confessed, "but I think it will work out fine."

"You've always had such fun with your ANGELs and made such a difference in their lives. I'm sure this group won't be any different," Louise said reassuringly.

"Speaking of groups, I see that some guests have arrived."

Louise nodded. "I just showed two of our guests to their rooms. They're good friends, both working on their graduate dissertations. They expressly asked that we keep it as quiet as possible while they work."

"Oh dear. We're fairly quiet people, of course, but don't we have two families arriving. . . with children?"

"Yes. We'll have to hope the parents make it clear to the young ones that they must be courteous toward our other guests."

Louise headed for the kitchen to check on some marinating zucchini. Alice lingered at the reception desk, checking future reservations and e-mail on Grace Chapel Inn's computer. When she heard footfalls on the staircase, she came out from behind the desk to greet their guests.

Two twenty-something women, one blonde, the other brunette, chatted amiably. The blonde wore thick black glasses and sweats. The brunette had pulled her hair back in a severe ponytail, went without makeup, and wore baggy jeans and a faded red T-shirt.

Alice cleared her throat to get their attention, but to no avail. "Ahem." She tried again, and this time they stopped talking and turned.

"I'm Alice Howard, one of your hostesses," she said, extending a hand. "My sister Louise said she checked you in."

"She did." The blonde smiled, shaking Alice's hand. "I'm Janette Frappier."

"And I'm Glenna Moline." The brunette shook Alice's hand as well. "This is a beautiful place you have, Miss Howard. And so quiet! We were looking for a small town. We saw the shopping area as we drove in, and it looks quiet as well."

"I've lived here all my life, and I can vouch that Acorn Hill is seldom noisy. As I recall, you'll be staying for several weeks."

"That's right." Janette nodded. "We're staying into August. We hope to get lots of work done on our dissertations, and it's too noisy in our apartment in Philadelphia to be productive."

"We received grant money to assist us, so we decided a

bed-and-breakfast in the country would be a great idea," Glenna finished.

"So it is," Alice said. "We've had several writers stay here. I'm sure you'll find that our librarian, Nia Komonos, will be glad to assist with any research needs you might have."

"Thanks," Janette said. "We'll probably need some help."

"I hope you've had a chance to get settled. Which rooms do you have?" Alice asked.

"The ones at the back of the house with the adjoining bath. We're used to sharing," Glenna said.

"I took what your sister called the Symphony Room, since I like music so much," Janette said. "I love the climbing-rose wallpaper."

"And I took the Sunrise Room," Glenna said. "I really like the colors. The patchwork quilt and the landscape picture make it feel so homey."

"I'm glad you like the rooms. Louise and Jane and I had fun fixing up the house for our guests."

Janette and Glenna looked at one another, then at Alice. "We were wondering... We're headed into town for some lunch. Can you recommend a place for us?"

"The Coffee Shop. The food is good and the price is right."

The young women thanked her, then headed toward the door. Alice watched them go. It wasn't her place to say, but she thought they bore some resemblance to her at-risk girls, with their unkempt clothing and hair. She could understand their wanting to be comfortable while they wrote, secluded in their rooms, but going out in public?

Alice shook her head. She was being too critical. Times had changed since she was their age, and she shouldn't be concerned.

Jane and Craig finished surveying the older subdevelopment near Acorn Hill and headed toward the eastern corner of the town. "Where to now, boss?" Craig asked.

Jane studied the map. "Take your next right."

Craig obediently turned the pickup. This time they were not in a rural area; however, it was a part of Acorn Hill where people seldom ventured because there was little commerce. They passed a lone video rental store that, judging by the weeds growing in the parking lot and the shabbiness of the marquee, had long since gone out of business. The same could be said of a small, aged drive-in, fast-food building with individual lanes that looked as though it had been popular during the 1950s.

"I remember that place," Jane said. "My father used to take us there occasionally when I was very young. The carhops—"

"Carhops?" Craig grinned.

"Waitresses who came to your car," Jane said. "You'd pull up to the speaker phone, place your order, and the carhops would bring your order out on a tray, which hooked on the partially rolled-down window of your car."

"Oh, I remember places like that," Craig said. "And the carhops were on roller skates?"

"Yes! All the teenagers would hang out there, which made me want to grow older quickly so that I could hang out with them as well. They always looked so sophisticated on dates."

"I wonder if your sisters ever went there, since they're older than you," Craig mused.

Jane grinned. "I'll have to ask them. What was the name of that place? The sign's so old, it's hard to see. Oh, wait, I have it. Cameron's. Cameron's Drive-In."

Craig shook his head. "There's certainly not much left in this area at all. It looks as though everything's been closed for quite a while."

"Not everything. Turn left at the next intersection."

A lonely gas station was all that stood at the intersection, and Jane wouldn't have thought it was still functioning except for the attendant she could see inside. "Are we going here?" Craig asked.

Jane shook her head. "That building just beside it. Pull into the parking lot."

Craig did so. The lot could comfortably accommodate at least twenty cars, but there was only one other car in it, an old Buick that had seen better days. Craig hunched down so that he could read the chipped, raised letters on the gray-brick building. "Three Seasons Community. Three? Why not Four Seasons?"

Jane shrugged. "I guess we'll find out."

They walked inside. A sixtyish woman with a bouffant blonde hairdo that had been popular forty years before smiled at them from behind a receptionist's window. Slightly plump, she was squeezed into a loud print dress, and Jane could see that her knee-high stockings were rolled down at her ankles. "Can I help you?"

Jane wondered if the woman wrapped her hair in a net at night to keep its shape. "We're here as representatives of Acorn Hill, taking a census." She introduced herself and Craig.

"May we speak to the residents here?" Craig asked.

The woman nodded and smiled. "You sure can. They'd

love to have some company. Nobody much visits here. Most of our residents don't have any family, or at least any family that cares about them. By the way, my name's Elena Nole."

"Nice to meet you." Craig shook her hand. "Should we speak to the manager of Three Seasons to make sure we aren't disturbing anyone's privacy?"

Elena drew herself up to her full height, which couldn't, by Jane's estimation, top four foot eleven. "Honey, I *am* the manager. I'm the manager, receptionist and sometimes even the dishwasher. Why don't I go with you?"

She disappeared for a moment, then reappeared through a door leading to the lobby. She adjusted her hair and straightened her dress. "There. Now I'm ready."

Though the lobby was filled with comfortable-looking modern sofas and chairs in matching autumn colors, the room was empty. An unseen music system played Big Band music at a soft level. "Some of our residents like to dance occasionally," Elena said. She gestured at the furniture for them to sit.

Jane and Craig sat on a rust-colored sofa. "Dance? Are most of your residents fairly mobile?" Jane asked.

"Oh yes, they're all ambulatory. We're not a nursing home —more like a dormitory set up for old folks who enjoy one another's company. Other than helping them keep track of their medicine, they're very much on their own."

"What happens if they need medical attention on a regular basis?" Craig asked.

"Then they must move to another facility." Elena sighed. "That's the problem. Many of our former residents have moved on to Potterston for better medical attention. I want to keep the costs down here, so I've had to let a lot of the staff go. I don't want to raise the cost for my people. Most of them are living on fixed incomes."

"How many residents do you have?" Jane asked.

"Only nine." Elena shook her head. "At one time we had fifty. Oh, this was a vibrant place then. There was always something going on. I had a wonderful activities director who was always planning fun events, but…"

"You had to let her go," Jane finished.

Elena nodded. "She was the last person to be cut from my staff, and we've missed her greatly. I try to plan things, but I'm not as young as I used to be either. So who would you like to meet? We have three couples, two women and one man."

"Whoever is available, I guess," Jane said.

Elena smiled. "We'll make the rounds. I'm sure they'll all be as interested in talking to you as you are to them."

She led them down a hallway painted in a warm, terra-cotta orange. Jane commented on the color of the paint, and Elena smiled. "So many schools and hospitals and nursing homes used to be painted in green because experts thought the color was soothing. We've found that warm, autumn colors keep our sweet people feeling vital."

Jane agreed and said so. She explained that she and her sisters ran Grace Chapel Inn and had given a lot of thought to the paint colors and design in each of their rooms.

"Then you know exactly what we strive for here," Elena said, smiling. "We allow our residents to choose their own decor. We even used to have an interior decorator in to help them." Her smile fell.

"But you had to cancel that," Craig offered sympathetically.

Elena rapped on a partially open door. "Exactly. Hello! Mr. and Mrs. Stonehouse, I have some visitors for you."

"Oh my! How fun!" a high feminine voice said. "Come in, Elena. And bring your friends."

Elena opened the door to a large room. It reminded Jane of studio apartments in San Francisco—one large bedroom with a small sitting area and a bathroom to the side. The room was decorated in a Victorian style—wallpaper with a small flower-bouquet print on a white background, hurricane lamps on heavy oak furniture and a large white iron bed topped with a white ruffled bedspread.

Mr. and Mrs. Stonehouse seemed to fit the decor as well. Mrs. Stonehouse had pinned her long silver hair on top of her head. She wore a long print dress and heavy black shoes. Dressed in a suit and tie, Mr. Stonehouse sat on a striped settee, reading a newspaper as though waiting for a job interview. Mrs. Stonehouse put her hand on his shoulder. "Dear? We have guests." She smiled at Jane and Craig. "He's a little hard of hearing."

Elena moved in front of him to gain his attention. "Mr. Stonehouse?" she said, raising her voice.

He looked up, startled. "Oh, Elena! I didn't see you there."

"There are some others here too." She gestured toward Craig and Jane. "These nice people are here to talk to you."

"Really?" He folded his paper and rose. "Well, have a seat, have a seat. So nice to meet you. I'm Irwin Stonehouse."

Craig shook his hand and introduced himself and Jane. They shook hands with Mrs. Stonehouse as well while Elena said, "This lovely lady is Irwin's wife, Irina Stonehouse."

"We've been married for over sixty years," Irina said. "Please have a seat and tell us why Irwin and I are so blessed to have your company today."

Craig launched into an explanation of their mission, and Jane took the opportunity to glance around the Stonehouses' quarters. Though the place was clean and cheerful, the wallpaper was peeling from the ceiling down, the baseboards bore signs of scuffing, and several dents and chips marred the walls.

She also saw several bookcases filled with thick, academic tomes, a collection of Lladró figurines and numerous photo albums. The Stonehouses had obviously led an interesting life, and she looked forward to hearing about it.

After Jane and Craig learned a bit about the Stonehouses, they discussed the purpose of their visit. Elena then took them around to meet the other seven residents. Jane thought that each one was charming. The two other couples were just as sweet and in love as the Stonehouses. The two women shared a room and were as congenial as sisters, even though there was a ten-year difference in their ages. The lone man was a confirmed bachelor, but he had a way of beguiling the two unmarried women that made Jane think they were in competition for his attention.

Elena had been right that the residents' mental capacities were undiminished, and their physical ones only mildly so. Many of them spoke fondly of their former activities director, whose absence had apparently left a noticeable hole in their lives.

Surveys taken and responses noted, Jane and Craig walked with Elena back to the lobby. "What *does* everyone do for fun now?" Jane asked.

Elena shrugged. "They stay in their rooms much more now. They used to have organized games—bridge, dominoes, even poker—but no one can agree on setting up a schedule. The activities director also used to take the bus into Acorn Hill for shopping or sightseeing—even up to Potterston occasionally for a movie. My husband George took them out once or twice, but he has another job. We're co-owners of Three Seasons, but he's always left it up to me to manage it."

"Why is it called Three instead of Four Seasons?" Jane asked.

Elena smiled. "We wanted to emphasize that there was no fourth season in a person's life—no winter. It seemed too final and discouraging, so we focused on only three." She shifted in her chair, and her dress crinkled. "Did you get what you wanted?"

"I hope so," Jane said, consulting the clipboard in Craig's hands. "We'll report to Mayor Tynan next."

"If there's anything you can do for Three Seasons, we would all be most appreciative," Elena said. "These lovely people need something to stimulate their minds. I hate to have them sitting in front of the television every day watching soap operas."

"Of course you do." Jane patted her hand. "We're on our way now to meet with Mayor Tynan. I hope we'll have some good news to share with you soon."

Jane and Craig returned to Town Hall and Lloyd's office just after eleven o'clock, giving them adequate time to chat. Bella had taken an early lunch, and Lloyd was at his desk, munching on a tuna-fish sandwich, a napkin tucked in his shirtfront.

"Gotta keep my blood sugar up," he said, by way of apology, gesturing to the sandwich.

"You don't have any diabetes problems, do you, Lloyd?" Jane asked, worried for her friend.

Lloyd shook his head and swallowed. "Just an energy problem when I don't eat enough breakfast. I start getting lightheaded around this time." He took another bite.

"*Mmm.* June really knows how to make a mean tuna sandwich." He glanced up. "No offense, Jane. I know you're a mighty fine chef yourself."

She smiled. "No offense taken. Would you like some water?"

Lloyd nodded. "Thank you."

Jane saw that the coffee mug on his desk was clean, so she filled it with spring water from the cooler in the office. She and Craig watched as Lloyd hurried through the last of his early lunch, wiped his mouth and hands, then took a long sip. "Ahh. Thank you, Jane. I feel refreshed." He opened a leather notebook on his desk to a blank page and uncapped a fountain pen. "Let's get started."

"Where are the other volunteers?" Craig asked.

"They're still out canvassing, but I'm not sure that they're finding many needy folks, since they're talking mostly to the people living closer to the town center who already seem to avail themselves of city services when necessary. So far, I haven't received many suggestions."

"We have some," Craig said, laying his clipboard on the desk. "We've already mentioned Bernice Sayers, of course."

"Yes, I've been thinking about her." Lloyd scribbled a few notes. "She needs someone to help her get groceries every week, house cleaning, home maintenance, yard work, dog care . . . health services?"

"I don't know that she needs all that," Jane said, "but I suppose she gets lonely, particularly being blind."

"The people at Three Seasons could use some help too," Craig said. He explained about the retirement home for Lloyd's benefit, giving names, ages and pertinent information.

Lloyd nodded as his pen scratched across paper. "Sounds like they need someone to help with activities," he said.

"And perhaps some way to feel useful," Jane added. "They *are* in good health."

Lloyd nodded, taking down all the information. "How about some of the other folks you met?"

Jane told him about Bonnie Ethedridge, Bernice's neighbor with the three small children. "They don't seem to need any help," she added, then described Inge Starr, who lived with her parents, Thomas and Dotty Gilpin. "When I mentioned the possibility of their driving to town, they seemed uncomfortable."

"I noticed that too," Craig said. "They were a great family, though. Thomas likes to tinker with model trains."

Lloyd finished writing, then laid his pen on the desk and reviewed the notes. "*Hmm.* I see people here with lots of needs, but I'm not certain what Acorn Hill, as a local government, can do for them."

"What about a Meals on Wheels program for Bernice and any other shut-ins?" Jane asked.

"That would be the role of a nonprofit charity, not government," Lloyd said.

They heard someone enter the door to the reception area, then Bella stepped into Lloyd's office. "I'm back from lunch. Don't forget you have an appointment with Carlene Moss in five minutes. She wants to interview you for the latest *Nutshell*."

"Oh, right, right. Thank you, Bella." Lloyd closed his notebook and addressed Craig and Jane. "Thank you for the information. Keep up the good work. We're developing a better sense of what our citizens' needs are. I'll think about what our local government can do to help."

"Thanks for your time, Lloyd," Jane said. She and Craig said their good-byes, then stepped into the reception area, where Carlene was chatting with Bella.

"Go on in, Lloyd's ready for you," the receptionist said to Carlene.

"I will, thank you. Craig, Jane ... I'd like to interview you two about the work you're doing for Lloyd, if that would be all right."

Without consulting each other, they shook their heads. "The canvassing isn't about us," Craig said. "We're just trying to bring help to some of Acorn Hill's citizens."

"And we still don't have many details ironed out," Jane added.

Carlene looked crestfallen. "Perhaps when you do, you'll be willing to talk to me...?" she asked.

"*If* we do," Jane said. She hated to add the conditional term, but right now it didn't appear as though she and Craig were making much headway.

Chapter Six

*J*ane returned home and with her sisters' help prepared a light lunch of panzanella salad made with bell peppers, summer squash and tomatoes. "*Mmm*, I love this dressing," Alice said. "This is definitely not only light enough for summer fare but delicious as well."

"I couldn't agree more," Louise said.

"Well then, all of us are pleased." Jane smiled.

Just as the three sisters finished cleaning up, their next guests arrived. Grace Chapel Inn was all confusion as two families checked in—Rudy and Roxanna Ducey and their friends, Malcolm and Loretta Westrich. Both families were young couples, each with a boy toddler who seemed unwilling to stay still long enough for their parents to check in.

"They're tired from the road trip," Roxanna said after apologizing for the second time that her son Randy would not stop running around the circumference of the front hallway, trailing his hands along the cream-and-gold wallpaper.

Crash!

Louise winced. "Randy!" Roxanna raced to her son, who rose, unhurt, from where he'd knocked over the coatrack. "Are you all right, sweetheart?"

Louise righted the coatrack, a nineteenth-century antique beech fixture. She was grateful that no harm had come to the little boy...or the coatrack.

"I'm so sorry," Roxanna said. "He's tired. Maybe if you showed us to our rooms, I could put him down for a nap."

"I'll go too," Loretta Westrich said, "but I don't know that my Mikey is tired out enough."

"Right this way," Louise said, feeling as though she were leading a parade up the staircase, what with two weary mothers, two silent fathers and two rather noisy toddlers. On the second floor, she opened the door to the first front bedroom. "Mr. and Mrs. Ducey, this is the Sunset Room. There's an attached bath."

Roxanna oohed and ahhed over the room's terra-cotta ragged faux paint, creamy antique furniture and impressionist prints. "It's so soothing." She sat on the bed to test it, then smiled. "And comfortable." Rudy Ducey set their luggage and a portable crib for Randy on the floor.

Louise led the way to the Westriches' room. "And this is the Garden Room. It also has an attached bath."

With a howl, Mikey raced to try the bed. Loretta

admired the room and ran her hands along the rosewood bedroom suite as though in amazement. "It's beautiful. How nice it is to get away for a while."

Malcolm Westrich sighed. "All these beautiful furnishings. Let's just hope Mikey behaves."

Louise silently agreed.

⌒

Janette and Glenna returned from lunch to get down to serious writing. The two young families had gone on a walking tour of Acorn Hill, since Randy and Mikey refused to take a nap. All was quiet in the house, and the Duceys and Westriches returned only long enough to change clothes in preparation for dinner at Zachary's Supper Club.

The sisters were having their dinner in the kitchen when Roxanna Ducey tiptoed in. "I hate to bother you ladies."

"It's all right. Anything wrong?"

Roxanna wrung her hands. "Randy and Mikey fell asleep just now. Since they didn't have naps today, we're afraid they're ready to sleep through the night."

"Would you like us to watch them while you go to dinner?" Jane asked. "That would give you adults some quiet time."

"Would you mind?" Roxanna asked, looking relieved.

"Louise will be out tonight, but Jane and I will be home."

"We have baby monitors that we can hook up for you," Roxanna said. "You wouldn't have to stay up there."

"We can certainly call you at Zachary's if either of them does wake up and needs you," Alice said. "I know the restaurant wouldn't mind boxing up your food if you need to come home early."

Roxanna sighed, then smiled. "That would be so wonderful, ladies. The four of us have been good friends for more than ten years. We live near each other and do a lot of things together, but this is the first time that any of us has gotten away since our kids were born."

"Don't worry about a thing," Louise said. "Alice is also a registered nurse, so your children will be safe."

"Thank you again. You're all saints." Roxanna disappeared, presumably to share the good news.

An hour later, promptly at seven as specified, Louise hesitated outside the glass doorway to the Potterston Rec Center. Why on earth had she agreed to participate in a dance competition? What if she couldn't even remember the steps to the different dance styles?

Someone rapped on the inside of the door, startling her. Gail Cohen smiled back at Louise.

Louise pulled open the door and stepped inside. "You must be Louise. You're just as Ben described you," Gail said, shaking Louise's hand. "It's nice to meet you."

"It's nice to meet you too."

Gail smiled. "Are you nervous?"

"A bit," Louise admitted, knowing that it was an understatement.

Gail put an arm around her and walked her down the hall toward the studio where dances and dance classes were conducted. "We're just here to have fun, and you, especially, are here to help someone else learn how to have fun. You like to dance, yes?"

Louise nodded. "It's been so many years, though."

Gail grasped the handle of the studio door and leaned toward Louise. "Think of it as riding a bicycle." She winked again and pushed open the door.

The room was filled with people of all ages gathered in groups, some chatting, some demonstrating dance moves. Many looked nervous, Louise noted, particularly the men— both young and old.

"So you found Louise after all." Rabbi Cohen called out as he approached the two women. "Welcome! We're delighted you could come." He raised his voice. "Everyone, I think we're all here now. Would you please take your seats?"

"Do you mind if I sit with you?" Gail asked as she and Louise headed for the chairs lining the room.

"That would be delightful." Louise was grateful for the company. She'd scanned the room without recognizing anyone she knew.

Rabbi Cohen moved to the microphone on the stage at the head of the room. He tapped the mike, and when he heard the appropriate feedback, he smiled. "Welcome, Potterston Ballroom Dance Club members, and welcome, special guests. We're trying something different this summer that we hope generates a lot of enthusiasm for our favorite 'sport.' You all know that we're pairing an experienced dancer with a novice, and we'll have a final competition to determine which couple has progressed the most. There will be a plaque for the winning novice, but more than competing for any trophy, we want you to have fun."

The crowd applauded, some nodding, some looking skeptical. Louise found her inward response to be somewhere in between.

"We're here tonight to pair up," Rabbi Cohen continued. "Once you know who your partner is, it is your responsibility to practice together. We suggest at least once a week, but if you're truly competitive, you will probably want to do more. What, you think maybe you're going to be Fred or Ginger overnight?"

Everyone laughed, then Rabbi Cohen continued. "So make your arrangements as soon as possible, or as we at the dance club say, 'Dance early, dance often.' The rec center studio is available for practice if you can't find anyplace on your own, and you can sign up at the front desk."

The rabbi never stopped smiling. "The dance club has put a lot of thought into the matches, but if you want to complain, speak to Gail or me. We made the final decisions. And so"—he held up a sheet of paper—"let us begin. When I call your names, please come up to the front so that you can be introduced to each other if you're strangers."

While he called off the names, Louise turned to Gail. "So you really did pick a partner for me?"

Gail nodded, smiling. "I think you'll like him. He's a nice man. Athletic, remember?"

"Louise Howard and Roman Delwaard."

Louise hesitated. "Go ahead," Gail whispered. "Trust me. You'll like him."

She found herself on her feet walking steadily toward the stage. Everyone else was so engrossed in conversation that she realized no one was paying attention. Still, she felt conspicuous. Where was her partner?

Rabbi Cohen had finished calling off names and saw her searching. "Here comes Roman," he said, gesturing behind her.

Louise turned. There striding confidently toward her was a tall, white-haired man with a warm smile. "Louise Howard?" he asked. "I'm Roman Delwaard."

She nodded, unable to speak. Somehow she managed to shake hands, her hand nearly engulfed in his larger tanned one. It was a firm shake, but comfortable. He certainly did seem athletic—muscular, tanned and trim. Golf? Tennis? "It's nice to meet you," she said at last.

The mike onstage emitted feedback, and Louise realized that Rabbi Cohen had something else to say. "One last thing," he said. "There are refreshments in the next room, or you can begin your practice tonight if you wish. The rec center has asked us to leave by ten o'clock."

Roman's eyes, the color of faded blue denim, shone as he smiled at Louise. "Would you like some punch? Maybe we could get to know one another over a treat."

"I'd like that."

Roman led the way to the next room, where some of the participants had already wandered. He and Louise put petits fours on their snack plates. Then he procured two glasses of pink punch.

Louise sipped hers. "*Mmm.* Pink lemonade," she said, then wished she could take back the words. She probably sounded thirteen years old.

Roman laughed. "It tastes pretty good, doesn't it? Reminds me of being a kid. Let's have a seat at one of these tables."

They sat at a table for two. Louise daintily arranged her napkin in her lap and looked up to find Roman watching her. "You're a piano teacher, aren't you?" he asked.

"Why, yes. How did you know?"

"I hear lots of talk about people from my kids."

"Oh, do you have children?" Louise sipped her punch.

"I have a son and a daughter, but they're both grown and living on the other side of the country. No, I was talking about my kids at school. I teach at Franklin High School."

"How interesting. What do you teach?"

"Freshman biology part of the day, but my true love is football."

"Are you a coach?" Louise asked.

Roman smiled. "I'm afraid I'm guilty of being the head coach for the Franklin Patriots football team."

"Oh…my." A football coach? She had some vague recollections of seeing a picture of Franklin's coach, probably in the local paper. Louise knew little about high school sports—or any sports, for that matter. What on earth would they talk about during their dancing lessons?

"That's an interesting profession," she said. "You must enjoy working with youngsters, just as I do."

"Oh yes, ma'am," he said. "I'll admit that teenagers can be a bit irritating at times, but most of the students at Franklin are good kids. As far as the football team goes, they want to be there, so they behave. If they don't, they know they can be booted off the squad."

"I don't keep up with Franklin High as much as I'd like," Louise confessed, "but do I recall reading in the *Nutshell* that the football team does quite well year after year?"

"We certainly do," he said proudly. "We may not always be the biggest team, but I make sure those boys know that when they put on a Patriots uniform, they'd better also put on a lot of pride and willingness to work hard and play fair."

He took a sip of punch. "But that's enough about me. How about you? You also run a bed-and-breakfast, don't you?"

Louise nodded, explaining how she had moved back to town to be near her sisters and help run Grace Chapel Inn. "Of course I grew up in Acorn Hill, so it wasn't a difficult relocation. Perhaps I should have made the move sooner."

Roman nodded as if he understood. "I'm sure your sisters are delighted to have you home again. And I'm delighted that you're willing to teach this old athlete how to cut a rug."

Louise couldn't help the smile that curved her lips. "I have to confess that it's been many years since I've *cut a rug*, as you say, but I'm willing to try. I used to belong to a similar dance club in Philadelphia. Do you have any dancing experience?"

Roman shook his head. "None whatsoever," he said cheerfully. "Well, I've been roped into doing the 'Cotton-Eyed Joe' once or twice at a honky-tonk, but a person doesn't exactly have to know any fancy steps for that one, if you know what I mean."

"I believe I do," Louise said. "Nevertheless, I'm confident that you can learn some of the basic dances—the waltz, the fox-trot, the Lindy Hop—"

"Whoa!" he said, holding up his hands. "I think we'd better take them one at a time. We only have a summer, you know."

"Of course," she said. "I'm sorry if I got carried away. When would you like to begin?"

"How about tonight?" he asked. "You've driven from Acorn Hill to get here. Why don't we take advantage of the time already booked at the rec center?"

"Very well," she said.

Roman rose and held out a hand as though he were a prince inviting her to dance. She appreciated the gentlemanly touch and let herself be led back to the ballroom.

"We're going to start with the waltz," Louise said, facing Roman on the dance floor. "International style."

"International? Like the pancakes?" he joked. When Louise merely smiled, he said, "I'm sorry. I promise I'll be a serious student. But honestly . . . is there any other kind of waltz?"

"There's the American version, but I prefer the international. It's more traditional. It isn't taught much in our country, so it might provide an edge for winning as well."

"What's the difference?"

"The international has only closed positions."

"Excuse me?" Roman said, smiling. "I'm afraid I need more explanation. Remember that I'm new at this."

"Certainly. I'm sorry," she said. "A closed position is

when the dance partners maintain close contact." She blushed at what she had said. "As a teacher yourself, you might be interested to know that it was originally considered quite a scandalous dance, particularly in England, when it was first introduced."

"Didn't it originate in Vienna?"

Louise nodded. "In the late eighteenth century. It became the inspiration for other ballroom dances."

"Which we may or may not learn, depending on how I manage this one, right?"

"I'm sure you'll do fine." Louise smiled. I think the waltz is easy because it's in three-quarter time."

"Sure, I've heard of it. One-two-three, right?"

"There's a little more to it than that, but that's a good start. Speaking of which, hold out your left hand and take my right, then put your right hand at my back. My left hand goes on your shoulder."

They faced each other, and Louise drew a silent breath. "The waltz"—she cleared her throat and tried again—"the waltz begins with a strong downbeat, followed by two lighter beats."

Roman laughed. "I'm not much of a musician, Louise. I don't play any instruments, and I can't even carry a tune in a bucket. Maybe you'd better just show me."

"Very well. We are in a closed position. On the first

beat, move your left foot forward. On two, move your right foot to the side and slightly forward. On three, your left foot closes to the right."

"And you'll do just the opposite?"

Louise nodded. "Shall we try it?"

"No turns?"

"Let's just try this first movement," she said, smiling.

They tried it, and Roman stepped on her foot. "I'm so sorry! I was supposed to lead off with my left?"

"Yes." Louise grimaced. "Let's try it again."

This time they managed with a better result. "Good!" Louise said. "Let's try that again."

Roman beamed. He clasped Louise's hand tighter, and soon they were moving diagonally across the floor with greater ease.

Louise was exhausted during the drive home. She wearily parked her car and headed inside, not surprised when she found Jane and Alice waiting for her in the living room.

Jane was all smiles, though she seemed to try to conceal the fact. "How did it go?"

"For a first lesson, it went fine." Louise plopped down

on the sofa beside Alice, who set aside a novel. "How did things go with the toddlers?"

"Just fine. They never woke up, and their parents had a wonderful, quiet dinner by themselves. So tell us more about your evening," Jane said.

"There's not much to tell. I met my partner, and we had our first waltz lesson."

"Who's your partner?" Alice asked.

"Oh, the Franklin High football coach." Louise suppressed a grimace, waiting for the inevitable fireworks.

She wasn't disappointed. *"Roman Delwaard?"* Jane asked.

"Do you know him?"

"I've never met him, but I've seen him and heard a lot about him. He's supposed to be a nice guy, and he certainly is good looking."

"How interesting that a football coach would sign up for the competition," Alice said. "Did he mention why he wanted to learn to dance?"

"I never thought to ask," Louise said. "We didn't share much information. I know that he has a son and a daughter who live out west."

"I think he's widowed, or maybe he's divorced," Jane said. "But I'm with Alice. I wonder why a coach would want to learn how to dance."

"Perhaps it will come up in conversation," Louise said, almost to herself. "We're meeting again soon for another waltz lesson."

Alice had arranged to meet with her girls alone two days later. Lilia and she had agreed that it was time for Alice to take charge of the group. At the previous meeting, they had made a list of activities they wanted to pursue, and Alice intended to finalize their plans.

The girls' homes were spread out between Acorn Hill and Potterston, and Alice had cleared it with Rev. Thompson to meet in the basement of Grace Chapel.

"I don't have a ride," Esmeralda had said flatly.

"You can ride with me," Isidra said. "My mom will pick you up. You know that."

Esmeralda sighed. "Fine. But I hope we don't plan to meet at a church often."

"I'd invite you to Grace Chapel Inn, but we have guests staying with us," Alice said. "I'm not sure if they're going to need the living room. We'll meet there another time."

Near Grace Chapel Inn, Grace Chapel was built into a small hill. The lower level was accessible in back with a staircase from the chapel to ground level and from ground level to the basement. Beneath the church proper, Alice arranged chairs in the Assembly Room, where her ANGELs and other groups often met. Today her new girls' group would meet, and she hoped the familiar location would make her feel more at ease.

Julie Pepperell was the first to arrive, her head down as always. "Hello, Miss Howard," she mumbled, studying the tips of her tennis shoes.

"Hello," Alice said. "How are you today?"

Julie shrugged. "Okay, I guess. I'll be glad when school starts."

"Really? I find that most of my middle schoolers enjoy being off from school, even those who generally like the academic work."

"There's nothing to do during the summer. My mom works, so I'm home by myself. That's why I'm in this group, I guess."

She selected a folding chair and sat, clutching her hands in her lap. "I don't want to sound mean since you're nice enough to work with us, but I'm not too big on sports or things like that."

Alice sat in the chair beside her. "I'm glad you told me that, Julie. We don't have to do sports all the time. I want you girls to do different types of activities. Is there anything in particular you'd like to do?"

"I—"

"Hey! Hello? Anybody home?" Esmeralda and Isidra stuck their heads through the doorway, and when they saw Alice and Julie, entered. "This must be the place," Esmeralda said.

"Come in and have a seat, girls," Alice said. She noticed that Isidra and Esmeralda wore longer shorts and more appropriate tops. "We'll give Sabrina a few more minutes."

"I'm here," she said, panting. "I asked my ride to drop me off up the street and I jogged the rest of the way."

"Well then, everyone find a seat."

The girls all sat. Only Sabrina said hello to Julie. Isidra opened her mouth to say something, but Esmeralda shot her a look that made her hold her silence.

"Today I wanted to finalize our plans for the rest of the summer," Alice said. "We came up with some good ideas, but perhaps we don't want to focus only on sports."

"I do," Esmeralda said. "If we have to do anything at all, it might as well be something that keeps us busy and gets us tired."

"I like sports," Sabrina said.

"What else did you have in mind?" Isidra asked.

Alice glanced at Julie. The girl glanced up, then put her head down again.

"Do any of you have suggestions?" Alice prompted, hoping Julie would say something.

"Movies?" Isidra said. "We could rent DVDs and make popcorn."

"That would be fun," Alice agreed, "but our main goal this summer is for us to do active things together. To work as a team and bond."

"Can we talk about the sports first?" Sabrina asked. "I'm hoping for swimming and rock climbing."

"We can do that," Alice said. "How about rafting?"

"Yeah, that sounds like fun," Esmeralda said, yawning. "About as much fun as watching paint dry."

"I'm putting it on our list of things to do because I think it will be good for us to learn to raft as a team," Alice said. "And to be honest, I've never done it before. I think it would be a good challenge. Have any of you girls ever gone rafting?"

They all shook their heads. Alice smiled. "Then it will be an adventure for all of us."

"Could we…," Julie said tentatively, then lowered her head.

"What, Julie?" Alice said gently.

Julie raised her head long enough to ask quickly, "Could we do makeovers?"

"Yeah!" Isidra said. "Hair and makeup. That'd be fun."

"I think it sounds stupid," Esmeralda said.

"Not me." Sabrina laughed. "My hair never looks good. And I've seen those TV shows where they totally redo a woman. I would *love* for someone to do that to me."

"I can certainly look into it," Alice said.

Esmeralda sighed, crossing her legs.

"And fashion?" Isidra asked. "Can someone tell us about that? Lilia's always getting on me for wearing stuff that she calls inappropriate. I've seen TV shows where they do women's hair and makeup *and* give them a credit card to spend a fortune on clothes."

Alice smiled. "I can't give out credit cards, but maybe someone who knows something about fashion design could come to us. My younger sister sometimes accuses me of needing a fashion makeover myself."

The girls laughed. "Do you have a lot of sisters?" Sabrina asked.

"One older and one younger," Alice said. "How about you girls? Do you have sisters and brothers?"

"I have three older brothers," Sabrina said. "They were all football stars at Franklin High. They're in college now."

"I can see athletic talent runs in your family." Alice smiled. "How about you, Isidra?"

"Three younger brothers and sisters. They're all in grade school," she said. "It's my mom's second marriage. For a long time it was just her and me."

"I have an older brother and two younger sisters," Esmeralda said. "A lot of times my mom wants me to watch them. That's why I'm so good at working in the day care," she said proudly.

Isidra and Sabrina laughed. "She *is* good. All the little kids love her."

Alice made a mental note to find out more about that. Maybe kids were Esmeralda's soft spot, a possible antidote to her tough-girl exterior. "What about you, Julie?"

"I don't have any brothers or sisters," she said, twisting her hands in her lap.

Alice wondered if the girl had any friends either, but wisely decided to change topics. "All right, we've got some sports, and we've got some beauty makeovers. Anybody else?"

"Maybe we should try to do some community service besides day care," Sabrina said. "My brothers have told me that colleges want to see stuff like that on applications. I definitely want to go to college, and we can help more people in town."

"Why would I want to help anybody else, anyway?" Esmeralda's face showed hostility.

"I think it's an idea we could examine further," Alice said. "When we help others, we tend to forget about our own problems."

Esmeralda crossed her arms and looked Alice squarely in the face. "I don't have any problems."

"No one said that you did, Esmeralda," Alice said. "I just meant—"

Esmeralda straightened. "I know what you meant. You think we're all troubled girls. We're labeled *at risk*, aren't we? Just because we're teenagers doesn't mean we're messed up, okay?"

Alice found herself smiling.

"What?" Esmeralda demanded.

"I was thinking about how a lot of adults would say these are the best years of your life. Do any of you think that's true?"

The girls glanced at one another. Sabrina laughed. "No."

"They're pretty horrible," Isidra agreed.

Esmeralda and Julie remained silent.

"If I didn't believe that things were bound to get better," Isidra continued, "I'd be pretty unhappy."

Sabrina counted off on her fingers. "You worry about how you look, about your grades..."

"Boys," Isidra added.

"Your family," said Julie.

Everyone turned to look at the shy girl.

"Do you worry about your family?" Alice asked gently.

Julie shrugged. "Sometimes."

"What about?"

Julie glanced at the other girls, then lowered her head. "I really don't want to talk about it."

Chapter Seven

*L*ouise and Roman had agreed to meet Friday afternoon to practice. Because Roman had the summer off, they only had to work around Louise's piano teaching schedule, as well as any duties at Grace Chapel Inn.

And this Friday was open for Louise. Alice had met with her girls and headed for her work at Potterston Hospital, and Jane puttered in the kitchen, working on that evening's meal. Glenna and Janette had said they were going to be holed up in their rooms all day to spread out a vast quantity of note cards for their research. The Duceys and the Westriches had driven to Potterston to take Randy and Mikey to a children's-themed pizza restaurant. "With luck, they'll tire themselves out," Loretta had confided to Louise.

Louise certainly hoped so. The boys had slept soundly at night, but she worried that such would not always be the case. She remembered when her own daughter Cynthia was quite young, and how rambunctious she could be. Louise worried that the toddlers would disturb Glenna and Janette, but so far all seemed to be well.

She had spent several hours writing down dance steps and how to explain the turns. It had taken her a while, since she was accustomed to dancing the ladies' part, but she simply reversed everything for Roman's benefit.

Roman was waiting at the rec center studio for her when she arrived. She brought Grace Chapel Inn's portable CD player and several appropriate CDs. He smiled when he saw her and took the player from her hands. "Let me carry that."

"That's quite all right, thank you. It's really not heavy," she said but secretly thought him quite the gentleman for offering to carry the player. So many men today wouldn't.

He set it on a bleacher and turned to her. "You look well, Louise. May I call you Louise?"

"Of course," she said. "And thank you. How are you enjoying your summer?"

"So far it's been nice. But I'll feel better when I know how to dance a few steps...never mind actually winning the competition."

"You don't have any desire to do that?"

"Oh, I want to, all right, but I'm just afraid that these

two left feet of mine will disqualify me. You've probably noticed I'm not very graceful."

Louise had noticed nothing of the kind. "I thought you did just fine the other night."

"We didn't actually do any turns though," he pointed out. "I imagine that's a little trickier than just scooting straight across the floor."

"It is," Louise admitted, "but I see no reason why you can't learn it. In fact, let's start with the steps. Here's how it goes."

She held up her arms, but Roman asked. "Wait a minute, teacher, can we talk a minute first?"

"We really don't have much time," Louise said. "We should take advantage of every minute."

"I agree," Roman said. "But it seems too formal to dance without chatting a bit first. I know certain things about you, of course, but not enough to call you my dance partner."

"Very well. What would you like to know?"

"For starters, how are you doing today?"

Louise was taken aback at the question. "I am well, thank you."

"Are you enjoying *your* summer?"

She smiled. "I'm enjoying the warmer weather, yes. But unlike a school teacher, a piano teacher's schedule doesn't vary much during the summer. I have a few students who take June through August off so that they can enjoy their vacation, but not many."

"Still, you must feel a difference in the air. That something special that makes you want to take off your shoes and run barefoot through the grass like a kid again," he said.

Louise blinked. "I beg your pardon?"

Roman laughed. "Just checking to see if you were listening."

"Perhaps we should begin."

"You're the teacher," he said, holding out his arms in the waltz position. "What do I do?"

She faced him, putting her right hand in his left, her left hand on his shoulder. "We start in closed position like this. Let's walk through it slowly, until you get the hang of the turns. It actually takes six steps to make a complete turn."

"Whatever you say." Roman grinned at her, and she wondered whether he was even paying attention.

She cleared her throat. "Everything I tell you will be from your perspective. Ready?"

He nodded.

"All right then." Louise began her explanation of executing a turn.

"Like this?" He turned them nearly one hundred and eighty degrees.

Louise put her hand over her heart. "Goodness! If you turn your partner that fast, she may become dizzy."

"Sorry. Shall we try it again?"

"Of course." Louise smiled. "And remember, just a quarter turn in between counts two and three. Then—"

"Louise?"

She had been staring at their feet, but she looked up at the sound of his voice. "Yes?"

He dropped his hands. "I'm a football coach, right?"

She nodded.

"When I want one of my boys to learn something new, I've found that telling him never does any good."

Louise frowned. "I don't understand."

"I show a boy what to do, then let him do it. Over and over, usually, until he gets it. The body has to learn the motions, not the head."

"I see," she said. "What would you like me to do?"

"Can you dance your part—from the lady's perspective —and lead? I think I can follow if you go slowly enough."

She smiled. "That probably would be easier, wouldn't it?"

He nodded. "I'd appreciate it if you'd count out loud though. That helps."

She held out her hands. "Ready to give it another try then?"

He smiled, taking her hand. "Ready."

She walked them through it slowly, counting, and sure enough, after only a few attempts, he seemed to get the feel for it. "That's it," she said when they had accomplished their first successful turn. "You're waltzing."

"You mean *we're* waltzing."

Louise stopped short. "Yes, I suppose we are."

Roman smiled, his blue eyes warm. "Can we try the turns again?

"Of course."

They executed the turns several times. Louise scarcely noticed that there were other people in the practice room, so intent on the dance was she. Roman missed a few steps and apologized profusely each time, but his athletic ability was evident. His movements were more fluid than she would have imagined for such a large man. He was so tall that he had to look down at her.

After forty-five minutes of practice, Roman asked, "Would you like something to drink, Louise? I saw a soda machine nearby."

"I normally don't drink soda, but I *am* thirsty," she admitted.

"Follow me."

Roman led the way back to the room where they'd had refreshments at the last meeting. He bought cans of soda from the machine and gestured toward the table where they'd sat before. "You know, you lead pretty well," Roman said jokingly. "Have you taught dancing before?"

Sipping from her drink, Louise shook her head. "My husband and I were in a dance club in Philadelphia years ago."

"Are you divorced?"

"Widowed. My husband died of cancer."

"I'm sorry," he said. The gentle expression in his eyes said that he truly was, and she relaxed.

"What about you?"

"I'm a widower. My wife also died of cancer."

"Now it's my turn to be sorry."

"It's been ten years now. I miss her, of course, but I've learned to move on with my life."

"What do you like to do besides teach and coach?"

"I like sports. Racquetball and working out, mostly."

"I would have imagined you were a tennis player."

Roman smiled. "I don't have any patience with keeping the ball between the lines. Racquetball is more about playing the angles."

"What about golf?"

He shook his head. "Too slow. Too time consuming. I like fast-moving sports."

"And dancing? Some people might think it's too slow. Particularly the waltz."

He leaned back in his chair. "Would you believe that I need an activity with some grace?"

She studied him critically. "I *might* believe it. But should I?"

"Yes." He grinned. "That and the fact that my daughter challenged me to take some dance lessons. She's never let me live down the fact that I didn't know how to dance with her when she got married ten years ago."

"So why did you let her talk you into it now?"

"I lost a Super Bowl bet with her, and I promised I'd take the dance lessons before football season started again. Rabbi Ben's a good friend, so when he told me about his club's competition, I thought it might be a fun way to learn."

"I hope it is," Louise said. "I have to confess that I haven't danced in years, and I feel a little rusty."

"You're doing fine as far as I can tell." Roman drained the soda from his can. "Are you ready to try it again or have you had enough?"

"I'm ready." Louise sipped the last of her own beverage. "Let's try the turns a few more times, then I think we're ready for a spin."

Roman smiled. "Sounds like fun."

$\backsim$

That night, Alice invited Vera Humbert to dinner. Fred was working late at the hardware store, restocking. Alice and Vera had walked that afternoon, something they tried to do several times a week, and when Alice learned her friend would be alone for the evening, she invited her to dine at Grace Chapel Inn.

Jane prepared grilled country ribs with mustard marinade, which had them all ecstatic.

"This is delicious, Jane," Vera said. "Fred would love these."

"I'd be glad to write down the recipe for you. They're not difficult to make."

"Maybe not for you, but I'm not as talented in the kitchen—or with a grill—as you are."

"You underestimate yourself, Vera. By the way, have you and Fred decided on a vacation?" Alice asked.

Vera sighed. "I can't get that man to stand still long enough to talk about it, let alone actually take one. I'm thinking about going to visit my sister out of state, if nothing else. I've even been on a diet, trying to fit into a swimsuit."

"Isn't it just as much fun to stay at home?" Louise asked, smiling.

"Don't get me wrong." Vera laughed. "I love Acorn Hill, but I'd like to get away for a while. Since I'm a teacher, it has to be during the summer or at Christmas break."

"What sort of vacation would you like to take?" Jane asked. "A cruise? A guided tour?"

"A visit to a bed-and-breakfast?" Louise asked teasingly.

"Yes, yes and yes. Anything." Vera sighed.

"Maybe you and your sister could go someplace together," Jane suggested. "Lots of women take vacations without their husbands. A girls-only outing."

"I've done that before, and it's fun, but I want to go someplace with Fred. We haven't taken a trip together in years."

"*Ohhh*. You want a *romantic* vacation." Jane's eyes sparkled. "I see."

Vera blushed. "Well…it would be nice to have Fred all to myself for a while."

Alice crossed her arms on the table. "What if Fred could find someone to fill in for him at the hardware store? Do you think he'd go for a vacation then?"

Vera considered. "He might. Do you have anyone in mind?"

"No, but I'll put my thinking cap on. The summer is young."

"Unfortunately, the same can't be said for me." Vera laughed.

Jane rose and started to clear their empty dishes. "Who's for dessert? I have a jumble-berry pie."

"A what?" Vera stared blankly. "I can't recall you ever baking that before, Jane, whatever it is."

"Jane is trying new recipes this summer," Alice said.

"That's right." Jane removed the last dish from the table and replaced it with a slit crust pie, nicely browned. "There's peach-and-brown-sugar ice cream too."

"Good-bye, diet," Vera said. "I'm not going to get to go on a cruise anyway, so no point in wasting the opportunity to try this, um, this. . . what did you call it, Jane?"

"A jumble-berry pie. It's made with summer berries—blackberries, raspberries, blueberries..."

"Oh, I suppose I'll have a slice," Louise said.

"Alice?" Jane asked.

"It would probably be wise for me to keep up my strength," Alice said, winking at her younger sister.

"Four servings, then, coming right up," Jane said, laying out clean plates.

The back door opened. "*Yoo-hoo!*"

Jane laid out an extra plate. "Better make it five. Aunt Ethel's here."

Ethel Buckley strolled into the room, smiling at her nieces and Vera. Her eyes widened at the sight and smell of warm, fresh-baked pie. "I didn't mean to interrupt your dessert."

Louise vacated her chair. "Have a seat, Auntie. I'll get another chair."

"If you girls don't mind," she said, sitting without waiting for their response. "Do you have enough pie to go around, Jane? I don't want to take anyone's portion."

"I have plenty for all," Jane said, slicing into the pie with a knife.

"We're glad you could join us, Aunt Ethel," Alice said. "With Vera here, too, we have a regular little party."

"Who's for taking dessert out to the porch?" Jane asked. "I love eating alfresco during the summer."

Ethel took a bite of the pie. A dreamy look came over her face. "I don't know what alfresco is, but it can't be as delicious as this pie, Jane."

Jane smiled. "No, Auntie, alfresco means—"

Louise put her hand on Jane's arm. "How about some fresh air with our pie? Jane's right. We should take our plates to the porch."

The women adjourned to the porch, where they took seats on the wicker furniture. Jane stayed in the kitchen long enough to collect decaf and tea, which she brought out on the inn's silver service.

They were silent for a while, listening to the summer noises—crickets chirping, the wind blowing gently through the elms, the sound of a screen closing somewhere in the distance. Vera sighed. "It almost seems a shame to enjoy such refinement on a beautiful summer night, doesn't it?"

"What do you mean?" Alice asked.

"Our enjoying this lovely dessert seems so…grown-up, somehow. I have this urge to collect fireflies in a jar."

"And pitch a tent in the backyard," Jane added.

"Run barefoot through a sprinkler," Ethel said.

"Yes, childhood things," Vera said. "Maybe it's because I'm a teacher, but the day that I don't want to do those things during the summer is the day that I'll know I'm too old."

The others laughed gently. Alice put her hand on Vera's arm. "You'll never be too—"

A shriek from inside the house split the air. "What on earth?" Louise asked, rising. Another shriek sounded, this one more high-pitched, and she dashed toward the front door. The others followed, leaving plates and cups behind. They made it inside just in time to see pajama-clad Randy, closely followed by a similarly dressed Mikey, racing down the stairs, followed immediately by their mothers.

Alice was terrified that one or both of the toddlers would fall and hurt themselves, so she raced toward them, scooping up first one, then the other like a softball catcher. She sat down on the stairs, a child under each arm, until their mothers could reach them.

"Oh, thank you," Loretta said. "Mikey, you could have fallen down the stairs."

"Same for you, Randall James Ducey." Roxanne scooped her son into her arms. Her voice scolded, but her eyes flashed relief and thanks in Alice's direction.

Loretta cradled Mikey for a moment, then turned to Alice. "I am so sorry. Thank you for stopping them."

Roxanna nodded her agreement. "Yes, thank you."

"I'm glad they're all right," Alice said.

Rudy and Malcolm observed them from the top of the stairs, and Louise, Jane, Vera and Ethel from the bottom. They all murmured their relief and were still commenting on the scare when Janette and Glenna moved past Malcolm and Rudy. "What happened?"

Alice opened her mouth to speak, but Roxanna beat her to it. "Our children got away from us and might have tumbled down the stairs—"

"But Alice stopped them in time," Loretta finished.

Janette and Glenna looked at one another. "We heard the screaming," Glenna said.

"Several times," Janette added.

"I'm sorry," Roxanna said. "Our boys were both having trouble falling asleep. They've been so wound up today. Did they bother you?"

"Well…"

Roxanna sighed. "I am *so* sorry. You girls are working on papers, right?"

"Dissertations," Glenna corrected.

"We really do need quiet," Janette added.

Jane ascended the staircase until she was at Alice's level. "You're welcome to use the library."

Janette frowned. "Aren't they closed at night? We have all our notes here, too, all spread out."

Jane shook her head. "I meant the library here. It was my father's, and it might suit your purposes even better than your rooms can. There's a large desk you could use for spreading out your notes. It's on the first floor, as well, so it should be a little quieter."

"Thank you," Glenna said. She yawned. "I think I'm

about ready to sleep anyway. Maybe we could check it out tomorrow?"

"Of course," said Jane.

"Good night then," Glenna said.

Janette smiled at the two young mothers. "I'm glad the boys are all right."

"Thank you," Roxanna said. She and Loretta rose, cradling their precious cargoes, who were now yawning. "I think these little guys are ready for sleep too."

"At last," Loretta said. "I'm sorry about the fuss, ladies. Thank you for coming to our rescue."

"You're welcome," Alice said. "Have a good night."

A crisis averted, all the guests retired to the second floor. The women downstairs made their way back to the porch. Murmuring over the turn of events, they finished their dessert.

"I suppose Fred's home by now," Vera said. "I'd better get there myself. What a lovely dinner, Jane. It's always delightful to spend time with you ladies, but I have to say the meal was extra special tonight."

"You're welcome any time," Jane said, stacking the cups and plates onto the tray. "I promised Louise and Alice more variety with their summer meals, and I plan to make good on it."

"What's this about summer meals?" Ethel asked.

Alice explained Jane's decision to shake up the menu with new summer dishes. Ethel's eyes widened. "I'm not one to invite myself or anyone else, but Lloyd and I would love to sample your efforts…if you need a second opinion, that is."

Jane put her arm around her aunt. "I'd be delighted to have either or both of you, Ethel. Pop over any time, and we'll set out extra plates."

Chapter Eight

*M*onday morning, Jane realized she didn't have any special plans. She and Craig had only one more place to survey, but because of a business rush, he couldn't make it until later in the week. She considered how to use her time—search for a new recipe? Make sure the house was clean? Louise was giving a piano lesson, and Alice was at work. Janette and Glenna had headed toward the town library, and the young families were out somewhere touring.

Jane hated feeling cooped up, especially on such a lovely day. She thought about taking an early jog when she realized what she really wanted was human interaction. By nature an extrovert, she felt recharged when she was around other people. Smiling, she packed a picnic basket with goodies, then scribbled a note for Louise and Alice about her whereabouts and also about their lunch in the refrigerator. She grabbed her car keys and the basket and headed for the edge of town, noting that it was still well before noon.

She pulled up outside Bonnie Ethedridge's trailer. Bonnie was surprised to see her when she answered the door, but she smiled at Jane's suggestion. "Give me a minute to gather the kids and we'll be right there."

"Do you need a ride?" Jane asked.

Bonnie shook her head. "Walking is part of the fun. We may stop to explore ants or trees or whatever we see—you know how kids are. But we'll be there."

Jane got back into her car and drove down the road to Bernice's. The idea of being around new friends excited her, but doubt poured in. What if Bernice didn't want company? What if she preferred to be left alone?

Birdie the black lab wasn't outside when Jane walked to the trailer. When she knocked, however, she heard barking. She could hear Bernice shushing the dog as she made her way to the door. "Yes?"

"Hi, Bernice, it's Jane Howard. Remember me from the census?"

"Of course I do, my dear," Bernice said, her face brightening. "Do you need more information? And where's that young man you had with you last time?"

"Craig had to work today and I was lonely. I thought maybe you and your neighbors might want to have lunch with me." Jane held up the basket even though she knew it would be, at best, a blurry image to Bernice. "I brought a picnic."

Bernice clapped her hands. "Wonderful!" She held the door open. "Stay inside, Birdie. Jane has come to visit."

Birdie seemed happy to see Jane, for she nuzzled against Jane's free hand. "Hang on, Birdie," Jane said. "Let me find a place for this basket."

"I think there's space on the counter." Bernice moved into the kitchen and felt with her hands for a free space. "Yes, right here."

"Thanks." Jane set the basket on the counter and opened it up. She stopped and said with a worried voice, "I hope you don't mind that I invited your neighbors. I thought Bonnie Ethedridge and her children might like to join us."

"What a marvelous idea! You think of everything. I love having children around. It makes me feel so full of life." Bernice smiled, then leaned over the basket. "What did you bring for us to eat?"

"Peanut butter and jelly sandwiches—no crusts. I thought the kids might like those. Some cucumber sandwiches for light eaters, and hearty roast beef sandwiches for meat lovers."

Birdie barked.

"Oh, all right, you can have some," Jane said to the dog. "I'm sure you're a meat lover."

Bernice laughed. "She has her own food. You don't have to waste your good cooking on her."

"I also have some homemade potato salad and peach cobbler—still warm—for dessert."

"My goodness, you'll spoil an old person." Bernice laughed. "But you didn't have to bring any food. I would have been happy just to chat with you again."

"We can do that too," Jane said. "But since it's getting close to lunchtime, I thought it'd be fun to share a meal."

"You're so thoughtful," Bernice said. "Where should we take our picnic?"

"Is there a good place to lay out a picnic cloth?"

Bernice thought for a moment. "The large elm tree out back might be nice. It would give us good shade, anyway."

"Sounds good. With the chain-link fence, we can see Bonnie and her kids coming too," Jane said. "There's one thing I don't have for lunch, Bernice, that I'm hoping you can provide."

"What's that?"

"Lemonade. I've hand-squeezed it lots of times, but I've never been able to get it to taste as good as yours."

"I'll be glad to mix some up," she said. "Anything to contribute to such a wonderful lunch."

"Do you mind if I watch while you do?" Jane asked. "You don't have a secret recipe, do you?"

"As a matter of fact, I do." Bernice laughed. "I'll be glad

to tell you what the secret is. I always add the juice of one lime. It gives the lemonade a little something extra."

⁂

When Alice finished her nursing shift, she changed into more comfortable clothes. She and the girls had agreed to meet at the rec center for rock climbing. She hadn't been sure what clothes to bring but settled on loose drawstring pants and a short-sleeved cotton shirt.

The girls were already waiting for her when she arrived. All four were clad in shorts and T-shirts. "Hi, Miss Howard," Sabrina yelled across the room when she saw her. "Doesn't this look fun?"

Alice glanced at the three gigantic simulated rock walls. The idea of scaling a rock face had always intrigued her, but up close, she could see that the task might prove more formidable than she had imagined. Several people were already hard at work hoisting themselves up the wall, grabbing on to toe- and handholds. She was glad to see that each climber had a rope attached to a belt around his torso, and someone stood on the ground holding the rope's end. She'd heard that they could stop a falling climber.

"Nervous?" Sabrina asked.

"A little," Alice admitted, eyeing the wall. "But I only

plan to attempt a very cautious ascent. Can the people standing on the ground really catch someone who falls?"

"Well, they don't *catch* them, but they stop the fall," Isidra said. "And sure, it happens. I've seen them help someone lots of times. They're called belayers, by the way, and the belt around the climber's waist is called a belay."

"I can see why you're scared," Esmeralda said, sidling up to Alice. "You must be pretty old, huh?"

Alice couldn't help but grin. "I'm sixty-two."

Esmeralda let out a long whistle. "You sure you want to do this?"

Alice tilted her head back and studied the top of the wall. Did she have the strength...the stamina...the *courage*?

"I do," she said firmly, smiling at Esmeralda and the other girls. "But only after you four go first, deal?"

Esmeralda nodded. "Sabrina's the only one who's done this before, so it will be a challenge for the rest of us."

Alice drew a deep breath. The wall looked to be thirty-five feet high. *Indeed it will be!*

A young man from the rec center explained the procedure and agreed to be the belayer for each girl and for Alice. Sabrina donned a helmet and hooked herself into the belay harness and took off for the top. In no time at all she grinned down at them from above, waving. "It's easy!" she shouted down to them. "Come on up, it's fine."

"I'll go next," Isidra said. Alice noticed that the girl looked a little nervous, but she listened carefully to last-minute instructions from the belayer, then started up the wall. She moved slowly at first, finding her toeholds carefully, then her handholds, but as she got closer to the top, she seemed to find her confidence and soon joined Sabrina.

"Y-you can go next," Julie said to Esmeralda.

"I planned to." Esmeralda adjusted the strap on her helmet. She took a deep breath, then started climbing.

"That's it!" Isidra shouted. "You can do it!"

"Yeah, come on, girl. That's the way!" Sabrina joined in with encouragement.

Slowly and steadily, Esmeralda made her way up the wall. When she reached the top, Sabrina and Isidra cheered.

"She made it!" Julie whispered. She turned to Alice, her eyes panicked. "Now it's my turn."

"Your friends made it and you can too," the rec center employee said, hooking her into the harness. "Piece of cake."

"Right…a piece of cake," Julie said as if trying to convince herself. She stared up at the wall and trembled.

Alice heard Esmeralda snicker. "I told you she'd be too scared. She can't do it."

Julie looked at Alice. "She's right. I *am* scared."

"Fear can be a good thing," Alice said. "Sometimes we need to conquer our fears. It makes us stronger."

Julie stared up at the wall again, then removed her helmet. "I can't do it, Miss Howard. You go ahead and I'll wait here."

Alice, who had thought that she might climb halfway up the wall, found herself facing a greater challenge. She shook her head. "I'm not doing it without you, Julie."

"B-but I can't." Julie's eyes watered.

Alice turned to the belayer. "Can you get a second person to help us?"

"Sure. I'll be right back." He left to find another employee.

"Julie, let's do this together," Alice said in a low voice. "We can encourage each other. I'll stay beside you the entire time, all right? We'll reach the top together."

Julie brushed her eyes. "Do you really think I can make it?"

Alice smiled. "I know you can. Frankly, I'd appreciate the company. I'm a little nervous myself."

"R-really?"

Alice nodded. "What do you say?"

They heard the girls' loud voices from the top of the wall but couldn't distinguish what they were saying. Julie looked at Alice full in the eyes, then nodded. "Okay," she whispered.

The rec center employee returned with another young man. "We're both going at the same time," Alice said.

"Great!" the employee said. "I know you can do it." The second employee nodded.

Helmets on and belay ropes attached, Alice and Julie approached the wall. "Ready?" Alice asked. Julie nodded.

Together they put a foot in the first toehold, then the other, then reached for a handhold. "That's how we're going to do this," Alice said. "One toe at a time, one hand at a time."

"One toe, one hand," Julie repeated, hoisting herself up.

"Right. Toe, toe, hand, hand," Alice said, verbally mimicking their action.

"Toe … toe … hand … hand …"

Slowly, carefully, they climbed. The voices of the girls above grew louder, and Alice realized they were shouting down encouragement. She was grateful for the regular exercise that kept her in good enough condition to attempt such a climb.

"Atta way!" Sabrina yelled. "You got it!"

"Keep going!" Isidra chimed in. "You're doing great."

Julie ignored them. "Toe … toe … hand … hand …," she whispered.

Alice's stomach felt like a cage for a thousand nervous butterflies. She refused to look down, concentrating instead on each black plastic life hold. "First the toes, then the hands," she said to herself. *Where is the top of the wall? Shouldn't we be there by now? Surely it didn't take the other girls this long to reach it.*

She concentrated so hard on her climb that it was a moment before she realized that Julie had stopped. Alice realized they were three-quarters of the way to the top, but the girl was no longer moving. Alice could see her shaking, seemingly paralyzed. "Julie? Are you all right?"

"I … I can't make it, Miss Howard. I looked down, and …"

"Don't look down again," Alice said soothingly. "Concentrate on getting to the top."

"I … I can't!"

Alice moved sideways across the wall, closer to Julie, picking her way with the toe- and handholds. "I'm right here," she said gently, as she would to a patient. "I'll stay closer to you, all right? We can do this together. Julie … all right? Remember, toe … toe …"

"… hand … hand," Julie whispered.

"That's right," Alice assured her. "Just like climbing a ladder. You can do that, right? Just one foot after another, then one hand after another."

Julie stepped one foot up, then the other. "Foot…
foot…"

"…and hand…hand. That's it, Julie. You can do it!"
Alice said.

The girls above cheered. "Yay, Julie! Come on. It's great
up here."

Hold by hold, toe by toe, hand by hand, Julie and Alice
made their way to the top. Alice felt her fingers screaming
with pain from gripping the plastic, her calves trembling
with exertion. At last, however, she saw Julie reach the
top, and Sabrina pulled her up over the wall. "Yay! Good
going!"

The belayers shouted their congratulations from below.

Alice reached the top soon after, and Isidra gripped her
arms. "Way to go, Miss Howard!"

Trembling, Alice sank to the platform at the top of the
wall. "Thanks," she murmured.

"Have a seat over here," Isidra said, guiding her to a
bench. "You two did great."

Alice gratefully took a seat, and Julie sank beside her.
They both breathed hard for a moment, wiping the perspiration from their foreheads with towels someone handed
them. They glanced at each other in triumph. Julie's face
beamed, her eyes shining. She nodded at Alice, who smiled
back at the girl.

"That was all right," Esmeralda said. "I didn't think you'd make it, but you two did all right."

Alice looked the girl straight in the eye and smiled. "Thank you, Esmeralda."

The teenager blinked, then looked away.

Late that afternoon, Alice parked her Toyota at Grace Chapel Inn and limped up the walkway. Jane met her at the front door and held it open for her. "I saw you coming. Are you all right?"

Alice winced as she stepped into the house. "I went rock climbing with my girls today." She put her hand at her lower back, then touched a calf, letting out a moan. "I'm afraid I'm a little sore."

"Come into the living room where you can put your legs up." Jane hustled her to a sofa. Alice had to bite her lip several times to keep from moaning again. Jane was an avid jogger and in good shape, but she could appreciate how painful the effects of overexertion could be.

"Have a seat and prop up your legs." Jane patted the sofa and Alice obediently sat. Jane gently helped Alice extend her legs on the sofa. "Rest here a minute and I'll be right back with some ice packs. I'd have thought you might do something less strenuous."

"Me too." Alice leaned her head back against a decorative pillow. Maybe Esmeralda was right. Maybe she *was* too old for such shenanigans.

She grinned at the ceiling. No, it had been worth it. Julie might not have made it to the top if she hadn't had someone climbing beside her, cheering her on. Julie's success alone had been worth it.

"All righty, here we are." Jane propped two pillows under Alice's calves, then laid a dish towel-wrapped ice pack between her legs and the pillows. "That should help. R-I-C-E for soreness, right?"

Alice nodded. "Rest, ice, compression and elevation. You'd make a good nurse, Jane."

Jane scuffed a toe against the rug and mimicked an old west accent. "Aw, shucks, ma'am. 'Tweren't nothin' at all."

"I don't think I need the compression, though, which usually means an elastic bandage. The ice and the rest will do me good."

"Want me to bring you a book?"

"If you don't mind, I have one in the parlor."

"I'll be right back."

She returned in record time and handed Alice the book. "Anything else I can get you?"

"I'm fine, Jane, really." Alice adjusted the ice packs. "I just need to catch my breath for a minute. After we climbed the wall, the girls wanted to try some of the other games at the rec center—bowling and indoor archery. They also wanted to go to a skating rink, but I promised we'd do that another day."

Jane smiled. "It sounds like you definitely put in a day's work. All that after working your nursing shift."

"Yes." Alice winced.

"Would you like to hear some good news?" Jane perched on the edge of the couch near Alice's feet. "Roman Delwaard called Louise and wants another dance lesson tonight."

Alice clucked at her younger sister. "I don't like the look on your face, Jane Howard. You're not cooking up any romance between those two, are you?"

"Who, me?" Jane asked innocently. "I just find it interesting that those two are paired up for this competition, don't you?"

"Interesting how?"

Jane shrugged. "Oh, interesting as in good. It's good for Louise to spend time with a male friend, don't you think?"

"I think whatever *Louise* thinks is what's best. I'm not sure that she thinks of Roman Delwaard as a special friend, Jane. Where is Louise, by the way?"

Jane grinned. "She's upstairs trying to decide what she's going to wear tonight."

Roman was waiting for Louise when she arrived at the rec center studio. He smiled when he saw her enter. "Thanks for agreeing to meet me tonight, Louise."

"I'm glad you're interested enough to keep coming back for more lessons."

"You're a wonderful teacher," he said. "If you're half as patient with your young piano students as you are with me, then you must have plenty of star pupils. I've often thought that a person's ability to learn isn't based so much on talent as it is on the quality of the teacher."

"Thank you very much. You're too kind, considering that this is my first time teaching someone to dance."

"Perhaps you should make a habit of it," Roman said, grinning. He took the CD player from her hands. "More waltzing tonight?"

"Indeed. Shall we see how much you remember?"

Two other couples were already practicing, one working on a fox-trot and another on a tango. Louise and Roman moved to an unoccupied area of the floor and set the CD player on a folding table. "Ready?" Louise asked, placing her finger over the play button.

Roman nodded, holding out his hands. Louise hit the button and took Roman's hands. The music began and she began to lead. "One, two, three," she counted softly for his benefit.

Roman followed smoothly as they took several turns to the music. "Can we try a spin?" he finally asked.

Louise obliged, and he followed through. "Very good," Louise said. "You're really doing very well, Roman."

"Thank you." He paused. "Can we take time-out for a minute?"

"Certainly. Are you tired?"

"No, not at all." He gestured toward two folding chairs.

Bewildered, Louise sat. "Is something wrong?"

Roman clasped his hands between his spread knees. "Can I be honest with you?"

"Of course."

"I know that learning a new dance step requires that you take the man's role for a while, but it's a little demoralizing for me. I'm a football coach, and I'm used to showing others what to do."

"This must be a fairly humbling experience," she said, "and I can see your point. But I don't know what else to do."

"Neither do I. Do you think I'm doing well so far?"

"Very much so."

Roman grinned. "Then do you think I could lead from now on? At least until you teach me a new step or we move on to a different dance?"

Louise sighed with relief. Despite his kind words earlier, she had thought him displeased with her teaching. "Is that all that's bothering you? Of course you may lead. I think you are more than ready and capable."

"Great!" Roman smacked his palms against his knees and rose. "Shall we try it?" He held out his hand to her.

She placed her hand in his and rose alongside him. "If that was an invitation to dance, Mr. Delwaard, I'm delighted to accept."

This time Roman pressed the start button on the CD player and led them off. Louise mentally counted one-two-three, but wisely kept silent. He seemed a little nervous, a little mechanical in his movements, but he led beautifully. She was able to follow without any difficulty. Neither of them stepped on the other's feet.

By the time the music ended, Roman had maneuvered them back to the CD player. He clicked it off with a flourish, smiling. "How'd I do, Teacher?"

"Wonderfully," she said. "I think you have a real shot at winning the competition."

"You mean *we* have a shot. I can't do it alone." His eyes twinkled.

She smiled in return. He was a pleasant person to be with and an eager student. Roman Delwaard was a kind, considerate man.

Suddenly his face went serious. "Louise, do you drink coffee?" he asked.

"Yes. Why?"

He smiled again. "Would you consider meeting with me Wednesday evening?"

What on earth did coffee have to do with anything? "You mean another dance lesson?"

He shook his head. "Coffee and dessert. Just a chance, perhaps, to get better acquainted."

His intention sunk in, and Louise's heart beat a little faster. *A date, that's what he means.* The idea didn't seem as foreign as it once might have. She wasn't sure if she should feel unnerved at that realization. "Why, I think that would be very nice, Roman. Where should we meet?"

He grinned as though she were a teenager unfamiliar with dating rituals. "I'll pick you up at seven thirty...if that's all right."

"That would be fine." She gave him the location of the inn. "Are you familiar with Acorn Hill?" she asked, knowing that he lived in Potterston.

"Your inn is near Grace Chapel?"

She nodded.

"Then I won't have any trouble finding it. Now, shall we dance some more?" He held out his hand.

Louise nodded, placing hers in his.

Chapter Nine

ednesday morning found Jane and Craig sitting in Lloyd Tynan's office discussing the census and their ongoing efforts to interview residents. Lloyd looked over pages of notes on his desk and squinted at the writing. "It appears that our census is complete. As I had guessed, getting a count on the folks who live in Acorn Hill proper wasn't too much of a problem."

"Did any of the others find needs that aren't being met?" Jane asked.

Lloyd nodded. "Yes, they met some folks who need assistance."

"I wish Craig and I had found better situations." Jane sighed. "Have we determined what Acorn Hill can do?"

Lloyd stood a ballpoint pen on end against his desk, then swiveled it in his fingers thoughtfully. "I've been looking over the budget, and I'm not sure that we have anything extra. We could, of course, consider raising taxes."

Jane opened her mouth, but Lloyd held up his hand. "I do, however, have another idea."

They heard a *harrumph* from the reception area.

"All right, it was Bella's idea," Lloyd said, smiling. "But it's a darn fine one, I say."

"What is it, Lloyd?" Craig asked.

"Bella suggested asking for voluntary contributions in the quarterly reports sent out to our citizens. One dollar per family would go a long way."

Jane mentally calculated the number of Acorn Hill citizens and the maximum that could be received. "That could help out, Lloyd. It's a good idea."

"It's definitely a start," Craig said. "Do you think the council will agree to it?"

"We'll put it up to a townwide vote, if need be," Lloyd said. "Since it's strictly voluntary, though, I don't know why anyone would object." He rested the pen on its side and leaned back. "It probably won't be enough on a regular basis for what you two probably would like to do, so Bella and I did some more brainstorming."

"And?" Jane leaned forward, anxious.

"What if all the churches in the area could get together and form a committee?"

"Ah, using private resources instead of public," Craig said. "I like the idea."

Lloyd nodded. "Most churches have some sort of

charitable group within the congregation anyway. That'd be a logical place to start."

"Grace Chapel has the Helping Hands ministry," Jane said. "I would hope they'd be interested."

"Can you check with them?" Lloyd asked. "Word can go out to the other churches, and we'll see if a representative from each congregation would be willing to participate in the group at large." He paused. "And that's where you two come in. I'd like for you to head up the group, as well as manage the voluntary contributions from citizens."

"I'd be happy to, Lloyd," Jane said.

Craig nodded. "Absolutely. Count us in."

"Splendid!" Lloyd leaned forward. "If we can get other people involved, that would be great too. My mother used to always say, 'Many hands make light work.' I've always found that to be true."

"Let's hope we can get many hands—and just as many hearts—involved in this project," Jane said.

Lloyd smiled. "I have every confidence that you and Craig can make it happen."

Alice had arranged to meet with her girls at Grace Chapel Inn early Wednesday afternoon. She hadn't told them what she planned, hoping that she wouldn't have any dissenters —meaning Esmeralda—at the last minute. When each girl was dropped off, Alice showed her into the living room until all were present.

Each one of them eyed the home with interest, but Sabrina commented first. "It's a nice house you have."

"Pretty cool for an older home," Isidra agreed.

"Can you show us the rest of the house?" Esmeralda asked.

"We have guests staying on the second floor, but I can show you the first floor if you're really interested."

The girls nodded. Julie stayed close to Alice and whispered, "I like older homes."

Alice smiled and showed them the parlor and the baby grand that dominated the room. Sabrina asked if Alice played. "Only my older sister, Louise, has the musical talent in the family."

"It's a beautiful piano," Julie said, running her hand along the keys without pressing them. She fingered the violet-and-ivory shawl draped over the piano.

Isidra admired the wallpaper with green ivy and pale-lavender flowers. Sabrina strolled the length of the room to study the antique, brass-faced mantel clock, the curio cabinets, a collection of antique vases and a porcelain doll collection.

"What's this?" Esmeralda flipped a switch on the

metronome. It began its rhythmic *click-clack, click-clack*. The girls smiled.

"It's to keep time when you're playing. It's called a metronome."

Alice led them out of the parlor and through the door with the plaque that said The Daniel Howard Library. "You have your own *library*?" Esmeralda's eyes widened.

"It was my father's study when he was alive. When we remodeled the house, we named this room for him."

"He sure had a lot of books." Isidra scanned the titles lining the bookcases on the wall.

"And a cool desk." Sabrina plopped down in the large leather chair, then glanced up at Alice guiltily. "I'm sorry, Miss Howard. I shouldn't be sitting here."

"That's all right," Alice said. "Would you like to see the sunroom?"

The word *sun* must have conjured happier images than the academic atmosphere of the study, for three of the girls bolted after Alice. Julie followed, showing more restraint. Alice led them to the glassed-in room with its wicker furniture.

"It must be fun to sit in here and read," Julie said wistfully, fingering one of the sofa's cushions.

"You're welcome here any time," Alice said, smiling at the girl. "All of you are."

"Really? I can just come here and read?"

Alice nodded. "As long as our guests aren't using this room."

Esmeralda popped up from her chair. "Who wants to read anyway? Let's see the rest of the place."

"Right this way." Alice showed them to the kitchen, with its black and white checkerboard floor tiles, the warm rusty-red cabinets and rows of colorful tile on the backsplash. The girls examined the maple butcher-block countertops, the soapstone sink, the eight-burner stainless gas stove and the stainless-steel dishwasher. Sabrina studied the Peg-Board on the wall holding cooking tools and a lamp. Alice noticed her glance. "Do you like to cook?" she asked.

Sabrina nodded. "I've been cooking for my brothers and me. My mom has to work late a lot."

"I bet you're a pretty good cook."

"Not really. I do a lot of boxed and frozen dinners. I've always wanted to learn how to cook, though."

Alice filed the information away. Every little bit she learned about the girls would help her to understand them better.

"Where are we meeting today?" Isidra asked.

"Yeah, and what are we doing?" Esmeralda folded her arms.

Alice smiled to herself. Esmeralda was nothing if not

straightforward. "We're meeting in here. She pushed through the swinging door that linked the kitchen to the dining room. Alice had already put a sheet across the mahogany table. "Have a seat, girls," she said, gesturing at the Queen Anne furniture. The girls stared at the sideboard set against one of the room's green walls. On it Alice had set the dish of pale pink, green and white Swedish mints that Jane normally left on the table. "Can we have some of those?" Esmeralda pointed to the dish.

Alice thought that perhaps it was an improvement that the girl had at least asked first. "Yes, you may."

Esmeralda dug in and came up with a fistful of mints, which she proceeded to pop into her mouth as quickly as possible. The other girls took a few, then returned to their seats. "What are we doing today?" Sabrina asked. "You've been very secretive about it."

Alice took a seat at the head of the table, around which the girls had gathered. "I hope you'll enjoy it. We're having a makeup artist come in today to talk to you girls about makeup and fashion."

"Oh boy!" Isidra and Sabrina squealed.

Julie smiled, then promptly frowned when Esmeralda glared at her.

The doorbell rang. "Excuse me," Alice said. "I think that's our teacher. I'll be right back."

The girls looked at one another, then watched the door expectantly until Alice returned. A woman in her late twenties followed her into the dining room. She held a leather-covered box and a garment bag in one hand and a portfolio sketchbook in the other. "Hi, girls." She smiled at each one in turn.

Alice cleared her throat. "Girls, this is Emilie Waters. I met her at the hospital where I work. She helps female cancer patients undergoing chemotherapy to update their makeup and fashion."

Esmeralda put her hands on her hips. "We don't have cancer."

"Of course not," Emilie said, flashing dazzling white teeth. "But I trained at a beauty school for many years and worked at the cosmetics counter in a department store in Philadelphia. When Alice told me that you girls were interested in makeovers, I jumped at the chance. I especially like working with teenagers."

"Why?" Esmeralda squinted.

"Honest truth?"

Esmeralda nodded.

"So many teens either use too little or too much makeup. The trick is to find just the right balance." She looked at each girl in turn. "Already I can see that each of you has your own natural beauty."

The girls beamed. "I mean that." Emilie rubbed her hands together. "Now, let me show you what I've brought."

She set the box on the sheet-covered table and pulled out several trays. Occasionally she would look up at each girl as if deciding what she needed. The girls, even Esmeralda, watched with fascination. Esmeralda pretended indifference if she thought anyone was watching, but Alice noticed that she peered with as much interest at Emilie's strange tubes and brushes as the next girl.

"Miss Howard?" Janette Frappier peered cautiously around the entry, with Glenna looking over her shoulder. "We were wondering if we could get a glass of water from the kitchen."

"Of course you may," Alice said. "Help yourselves."

Janette left for the kitchen, but Glenna paused. The girls were exclaiming over the makeup bottles and powder compacts Emilie laid on the table. Glenna smiled apologetically. "I hate to be nosy, Miss Howard, but what is going on here?"

Before Alice could answer, Emilie flashed her bright smile at Glenna. "We're having a sort of beauty makeover for Miss Howard's teenage friends. Would you like to join us?"

Glenna fingered her ponytail. "I'm not sure. Well, that is . . ."

"You're welcome to come in," Alice said. "Janette, too, if she'd like."

Glenna flushed. "We wouldn't be intruding?"

"Not at all."

"The more the merrier," Emilie agreed. "I have plenty of time, and as you can see"—she gestured at the cosmetic spread—"plenty of resources."

"Why don't you ask Janette?" Alice asked.

"Okay." Glenna headed down the hallway before Alice could tell her about the shortcut through the swinging door. They both returned soon, however.

"What's this about a makeover?" Janette asked.

"We're just having fun," Emilie said. "I'm showing the girls some new looks. If you want to participate, I have plenty of makeup."

"I'd like to," Glenna said.

Janette looked at her friend, somewhat with surprise, Alice thought. "Oh, why not," Janette said, pushing her thick black glasses up the bridge of her nose.

"Great." Alice made introductions while Emilie arranged bottles of foundation and sponges. "I'm going to start with the girls first. Then I'll do you two."

"That's fine," Glenna said. "We'll watch."

"Are you girls ready?" Emilie addressed the teenagers. "Who would like to go first?"

The four girls hesitated, glancing at one another. Finally, Julie timidly raised her hand. "I'll go. I'm probably the most needy."

"Why that doesn't describe you, Julie—not at all."

Emilie's enthusiasm was so obvious that Julie beamed at the praise. "Everyone pay attention. Julie, you sit closest to me. We'll use you as our model, but there are some things we'll all do together."

Emilie passed around small square packets for the girls to open. "The first thing you must do is start with a clean face. Be sure to wash in the morning when you wake up and at the end of the day before you go to bed. It's very important to remove all the day's grime and residual makeup. We're all going to take off any makeup we might have on now, so open your packets and wash your face with the cleansing cloth inside."

Alice declared herself merely an interested observer. After the others complied, Emilie pulled back Julie's hair with a hair band. She selected several cosmetics and applied them one at a time—"but only lightly, because you and your friends are young and don't need much makeup. You only want to enhance your natural beauty, not cover it up. Same for you, Janette and Glenna. You're a little older, but not by much."

The two nodded at each other and smiled.

When Emilie had finished, she handed Julie a mirror so that she could see the results. The girl blinked, then smiled widely. "Wow! I look...different."

"You look pretty nice," Esmeralda admitted.

Julie smiled.

Emilie held up a cosmetic brush. "Who wants to go next?"

"Me!" The three other teenage girls raised their hands. Janette and Glenna grinned at each other, then raised theirs too.

By the time Emilie had worked her styling magic on the four teenagers and two students, they were laughing and trading jokes and compliments about each other's improved looks. Alice did not have any interest in new makeup techniques. However, she did pay close attention when Emilie got out her fashion portfolio and discussed style with each girl. She assessed their body types and held up swatches of fabric to talk to them about what colors would be most pleasing for their skin tones. She also talked about mixing colors and textures to make an interesting fashion statement, tailoring her talk to the teens but adapting her advice a little for the more mature females.

"Jeans and T-shirts are fine for around the house or gardening," Emilie said to them all. "But when you go out with your friends, you want a bit more sophistication. You can pair nice jeans with a dressier blouse and some appropriate jewelry. And for a college or job interview, you definitely want to look your best—polished. So no jeans allowed."

"Thanks for letting us sit in," Glenna whispered to Alice. "Janette and I have been enjoying ourselves. We've been so busy working on our research that we haven't given much consideration to how we look."

Janette overheard and nodded. "We'll be entering the job market some day, but even before then, it's good to know a few tricks about looking nice."

"I learned a lot myself," Alice said. "My sister Jane sometimes encourages me to be a bit more stylish. I should listen to her more often."

"Your teenage friends seem happy too." Janette nodded at the four girls. They were fingering swatches of a silky material while Emilie held it up against wool swatches, presumably representing pants or a skirt.

Alice noticed that each of the girls seemed to sit a little straighter and hold her head a little more erect. Julie's eyes positively glowed. Sabrina smiled as always, and Isidra chattered away to anyone who would listen. No matter how lovely her newly made-up face was, however, Esmeralda still refused to smile, though she watched Emilie's every move with the fashion books.

Jane watched Louise choose her clothes for the coffee date with Roman Delwaard. "Let's see what you've got."

As Louise pushed the clothes hangers along the rack, Jane offered her opinions. "*Hmm*. Too sedate. Too church dressy. Too casual."

"We're only going to have coffee together," Louise said, bemused, "not meet the Queen of England."

"But it *is* a date." Jane studied a gray A-line skirt, then shook her head.

Louise felt her cheeks warm. "Do you really think it's a date? Do you think *he* thinks it's a date?"

"Did he ask you to have coffee with him?"

Louise nodded.

"Did he say he'd pick you up?"

Again, she nodded.

"Then you, my dear sister, have a date for this evening."

Louise held out a light blue twin set that she had selected. "*Hmm*, that will look great with your hair and your pearls. Do you have a pair of black flats?"

"Flats?" Louise repeated.

"Low- or no-heeled shoes," Jane said. "I know you have some."

"Certainly." Louise reached into the closet and removed a pair of low pumps.

"Perfect! Go ahead and get dressed, then I'll help you with your hair."

Louise laid the light knit top and sweater against the skirt on the bed. She removed her best set of pearls from her dresser, laid them against the ensemble and stepped back critically. It did look attractive. "This is a good pick, Jane," she said.

"Naturally." Jane held up the shoes to the skirt. "People should dress according to their own tastes. This will look good on you. Are you nervous?"

Louise paused to consider. "I don't think so, but you know I haven't been on a date since Eliot died."

"Then it's high time." Jane grinned. "But if the word *date* bothers you—"

"And it does—"

"Just think of it as a chance to make a new friend," Jane finished. "That's all first dates are anyway. You must like his company, or you wouldn't have accepted his request."

"I suppose you're right." Louise fingered her pearls thoughtfully. "I'm just worried that we won't have much in common. What will we talk about?"

Jane sat on the bed, careful not to muss the outfit. "Well, for one thing, you have dancing. You can talk about that. And you both have children."

Louise smiled. "And after fifteen minutes, what else will we discuss?"

Jane rose and patted her sister fondly on the shoulder. "You'll think of something. Meanwhile, it's time for you to get ready."

By the time the doorbell rang promptly at seven thirty, Louise was seated on the edge of the sofa in the living room. Alice sat beside her, as though in sympathy. Jane sat in a chair, grinning at anyone who would catch her eye. "Oh, you two are a couple of Gloomy Guses," she said as she rose to answer the door.

Louise smoothed her hair. She was grateful that Jane had not arranged it any differently from usual, but she had insisted on a squirt of hairspray here and there. Louise thought that the smell was probably noticeable from twenty feet away, though Alice assured her that it wasn't.

"She's right here," Jane said, leading Roman into the living room. They had obviously discussed something funny, for she was smiling, and he was chuckling.

"Hello, Louise," he said. "You look lovely."

"Thank you," she said, hoping that her voice didn't sound like the croak she imagined.

"This is our sister, Alice," Jane said.

Roman shook her hand. "I believe we've met before."

"Really?" Alice seemed puzzled.

"One of my football players sprained an ankle some years ago and I brought him to Potterston Hospital. I think you were on duty in the emergency room that day. Do you still work there?"

"At the hospital, yes, but I work in different areas where needed." Alice smiled warmly. "I believe I do remember you, Mr. Delwaard. It was one of your benchwarmers, wasn't it?"

"Yes, but he probably would prefer to be remembered as a standout defensive back." Roman chuckled.

"I can't remember the boy's name, but I remember him telling me how much he enjoyed playing for you, and that you had given him a chance on the team when no one else had."

Louise was pleased to hear this news. Many high school and junior high coaches were so concerned only with winning that many students grew disillusioned with sports.

Roman turned toward her and smiled. "Are you ready, Louise?"

"You two enjoy yourselves," Jane said. "I've got work to do on a new recipe."

"And I have to get to my ANGELs meeting," Alice said. "We're having an abbreviated session tonight."

"I assumed you wouldn't have a meeting since you're working with the teenage girls," Louise said.

Alice shook her head. "We're meeting as usual while their parents are at church services. I did warn them that I've been busier than usual lately, and we might revisit one of our old crafts and study sessions."

"I'm sure it will be fine," Roman said. "I've heard some of the girls at Franklin High recall your group with much fondness."

"Thank you, and it was a pleasure to meet you." Alice shook his hand again and headed for the door.

"I'm off too." Jane said. Louise couldn't be sure, but she thought her youngest sister winked at her. "It was nice to meet you, Roman."

Roman held out his arm, and Louise accepted it. "Good-bye, Jane," she said. "We'll see you after a while."

Roman led the way to the front of the house. Then they were outside, and Louise found herself on the steps of Grace Chapel Inn, embarking on the first date she'd had in a very long while. She was nervous, but she also felt a sense of excitement and adventure that she hadn't felt in many, many years. She hoped that Roman Delwaard felt the same way.

Chapter Ten

"Would the Coffee Shop be all right with you?" Roman asked. "I thought you might be interested in something close to home. My research indicated that they have delicious pie."

Louise laughed. "Your research is right on target."

As Roman led her toward his white, late-model Cadillac parked at the curb, she came to a stop. "Is something wrong?" he asked.

"You have the same car I do, only yours is much newer," she said.

"How old is yours?"

"Twenty years."

Roman whistled. "You must take good care of it."

"I try. For the most part, it's more lack of use than babying and pampering."

"And it's white?" he asked.

She nodded.

Roman grinned. "How about that?" He pulled out his keys and clicked the remote, then turned to her. "I didn't even ask if you would rather walk. It's lovely out tonight."

"Indeed it is. I think that a walk would feel good. It would certainly help us keep in shape for the dance competition."

"Well, walk it is." Roman clicked the remote once again, locking the car. "Which way, Louise? I'm not familiar with Acorn Hill. I'm a Potterston boy all the way."

Louise headed them in the correct direction. "Did you grow up there?"

"Born and raised," he said proudly. "You?"

"Acorn Hill. I lived in Philadelphia during college and afterward for many years, but it's been a delight to return home to be with my sisters."

"They're lovely," he said. "You three must work well together as a business team too."

"We've managed so far. Each of us brings unique talents and capabilities to bear—Jane with her cooking, Alice with her compassion and drive."

"And you?"

Louise laughed softly. "I'm more of the administrative expert. I manage the bills and many of the reservations, keep track of which guests are coming and which are going. It's a nice life."

Roman stopped for a moment under an elm tree, green leaves rustling above. "It sounds like it is, Louise. I envy you for having family here."

When they reached the Coffee Shop, he opened the door for her. "Any place in particular you'd like to sit?" he asked.

"Anywhere is fine."

Roman gestured toward a booth. Louise moved onto the red vinyl seat, and Roman sat opposite her. He took a menu and perused it for a moment, then shut it, shaking his head. "I should just ask *you* what kind of pie is good here."

Louise smiled. "My father was always partial to the blackberry."

"Blackberry it is, then."

Hope Collins appeared at their booth. "Hello, Louise."

"Hello, Hope. This is my friend Roman Delwaard."

Before he could say anything, Hope smiled. "Ah, this must be the gentleman who's your dancing partner."

"Word gets around as quickly here as it does in Potterston," Roman said, smiling back at the waitress.

"Roman, this is my friend Hope Collins."

"It's a pleasure to meet you," he said.

"We were thinking about two slices of blackberry pie." Louise hoped to forestall any further conversation about her companion.

"Two cups of coffee as well," Roman added.

"Make mine decaf," Louise said.

"Mine too. You set a good example. At this time of night, I'd never get to sleep with regular coffee."

"Coming right up." Louise thought Hope winked at her, but perhaps she was just imagining things. She *was* a bit self-conscious about being seen with a man—and a stranger to Acorn Hill at that.

Roman leaned back against the vinyl cushion. "Was it strange for you to return home after being away for so many years?"

Louise considered his question. "It was peculiar at first, yes. Part of that was because my father had recently died. My husband Eliot had died four years earlier. Alice was already living in Acorn Hill, though, and when Jane joined us, we felt like family again. It eased the pain of losing my father."

"How about your mother?"

Louise's recollection was bittersweet, even after all these years. "She died while giving birth to Jane. I was fifteen years old."

"That must have been difficult," he said softly. "You must have been attending Franklin High around that time."

"I was." She paused. "If you grew up in Potterston, you must have attended Franklin as well."

"I did, but I'm several years older than you, I think. I must have graduated before you were there. So you were saying your mother died when you were—"

"I didn't mean to monopolize the conversation,

Roman," she said. "Tell me about your family. Where do your son and daughter live?"

He smiled and gazed into the distance. "My daughter Sandra lives in Seattle. My son Luke lives in San Diego."

"Goodness! They're a long way from home."

Roman nodded. "They are indeed, but they've put down roots there. Sandra is an architect and Luke is a pastry chef. They're both happily married and have three children each."

"Grandchildren for you. How lovely," Louise said. "My daughter Cynthia is still single. I hope that she finds a good husband someday."

"And would you like grandkids?" Roman asked.

"It must be fun," she admitted.

"Everything grandparents say in that regard is true. It's even better than having kids. You can love them and spoil them and not have to worry about the day-to-day troubles of raising them. Of course, none of my grandchildren is a teenager yet, so we'll see how that goes when they get there."

Louise smiled. Roman was so easygoing that she couldn't imagine any relatives of his being difficult. "I'm sure they'll be wonderful. You must miss them terribly."

His smile fell. "That I do. I see them twice a year, some-times more. I have an old college buddy who coaches a small-college team in Colorado. We've been like brothers over the years. I try to see him to catch up on events and talk shop. Then I travel to the coast to see my kids. But my summers are pretty busy with practice for the coming football season. Then from September to June I'm teaching, of course. I try to visit San Diego or Seattle for Christmas, Thanksgiving, or a week or two during the summer, but it's never long enough. Same with my kids. They're busy with their families, and it's difficult to get away."

"Have you ever thought of moving closer to them?" Louise asked.

Roman nodded. "I've thought about it, but even though I only have them for four years, and every year I vow it will be my last, I get involved with the incoming freshman class. I love coaching football."

"I don't know much about sports, particularly at the high school level, but you must be delighted that you've had such success at Franklin."

Roman puffed out his chest. "That's because of my boys. Every year I get hard workers—boys dedicated to doing their best. We may not win every game, but we give it our all."

"Much like your dancing skills?" Louise smiled.

Roman chuckled and opened his mouth to say something. At that moment, however, Hope set two plates in front of them. "Here's your blackberry pie, and here"—she carefully lowered two cups and saucers from her uplifted tray—"are your decafs. Anything else?"

"I think that's all," Roman said. "Thank you."

Hope retreated, and Louise took a bite of pie. She savored the subtle, fruity taste of the shop's specialty dessert and sighed.

"It *is* good," Roman agreed, starting on his second bite. "Good pick. Now, you were asking about my dancing skills?"

Louise swallowed. "I wondered if you applied the same perseverance to your dancing skills as your football players do to their game."

"I hope so," he said. "If I teach them nothing else, I hope they come away with that lesson. I'm not the sort of coach who forces them to win at all costs, but I try to instill in them a sense of pride in persistence." He took another bite of pie, then paused to enjoy it. "Much like my dancing. I may not win a prize, but I'm determined to learn. I want to surprise my daughter when I see her next."

"I think she'll be pleased," Louise said. "You've picked up the waltz quickly."

"Do you think I'm capable of learning others?"

"I thought we might focus another lesson or two on the waltz, then try something else. Is there anything in particular you'd like to learn?" she asked.

"What others can you suggest? What are some of your favorites?

"There's the fox-trot, the two-step—"

Roman leaned forward. "But what's your favorite, Louise?"

For a brief moment, she was transported to a Philadelphia dance floor. Eliot smiled at her, their hands attached as they swung in time to the music. Several other couples stopped dancing to watch them, hands clapping with the beat.

Her eyes misted, and she set down her fork. "Eliot and I always liked the Lindy Hop."

Roman covered her left hand on the table. "I'm sorry I asked, Louise. I hope I didn't make you uncomfortable."

She brushed at her eyes, smiling, and he withdrew his hand. "I'm sorry," she said. "I'm fine. Sometimes the memories . . ."

"I understand," he said gently. "My wife's been gone for ten years, but sometimes it feels just like yesterday. It was very sudden. It was a blessing for her that she went quickly, but I didn't have nearly enough time to say good-bye. My kids had already moved out and away, and my parents had been dead for many years. Suddenly I was alone. Yet life is good." He leaned forward. "I know the Cohens wouldn't mind my mentioning this, but did you know about their child?"

"No, I did not."

"More than halfway through Gail's pregnancy they learned that their son would die soon after birth. Something about an irreparable organ, I believe. They agreed that they wanted to carry the child to term. Rabbi Ben said that God had ordained all the minutes of their son's days, and they were not about to cheat Caleb of any of them."

"How sad," Louise murmured.

Roman nodded. "Yet they grieved and moved on. I've watched them dance numerous times, and I finally realized that they enjoy life to the fullest, every minute, every possibility. Besides the fact that I lost a bet with my daughter, I figured I owed it to myself to learn how to dance before I passed on."

He dipped his spoon in his coffee and stirred, even though he had added no sugar or cream. "You see, my wife always wanted me to learn how to dance. I thought we'd have plenty of years after I retired to learn how, but it turns out I was wrong. I envy you for your memories of dancing with your husband."

"They *are* good memories, but I hope you don't feel guilty about not taking dance lessons with your wife."

"Sometimes I do," he admitted, "but I also know that there are often things left unsaid between two people who love each other, whether they are husband and wife, father and daughter, or whatever relation. We do the best we can while we're living."

"Indeed." Louise sipped her coffee. "So you teach football and you're learning to dance. What else interests you?"

He grinned. "Would you believe me if I said classical music and ballet?"

"I *am* a bit shocked."

"Because I'm a football coach?"

Louise nodded. "I must admit I had a preconceived notion about what coaches might be like."

"I also like to bake. Not cook, mind you, but bake." He gestured at the pie. "I have a real sweet tooth."

Louise blinked. Roman Delwaard was turning out to be an interesting man indeed. "Is there anything else I should know about you?"

"Just a couple of things that might surprise you." He counted on his fingers as he said, "I actually keep my whites and colored clothes separate when I do my laundry, I like cats instead of dogs, and, oh yes, I love watching old black-and-white classic movies."

Louise sat back. "I'm flabbergasted."

He grinned. "So what should I know about you?"

She tried to think. What was there to tell? "Besides teaching you how to dance and teaching my piano students, I suppose you should know that I play the pipe organ for

Grace Chapel on Sundays. I played a long time ago when I was a teenager, and I took over the duties again when I returned to Acorn Hill."

"And I'll bet they are glad to have you. I'll bet you're a wiz on the organ."

Louise thought about the aged instrument. "You haven't heard our pipe organ, have you?"

"I've never been to Grace Chapel. I attend church in Potterston. Why? Is there something special about the organ?"

"It's rather old. Very old."

Roman smiled. "You probably play very well. What else can you tell me about you?"

What, indeed? Louise thought for a moment. "I knit occasionally and love reading biographies and nonfiction. Mostly I think you should know how special it is to me to live in Acorn Hill and live with my sisters."

Roman took her hand again, and a tingle flashed where their fingers met. Louise wanted to ease her hand away, but he smiled at her so reassuringly and kindly that any discomfort she felt faded away. "I think that's wonderful, Louise," he said softly.

⌒

When they returned to Grace Chapel Inn, they were laughing. Roman told entertaining tales about his coaching experiences through the years. He was a natural storyteller, Louise decided, for even though she knew little about football, he highlighted some of the funnier plays he'd participated in both as a coach and as a player when he wore the uniform of Franklin High.

They ascended the porch steps slowly, each seemingly reluctant for the evening to draw to a close. "Thank you for a lovely evening," Louise said. "Would you like to have a dance lesson tomorrow night? There's always room for improvement."

"I'd like that." Roman cleared his throat. "I had a fine time, too, and I wonder if you'd consider going out with me Saturday night. Say, dinner and some music? I have two tickets to Potterston's summer outdoor concert."

Louise was surprised to find that the idea appealed to her—very much. "Why, I'd be delighted, Roman."

His blue eyes sparkled. "Are you sure you don't just want to go because of the concert?"

"Well, that's part of it," she admitted. "I love music, of course. But I'd love to spend more time with you."

"Off the dance floor?"

She nodded. "Off the dance floor."

"As in *date*?"

She thought about what Jane had said earlier about their coffee tonight being a date. "As in *date*," she agreed.

Roman smiled broadly and touched her hand. "Thanks, Louise. I'll see you at the rec center tomorrow night. Be prepared to waltz your shoes off."

He waited while she opened the door and entered. "Good night, Roman," she said. Whistling, he turned and headed cheerfully back down the steps. Louise watched until he entered his Cadillac, and only when he drove off did she close the door, a small smile lighting her face.

The next morning, Jane had an appointment with Ellen Moore, the woman who ran Grace Chapel's Helping Hands ministry. They had agreed to meet at Grace Chapel, and Jane fleetingly thought how appropriate it was that she would be asking for assistance from the very ministry that her father had started so many years ago.

"Hello, Jane." Rev. Kenneth Thompson met her inside the church building. "I understand you're meeting with Ellen Moore today."

"Hi, Ken. You're welcome to sit in with us," she said. "What I want to propose will probably require your assistance."

"Now I'm intrigued," he said. "Let's go to the sanctuary. Ellen's already waiting there."

Jane followed Rev. Thompson into the main room.

The creamy white walls seemed to soothe her, as always, and the rich stained-glass windows glowed in the morning sun. Even on a weekday the sanctuary seemed holy, and she felt she should whisper. "Good morning, Ellen."

"Good morning, Jane." Ellen nodded.

"I asked Rev. Thompson to join us if that's all right," Jane said.

"That's fine."

Rev. Thompson suggested moving downstairs to the vesting room, and he led the way there. Once they got settled, Ellen asked, "So how can I be of help to you, Jane?"

"I need assistance from the Helping Hands ministry," Jane said, then launched into an explanation of what she and Lloyd and Craig and all the other census takers hoped to accomplish. She told them about the people who lived on the outskirts of town, and the elderly, and the busy, and those who had been forgotten by Acorn Hill society. "And so," she finished after an outpouring of emotion. "We want to help."

Ellen sat back. "Of course you do. My goodness. I want to help too. What exactly can we in Helping Hands do?"

"Well, I made up a list of suggestions. I thought we might even ask the church to help, too, you know, members at large? It'd be lovely, for example, if some of the youth group wanted to visit Three Seasons folks on a regular basis. And if someone could help people like Thomas and Dotty Gilpin and Inge Starr occasionally. Or if someone could get groceries for Bernice—"

"Wait!" Ellen held up her left hand. Her right was busy scribbling furiously on a scrap of paper she'd pulled from her purse when Jane started rattling off ideas. "I'm trying to get all of this, but I'm afraid you'll have to slow down."

"She's a bit enthusiastic, isn't she?" Rev. Thompson asked. "I'm glad for it, Jane. And I'm glad you've brought these situations to our attention. I admire Lloyd's desire to get the city government to help, but I've always felt the church should be the first line of assistance for the needy."

Jane nodded vigorously. "I agree. So do you think Helping Hands can assist and also work with a committee of other Acorn Hill churches?"

"I don't see why not," Rev. Thompson said. "Ellen?"

She set down her pen. "We'd be delighted to work with anyone who wants to help, whether within this church or another. Just tell us what we can do."

"Good." Jane rubbed her hands together with enthusiasm. "Let me tell you about more of the people I've met and go over a few suggestions I have for helping them. Feel free to chime in with any suggestions of your own at any time. I'm completely open to ideas." She scooted closer to Ellen and Rev. Thompson. "You're going to love these people as much as I do."

When the meeting had concluded, it was nearly lunchtime, and Jane walked back to Grace Chapel Inn. She found Alice and Louise in the kitchen, already foraging for food. Louise was setting plates and silverware on the table. Alice had removed a covered bowl from the refrigerator. "I see you found the chicken salad I made for sandwiches," Jane said.

They turned, looking guilty. "I hope you don't mind that we started to get things ready," Alice said. "We didn't know how long you would be, and I have to work this afternoon."

"That's fine. I'm hungry myself." Jane poured glasses of lemonade for them all and set another side dish on the table.

The sisters sat down, and after Louise said grace, they spread the chicken salad Jane had made that morning onto sandwich bread. "How was your meeting?" Alice asked.

"Very good." Jane dished up some cucumber salad that she'd made earlier as well. "Ellen Moore with Helping Hands has agreed to assist with the project. Ken Thompson would like to see the rest of the church get involved too."

"I think you're the perfect person to coordinate the various churches and their committees," Louise said.

"You have a giving heart," Alice agreed. "What sort of ideas did you and Ellen and Rev. Thompson come up with?"

"We agreed that we should try to rotate assistance among the churches, if possible, so that no one gets burned out. I described the people Craig and I had met and what some of their needs might be. Then we made a list of possible solutions."

"Can you give us an example?" Louise asked.

"For starters, I thought that Three Seasons could use a little sprucing up. I'd be glad to serve as interior decorator, if I can get some helpers to work with the painting and so forth. Then we would want to have a rotating list of people to visit with the residents—people from all walks of life, so that the residents aren't always talking to the same folks. It'd be good to have young folks, maybe a visit from people who own pets—"

"Clara Horn and her potbellied pig would be good candidates. Clara loves to talk to people, and Daisy is such a novelty and so well-behaved," Alice said.

"That's a great idea." Jane got up and got a pad and a pencil. "Clara...Daisy..." she mumbled to herself, scribbling.

"What else?" Louise asked.

"We need drivers to take the Gilpins and their daughter into town when needed. None of them drives."

"What about that sweet Bernice Sayers you told us about?" Alice asked.

Jane nodded. "We need someone to shop for her—more drivers—and perhaps take her out occasionally. I'm not sure how long it's been since she last left her home."

"What about getting someone to supply Books on Tape for her, since she's blind?" Louise asked.

"Another great idea," Jane said, scribbling.

"Perhaps..." Alice began, then fell silent.

"What?" Jane asked.

Alice shook her head. "I'm probably just being too sensitive."

"What is it?"

"Perhaps you should ask people directly what they want or need. People like Bernice will be delighted with the books idea, I think, but some people might see it as charity and get offended."

Jane frowned. "Do you really think so?"

"I understand what Alice means," Louise said. "Some people have spent so much of their lives being independent that to rely on someone else might be humiliating."

"If I may venture to say so, dear Jane, I think *you* might be that way were you in their shoes," Alice said gently.

"Me?"

Alice nodded. "You are a very independent woman. If old age or infirmity rendered you less active than you are now, you might be resentful of someone's attempts to do things for you."

Jane sat back in her chair, thinking. *Would that describe how I might feel?* She tried to put herself in the place of some of the people she had met. *Bernice didn't seem resentful or defeated about her situation—far from it. She seemed to embrace her blindness in some way. The Gilpins? I don't even know why they don't drive. Is it possible that a mother and father and their daughter never learned? Would they resent someone's trying to handle the task for them?*

How would the retirement home residents—not to mention Elena—feel about strangers going in and taking over the redecoration of their home or scheduling activities for them that they might not want?

"You have a good point, Alice," Jane finally responded. "I obviously need to research this a bit more. Particularly to make sure that any help is actually wanted."

"I'm sure it will be in most cases." Alice smiled. "If you encounter anyone who's resistant but who truly does need assistance, sometimes it helps if you make them feel like they are doing *you* a favor by accepting help."

Jane scribbled Alice's last sentence on the final white space on her paper. "Thanks for the tip. It may come in handy."

Chapter Eleven

*A*lice had left her Friday schedule open so that she could meet with her girls. They didn't meet on the weekends so that they could spend time with their families at home. Because they had enjoyed the makeup and fashion lessons so much, she decided to encourage them to think about future careers.

Once again they met at Grace Chapel Inn. Jane had served breakfast to the other guests, then prepared a later sitting for Janette, Glenna and Alice's youngsters. The two students were happy to see their teenage friends again. Alice noticed that the older girls had taken to applying makeup and spending a little more time on their wardrobe. Instead of jeans and T-shirts, today they were wearing comfortable but stylish khaki capris and colorful scoop-necked blouses. Glenna had even wrapped a matching scarf around her neck, which accentuated her brunette hair. Instead of wearing it pulled back, she had left it loose and styled it to flip up at the ends. Janette still wore her thick black glasses, but Alice could see that a little makeup brought out the beauty of her eyes. She had also coaxed her blonde hair into natural waves that wisped around her face and softened the scholarly image created by the glasses.

"You guys look great," Sabrina said when she first saw them. "I mean it."

"You too," Janette said, nodding at the four teenagers in turn. "Those are terrific outfits you're wearing. And I love your makeup," she said to Julie.

The girl smiled and ducked her head self-consciously. "Thanks. I practiced what Emilie showed us."

"Well, it looks great." Glenna smiled.

The four girls looked at each other and giggled. "Do you really think so?" Isidra asked.

"Absolutely," Janette said.

Alice stepped forward. "Don't forget that it's not just how you look that makes you attractive."

"We know." Esmeralda sighed, though she herself sported some light makeup that enhanced her tanned skin. "It's what's inside. You know how to take the fun out of things, Miss Howard."

Alice couldn't help but smile no matter how Esmeralda might feel about her. "We did have fun with the makeup session, and I hope we'll have more fun today. At least we'll be getting outdoors, Esmeralda. I know you'll like that."

Esmeralda didn't respond.

"Where are you going today?" Janette asked.

"We're going to different businesses around town. It's sort of a career day for the girls to get some ideas about what they'd like to do when they grow up."

Esmeralda wrinkled her nose. "I hope you're not taking us to a plumber's shop. *Ewww*."

"Not at all. I've already arranged for you to visit the newspaper office, a seamstress shop, a bookstore, the florist and a coffee shop. That should give you a sample of various careers—professional, retail, food service." She turned to Janette and Glenna. "Would you two like to tag along?"

They looked at each other, then shook their heads. "It sounds like fun, but we'd better work on our dissertations today," Janette said. "We heard that the Duceys and the Westriches were going to be gone today, so we want to take advantage of the quiet."

"How have their boys been doing?" Alice asked. "Are they still making noise?"

The girls looked at each other again.

"If they are, you need to tell me or one of my sisters," Alice said. "We want all our guests to feel comfortable here."

"They're mostly quiet until bedtime," Glenna said. "Then they tend to make a lot of noise until they fall asleep, but we can bear it."

"I can only imagine how their parents feel," Janette said.

"Yes, the four of them do look fairly frazzled when we see them in the mornings," Glenna said. "The husbands have been working hard to keep their boys under control."

"Well, let's hope their early breakfast has given them the energy to succeed at that," Alice said.

Glenna sighed. "And now it's time for us to get to work, right, Janette?"

"Unfortunately. I'd much rather be on an outing."

Alice smiled. She could remember what it was like to be in school and want to be finished. She turned to her teenagers. "Are you girls ready to go?"

Esmeralda took a second Danish pastry, then glanced around guiltily. She thrust her hand behind her back as though she didn't want anyone to see; nevertheless, Alice had noticed.

"Sure," Isidra said. "Let's go."

Alice led the way out of Grace Chapel Inn, down the porch steps and on toward town. "We're going to visit the *Acorn Nutshell* first. Raise your hand if you read your local newspaper every day." No hands were raised.

"On Sundays? Even once a week?" Alice asked hopefully. The girls shook their heads.

"Perhaps when you see what running a paper involves,

you'll be more interested in reading on a regular basis," Alice said. "You should read to keep up with what's going on in the world in general and your community in particular."

"If I want to know what's going on in my area, I just ask my older brother," Esmeralda said. "He knows all the gossip about who's dating who and who's flunking out of class and who's gotten arrested for shoplifting."

The other girls giggled. Alice shook her head. "That's not exactly what I meant, Esmeralda."

She shrugged. "What's more important than all that?"

"Those things seem important to you now because you're young," Alice said gently, "but when you're an adult, you'll be more interested in the entire community, not just your friends. You'll want to know whether the city government is raising your taxes and whether the leaders of your town are doing what they've been elected to do. Of course you'll also want to think on a national and even global level about what it means to be a citizen of this country and of this world."

Esmeralda laughed. "I don't think I'll ever be that interested."

By the time they reached the office of the *Acorn Nutshell*, next to the post office, the girls were already intrigued by Acorn Hill. The town was much smaller than their hometown of Potterston, and they were impressed by the friendliness of the residents while they walked. More than one person stopped to greet Alice, who in turn proudly introduced her girls.

The newspaper office was located in a small brown-brick building and had a frosted-glass door with black- and gilt-edged letters spelling out *Acorn Nutshell* in old-style type. Alice opened the door, and, as usual, Carlene Moss sat at her workstation. Her L-shaped desk was covered with pages of printed copy, dictionaries, stylebooks and almanacs. A flat-screen monitor sat above her computer keyboard, and a terra-cotta pot filled with ivy and a bowl with freshwater fish made the work area seem homey. She stood when she saw Alice and the girls, twin dimples showing in the cheeks of her heart-shaped face as she smiled. In her midfifties, she still frequently wore her coarse, gray-flecked brown hair pulled back in a short ponytail.

"Come in," she said, gesturing them inside the room. "I'm so glad you could come. Friday is a wonderful day for me to give tours. The *Nutshell* releases each Wednesday, so I'm not terribly busy today. I've just started working on next week's issue."

Alice introduced each of her girls, who politely shook Carlene's hand.

"I'm Carlene Moss, and I'm the photographer, business manager, editor and publisher of the *Acorn Nutshell*. The first thing I want you to know is that you're standing in a very old building. We've been here for more than ninety years. We used to have a full-fledged printing press. Later we got moveable typesetting equipment. Do you know what that is?"

The girls shook their heads. "I'm not surprised," Carlene said, smiling. "It was way before your time. Nowadays most newspapers use computers to lay out their articles in the form that you see when you read. In the old days, operators would type out the articles they were given, and type would be set in rows to produce the newspaper."

She moved toward the back of the room, explaining about the progress of print from the Gutenberg press to modern-day desktop publishing. "This is the machine we used to use," she concluded, touching a machine set at the back of the room against a wall. "The trick was that all the type had to be set backward, because otherwise when the stories were inked and pressed onto paper, they would appear backward themselves."

Carlene demonstrated by typing out the girls' names, then handing each teen a metal strip with the raised letters of her name. "It *is* backward," Sabrina said, staring at the metal in her hand.

"That's called a slug," Carlene said. "Consider it a souvenir."

"Thanks," Sabrina said, and the other girls nodded.

Carlene talked to them about how she managed the newspaper, from gathering news stories to writing the articles and laying them out. She explained that she e-mailed the final product to a printer in Potterston, who delivered the newspapers each Wednesday.

While the girls marveled over their slugs and the machine itself, Carlene took Alice aside. "Speaking of gathering story ideas, I've been wanting to talk to Jane but haven't been able to get in touch with her. Do you think I could interview her about the work she and Lloyd and Craig are doing for the charity cases in town?"

"You'd have to ask her about that," Alice said. "I'm not sure they want to be known as charity cases, at any rate."

"Oh, I'm sorry, but you know what I mean," Carlene said. "Whatever you want to call it, Jane and the others are doing good for Acorn Hill. I'd like to focus on that. What do you say?"

Alice shifted uncomfortably. Jane was not afraid of the spotlight, but Alice knew her sister believed in simply doing what she was called to do, without fanfare. "It's not up to me, Carlene. You'll have to ask Jane. If she thinks it will help their efforts, I'm sure she'll agree."

"Miss Howard," Julie called.

Alice smiled at Carlene, concluding their conversation. "Yes?"

"Did you see this slug?" Julie held out the copy of her name.

"Would you believe I got one with my name on it fifty years ago?" Alice asked. "My grade-school class came here, and we got a similar tour."

"From my father, not me," Carlene added hastily, laughing. "He started working here when he was young and worked his way up."

"And that's what it often takes in the working world," Alice said. "Starting at an entry-level job and working hard to rise through the ranks. Girls, we'd better get going if we're going to see some other businesses."

"I'm so glad you came," Carlene said. "I never get tired of talking about newspaper work. It's an exciting profession where you let readers know what's going on in their world."

"Maybe my brother should start a gossip newspaper," Esmeralda said, laughing. "It'd save him a lot of time."

The other girls laughed, and after thanking Carlene, they were outside again. "That was fun," Isidra said. "Where to now?"

"Do any of you like to sew?"

Isidra raised her hand. "I do. Sometimes I make clothes for my younger brothers and sisters."

"Then I think you'll like our next stop. We're going to

Sylvia's Buttons. Sylvia is a friend and an excellent seamstress," Alice said.

They walked through town, greeting Acorn Hill citizens out and about, and at last they were at Sylvia's shop. As usual, Sylvia had a creative window display, this time a selection of colorful quilts and equally colorful sundresses for summer.

"Wow," Isidra said. "Did she make those quilts?"

"Let's go inside and ask," Alice said.

Sylvia greeted them at the door. An attractive woman in her midforties, her dark eyes shone with pleasure to see the girls. Her strawberry-blonde hair was pulled back in a tidy ponytail, and she had a tape measure around her neck and a number of pins stuck in the top of her apron. "I'm sorry about my appearance," she said. "I was working on a new sundress, and it's easier to keep everything right where I need it."

"Did you make the dresses in the window?" Isidra asked.

Sylvia nodded proudly. "I can't claim the quilts, however. They were hand-stitched by some of the Amish ladies near Lancaster. I sell them at my shop since that area already has an abundance of Amish quilts."

"They're pretty," Sabrina said. "I bet they take a lot of work."

"They do," Sylvia said. "Especially because they're all

stitched by hand. So what would you girls like to know about the seamstress business?"

"Isidra likes to sew too," Alice said, gesturing toward the girl. "She might have the most questions."

Isidra and Sylvia were soon lost in a discussion about fabrics and thread. Alice was pleased that she had decided to bring the girls here, for Isidra's sake if no one else's.

Sabrina tried to stay with the conversation, but Esmeralda and Julie wandered off. Julie examined a rack of ready-made clothing Sylvia had for sale, but Esmeralda leaned against a wall, sulking. "This is boring," she mumbled to no one in particular.

She said it just loudly enough, for Sylvia stopped talking with Isidra and raised her head. "What did you say, Esmeralda?"

"I'm bored," she repeated. "I don't like to sew. Besides, we're meeting people from Acorn Hill, and we live in Potterston. Nobody here understands what it's like to be us or in our shoes."

Sylvia stepped forward and laid a gentle hand on Esmeralda's shoulder. "I come from Potterston too. You're what some people call needy girls, aren't you?"

The other girls hung their heads or looked away, but Esmeralda met Sylvia's eyes defiantly. "Yeah, that's right. Does it show?"

Sylvia smiled. "Let's just say that I can relate to you. I was once a needy girl too. I was raised by a single mother and we were so poor that sometimes we didn't have enough to eat."

Alice thought about the extra pastry Esmeralda had taken. *Had that been the reason?*

Esmeralda shrugged. "Lots of folks have it rough. Should I feel sorry for you?"

"No, but I want you to know that you *can* make a better life for yourself. I did. My mother taught me how to sew, which I loved. You have to find what *you* love and use that skill or knowledge to make a person of yourself. Remember, it's not where you come from but where you're going that matters."

Esmeralda waved her hand as if to say *whatever*, but she didn't say anything.

Sylvia showed them a few more things around her shop, and when she bid them good-bye, she stopped Isidra. "Sometimes I can use a handy seamstress when there's extra work, like at Christmastime. Would you be interested in working part-time for me someday?"

Isidra's face was all smiles. "I sure would! Just let me know when you need me."

⌒

After they left Sylvia's, Alice took the girls to the Nine Lives Bookstore, where its owner, Viola Reed, showed them around. Julie was enchanted by the orderly shelves of books with labels indicating the various subject sections. She stared at the hanging portraits of Viola's favorite authors on the pale taupe walls—Kipling, Poe, Austen, Dickens, Shakespeare, Twain and one contemporary author—Billy Graham. Julie fondly recalled works of those authors that she had read during her English classes at Franklin High, and it was clear she felt in her element.

Viola explained how she ordered and received the books, then placed them on the shelves. She discussed some of the more recent popular books, and Julie hesitantly asked her about several authors whom she'd seen on the best-seller lists. Viola said that she didn't stock much contemporary fiction but that she did try to keep up with the times, and that certainly she could order any book that was still in print.

The other girls, less enthusiastic readers, enjoyed the variety of cats that prowled about Viola's shop. "I get it now —nine lives like a cat," Sabrina said as she stooped to pet a dark tabby. "I was wondering about that."

At the end of their visit, Viola gave each of the girls a slim volume of inspirational sayings. They thanked her, said good-bye and headed for Craig's florist shop.

"I think I'd like being a bookstore owner," Julie said during the walk. "I'd like recommending books for shoppers, so of course I'd have to read everything in the store."

"I can see you doing that," Alice said.

Julie smiled shyly, then looked at her feet.

At Wild Things, Craig showed them the floral prep area, described how he received his flowers from the wholesaler, showed them the refrigerator where arrangements were kept cool and fresh, then handed them each a colored carnation of their choice. Sabrina in particular asked a lot of questions and whispered to Alice at one point that she would like to work in such a cheerful place. "Everybody loves flowers, don't they?" she asked.

Alice couldn't disagree. The lovely floral smell, coupled with the enthusiasm with which customers purchased arrangements to cheer ailing friends or to celebrate birthdays, anniversaries or who knew what else would make a lovely working environment for anyone.

When they had said good-bye to Craig and were once again on the street, Esmeralda twirled her carnation upside down. "Is it time to go home? I'm tired."

"One more stop," Alice said. "And I think you'll like this one, Esmeralda."

"What is it? A mechanic's shop? A beauty parlor?"

"The Coffee Shop."

"Oh, I see." Esmeralda put her hands on her hips. "So

Julie likes the bookstore, Isidra likes the seamstress business, and Sabrina the florist shop, but I'm only good enough to be a lousy waitress?"

Alice stood still. Where had this girl acquired so much rage? "No, I thought you might like to get a soda, that's all. However, Hope Collins, the waitress at the Coffee Shop, is one of my friends. I don't think of her job as menial at all. She works hard and provides a much-needed service in this town. I don't appreciate what you're implying, either about yourself or her."

Alice wanted to say more, but she could feel herself shaking inside. She rarely let herself get distressed, but Esmeralda was definitely getting under her skin. She turned and headed toward the Coffee Shop without glancing back.

Julie followed her, and Sabrina was close at her heels. Isidra looked at Esmeralda for a moment. "Why are you so hard on Miss Howard?" she asked. "She's trying to make sure we have fun."

Esmeralda blinked. "She doesn't like me," she said, the excuse sounding lame even to her own ears.

"She likes you fine." Isidra turned and followed the others, obviously not caring whether Esmeralda followed. "You just don't like yourself."

That afternoon, Jane answered the ringing phone at the kitchen extension. "Grace Chapel Inn."

"Hi, Jane, it's Carlene. Do you have some time for me to pop over and interview you for the next issue of the *Nutshell*?"

Jane thought hard. "Um, what about, Carlene?"

The newswoman laughed. "Why, about your work with Lloyd and Craig on the census project. I know you said you had to think about it, but it's certainly news in this town."

Jane glanced at the colander in her sink. Among other tasks, she had to peel and devein shrimp before tonight's dinner, and she quickly calculated how long the process would take. There was no reason why she couldn't do her work and talk to Carlene at the same time, if necessary. "Sure. Come over any time," she said. "The sooner the better. I hope you won't mind interviewing me by our kitchen sink."

"Not at all. Thanks. I'll be right there."

Carlene, true to her word, was sitting at the kitchen table in less than twenty minutes. Jane offered her a glass of lemonade, which Carlene accepted before whipping out her notebook. "So tell me about this project."

Jane set about wielding the deveining tool against the first shrimp. "You've already talked to Lloyd, right? And Craig?"

"Yes, yes." Carlene waved her hand impatiently. "I want your side of the story. So start at the beginning."

Jane sighed inwardly but went step by step through the process of Lloyd's plan and how she and Craig had gotten involved.

"Tell me about some of the people and their needs," Carlene said. "That's what will make this story interesting."

Jane dropped a cleaned shrimp into a bowl. "Uh, the people?" she asked. "Well..." She thought for a moment, not wanting to be too specific about persons or situations, then spoke in general about some of the ones she and Craig had met and about their needs.

"What do you plan to do to help?" Carlene kept right on scribbling.

Jane explained how the town churches would get together and how she had talked with the Helping Hands ministry about representing Grace Chapel. "I'm looking forward to the work," she added. "There's so much that needs to be done in our town."

Carlene asked a few more questions, then wrote the last word in her notes with a flourish, tapping her pen against the paper. "And ... done. Thank you, Jane. I appreciate your help."

"You're welcome." She automatically stuck her hand out to shake Carlene's, then laughed. "Let's take a rain check. My hands are *fragrant* with shrimp. Can you see your way out?"

"Of course," Carlene said. "Thanks again. This article will be in the next issue on Wednesday."

"I hope it drums up some support," Jane said.

"I'm sure it will. Bye."

Jane turned to the last few shrimp and finished cleaning them. She planned to sauté the shrimp and serve them over rice, accompanied by a tossed salad and corn bread. None of that was difficult to prepare, but it was closing in on dinnertime, and she wanted to be ready. Had she given Carlene everything she needed for her article? No matter. Carlene would call to check on any details that might not be clear when she was writing her article.

Chapter Twelve

*B*ecause she knew it would please Jane, Louise allowed her sister to help her choose clothes for her date. Jane selected a light beige skirt and a pale green long-sleeved blouse.

"Your date is for dinner, then the outdoor concert, right?" Jane asked.

"Yes."

"Then you'll want something comfortable and durable, in case you have to sit on the ground. Don't people spread out blankets or sit in lawn chairs for those concerts?"

"I believe so," Louise said. She frowned. "I hope we don't have to sit on the ground. Oh dear."

"Now, Louie, it will be fine. You'll manage whatever comes with grace and poise, I'm certain."

Louise sighed, then smiled at her sister and thanked her.

When Roman arrived, Louise was waiting near the front door. "Hi, Roman, it's nice to see you," she said, opening the door and immediately stepping onto the porch.

Roman handed her a small bouquet of pink carnations. "You'll probably want to set these inside."

"Oh my, how beautiful!" she said, thinking how long it had been since a man had given her flowers. "I'll be just a moment. I think Jane is around, and she can arrange these for me."

In fact, Jane was just inside when Louise opened the door. Louise raised her eyebrows, and Jane smiled sheepishly as she took the flowers and promised to take care of them.

Louise returned to the porch.

Roman gestured toward the street where his Cadillac sat at the curb. "Shall we go?"

"I'm ready."

Roman walked beside her along the path. "Are you hungry? I know a good little Italian restaurant a few miles east of Potterston. It's close to the park where the symphony will be held."

"Sounds good. I like Italian food," Louise said.

Roman held open the door for her, then went around to the driver's side and climbed in.

He began to talk about Cadillacs, and Louise felt herself relax. During the ride they discussed mundane matters —an upcoming county election, a movie about a journey through France that both wanted to see, a talk show on a local radio station. Unexceptional though the subjects might be, Louise gradually realized that she cared about what Roman thought. He was well-versed in current events and seemed to enjoy history as well. The trip seemed to take only a few minutes, and she was surprised when he pulled into a parking lot. "Here we are," he said.

"Guido's," Louise said, reading the neon sign that rose above the brick building.

Roman put the car into park and shut off the engine. "It's not fancy on the outside, but they serve some of the best pasta I've ever eaten."

Before she could open her door, he was opening it for her, extending a hand to help her out. "Thank you," she murmured.

Roman placed his hand lightly at her elbow and guided her inside. To her surprise, a lone violinist played soft Italian music. The room was hushed with quiet conversation, the lights dimmed for atmosphere.

"Ah, *Signor* Delwaard." A large mustachioed man wearing a light summer suit met them at the door. "It's good to see you."

"It's good to see you, too, Guido," Roman said. "Is one of your best tables available?"

"Of course," he said. "Right this way."

He led them to the far side of the restaurant, passing

many round tables covered with white cloths. A Chianti bottle covered with hardened candle wax served as a candleholder on each table, the glow from the candles illuminating the faces of the diners.

"Here you are." Guido showed them to a corner table where they could see out over the back of the restaurant. Fairy lights lined a gravel path to a footbridge spanning a small pond.

"It's beautiful," Louise said, fascinated by the sight.

"Thank you," Guido said, bowing slightly as he handed them each a menu. "*Signor* Delwaard, I think I know what you want, but perhaps the lady would like time to decide for herself."

Louise glanced at Roman. "What do you usually order?"

"The Guido sampler. It has smaller portions of my favorite pasta—spaghetti, ravioli and lasagna—all of them specially prepared."

Louise handed back her menu. "It sounds good to me."

"*Grazie.* Someone will be right out with your water." Guido took the menus and departed.

Roman smiled at Louise. "Are you enjoying yourself?"

"Very much." She smiled. "I feel a bit like Lady in *Lady and the Tramp.*"

Roman put his hand over his heart in pretend shock. "I hope you're not implying that I'm a scoundrel."

"Oh no, not at all," she hastened to reassure him. "It just seems so ... so ..."

"Romantic?" he supplied.

"A bit, yes."

He took one of her hands. "Does that make you nervous, Louise?"

She smiled. "A bit, yes."

He leaned his head back and laughed. "That's what I like about you. You're honest to a fault. Straightforward too. Well, if it reminds you of *Lady and the Tramp*, then I'm pleased. It's a good, classic movie. You certainly are a lady. Those pearls you wear suit your personality to a T."

Louise smiled. Roman's comments were not displeasing. "Do you know what the concert is tonight?" she asked, deftly changing the subject to avoid any more talk about herself.

"They're doing a tribute to Gershwin."

"How wonderful! I hope they perform *Rhapsody in Blue*."

Roman grinned. "I knew it must be one of your favorites since you're a pianist. Actually, I believe it's the finale."

The pasta was every bit as good as Roman had claimed. The conversation continued on a pleasant basis as well.

Though Louise declared she couldn't eat another bite, Roman ordered one cannoli for them to split. While they were cutting into the crunchy, cream-filled shell with their forks, the restaurant's violinist appeared at their table.

"Is there anything special you would like to hear?"

"Louise?" Roman glanced at her.

She smiled, suddenly struck with a notion. "It's Italian, but it's probably not fitting for a romantic restaurant like this."

"What?" the violinist said, smiling. "Anything will do. Particularly if it's Italian."

She shrugged. "*Funiculì, Funiculà.*'"

"*Bella!*" The violinist paused for effect, then began to play. Several of the waiters heard the song and moved to their table, singing what Louise guessed were the original Neapolitan words to the lively tune.

Roman grinned at her, and they both waved their hands in time with the music, enjoying the fun. When the song was over, the waiters backslapped each other and congratulated the violinist. Roman and Louise thanked him profusely, and he bowed.

"Please, let me thank you," he said. "That's the most fun I've had all night."

"The music was…" Roman glanced at his watch. "The music! Louise, we're going to be late for the concert if we don't leave right now. Please tell Guido how wonderful everything was," he said to the violinist, then dropped several bills on the table. He unobtrusively tucked a few into the violinist's jacket pocket as well. "Thank you so much. That was the perfect end to a perfect meal."

"*Grazie*." The violinist bowed again.

Roman drove to the park and the ticket taker at the entrance assured them that they had plenty of time to set up. Roman drove down the dirt road, presumably toward the concert site. "What did he mean by *set up*?" Louise asked.

"You'll see." Roman grinned.

As they drove farther, Louise saw concertgoers carrying blankets and picnic baskets trudging down the road. "Why do we get to drive?" she asked.

"That's the surprise," he said. He turned onto another dirt road, and she saw a stage with a concert shell protecting an orchestral setup and a grand piano. Roman drove into a roped-off grassy area and turned the car around so that the trunk was facing the concert stage.

"This should do it," he said, consulting the rearview mirror before getting out. Louise tried not show how puzzled she was as he helped her from the car.

"Is this the parking area?" she asked, wondering why he had turned the car around. Maybe he wanted to be able to leave in a hurry to beat the crowds. A pickup truck pulled alongside them, and the driver also turned his vehicle around.

Roman smiled, popping the trunk of his car. "It may not be as nice as a velvet seat in a concert hall, but I've got two comfortable chairs for us to sit in. I also brought a cooler of bottled sparkling water and some fruit and cookies."

Roman retrieved two collapsible padded chairs from the trunk. He set them up, and Louise saw that they had headrests and even footrests. He arranged the chairs beside each other, then set a wicker basket covered with a linen cloth between them. He gestured at one of the chairs. "Have a seat and let me know if you're comfortable. How do you like the location?"

Louise sat, and after he showed her how to adjust the headrest, she admired the view. "This is wonderful, Roman. I can see the stage so clearly here. But won't we block the view for other people?"

"This is a special section. They allow two vehicles to park here so that people can watch in comfort and be close to the stage. The tickets for this area are a prize in a lottery, and I happened to be a winner. Naturally I thought of you, since you like classical music."

"I'm delighted to be here." Louise straightened, anticipating the music. It had been a long time since she had been to an outdoor concert. She felt young again, and Roman had thoughtfully provided all the comforts that would allow her to regard the concert as a truly special occasion.

He set a cooler next to the wicker basket and opened the lid. "There's plenty of everything here, Louise. Help yourself to whatever you like."

"I believe I'd like some water now," she said. "The pasta was delicious, but it always makes me thirsty."

"Me too." He retrieved two bottles from the cooler. As he removed the caps, the musicians took the stage and began to tune up.

What a lovely evening. What a thoughtful man. When he held up his bottle, she tapped hers against his in a cheerful toast. Then they settled in to await the music.

$\backsim$

During the ride home, they talked about the concert. They agreed that the organizers had made excellent selections, and Louise pronounced the pianist for *Rhapsody in Blue* one of the best she had ever heard.

"I imagine it's a difficult number to perform," Roman said. "Can you play it?"

Louise laughed. "There's playing, and then there's

playing. Mechanically, can I perform it? Yes. Emotionally? Not nearly as well as the pianist did tonight."

When they reached Grace Chapel Inn, Louise saw that one of her sisters had thoughtfully left the front porch light on for her. She glanced at her watch. "Goodness! I didn't realize it was so late." Jane and Alice had probably gone to bed.

Roman walked her to the door. "I can't remember when I had a more wonderful time, Roman," she said honestly. "Thank you for inviting me."

"Thank you for coming with me. I had a lovely time too."

"Perhaps we can practice again?" she asked. "You did so well with the waltz the other day that I think we can safely move on to another dance."

"I'd like that," he said. "Louise, I know it may be forward of me, but I'd like to see you again. Not just the dance lessons, I mean. If you have any objections, I'd rather know now."

"Why no, I don't," she said without having to think. Roman Delwaard had become more than her dance pupil. He had become a dear friend. "There's no reason why we can't see each other."

He looked relieved. "I'm glad, Louise. You're a fine woman."

To her surprise, he leaned over and kissed her cheek. Before she could react, he had straightened, then touched her hand lightly. "Good night, Louise. Sleep well."

"Good night," she said, watching as he headed back to his car. She turned the door handle and stepped into her home, nearly bumping into Jane.

"Oops! Sorry," Jane said.

"What on earth are you doing?" Louise asked.

Jane grinned. "Looking for a dropped contact lens?"

"You don't wear contacts."

"Oh. Well, then, I guess I was spying on you and Roman. I couldn't see anything through the door of course, since it's pretty solid. Did you know, Louie, that you can't hear anything from the other side, even if you press your ear against it?"

Louise folded her arms, pretending to be irritated.

"Well, then, uh, I guess I'd better head for bed," Jane said, her eyes twinkling. "Now that I know you're home safely."

"I suppose Alice had the good sense to retire long ago?" Louise asked.

Jane nodded. "Good night, Louise." She headed up the staircase.

"Jane?"

She turned back. "Yes?"

Louise smiled. "He kissed me on the cheek, if you must know."

Jane returned her smile. "Well, that *is* nice to know. Good night, Louise. See you tomorrow."

"Good night, Jane."

Louise turned out the porch light, then ascended the staircase herself, humming all the way to her room.

The next morning, Louise seemed to have an extra spring in her step as she prepared for church. As the organist, she tried to be at Grace Chapel before everyone else except Rev. Thompson. When she had a lot of extra time, she liked to run through the morning's hymns, the processional and the recessional.

"Good morning, Louise," Rev. Thompson greeted her when she rushed into the sanctuary. "In a hurry this morning?"

"Only because I seem to be running behind schedule," she said. "I'm sorry to be late."

Rev. Thompson smiled. "You're not late. I'm sure your organ playing will be inspiring as always. There are no last-minute changes to the order of our worship, so there won't be any surprises thrown your way."

"Thank you," Louise said, heading for her place at the organ at the back of the church.

She glanced over the music and ran her hands experimentally across the keyboard to see how the action was today. She winced when the organ wheezed a bit, but she knew the congregation was accustomed to the old instrument and wouldn't trade it for anything, not even the most expensive model currently made. It was a part of Grace Chapel's history.

Louise launched into a Bach prelude, nodding as members began to enter the church. After a while she lost herself in the music. Playing a keyboard had always been her best mode of expression as well as relaxation. Though the task required concentration, she often thought of it as daydreaming with tone.

At last the choir entered, then Rev. Thompson, who began the worship service. Louise adjusted her sheet music, and just as she arranged the next piece she would perform, she saw a familiar head of white hair among the crowd. When the man turned, she knew she hadn't been imagining things.

What on earth was Roman Delwaard doing at Grace Chapel?

As if he knew she had spotted him, he turned slightly and smiled. Louise smiled back, then chided herself. She would have to pay attention to the order of the service or she might make a ghastly mistake. Resolving to be diligent, she lowered her head so that she couldn't see Roman.

Naturally, she felt compelled to peek at him during the rest of the service. When she did, she noticed that he was sitting right between Jane and Alice. How on earth had *that* come about?

He didn't turn around any more, and she found it easier to concentrate. When the service concluded, she continued playing until the congregation dwindled to a few stragglers. Then she stopped, calmly arranged her sheet music and left the organ.

Rev. Thompson met her near the door. "There's someone waiting for you outside," he said.

"Thank you, Rev. Thompson. I saw him. Did he introduce himself?"

"Jane did the honors, but I met Roman at a charity sports function about a year ago." Rev. Thompson smiled. "As always, your organ playing was lovely, Louise. We appreciate you sharing your talents with us every Sunday."

"I'm happy to do so."

When she exited Grace Chapel, she found Jane and Alice deep in conversation with Roman. Jane waved when she saw Louise and gestured her over. "Look who's here!"

"I saw. Hello, Roman. What brings you to our church?"

"Good morning, Louise. I wanted to hear you play, so I made the trip. And I'm glad I did. You were wonderful." He smiled. "I see, or rather *heard*, what you meant about the condition of the organ, but you coaxed beautiful music out of it. The pastorale was lovely."

"Thank you very much. I'm glad you enjoyed it."

"Roman, would you like to have dinner with us? I have a pot roast waiting back at the inn," Jane said.

"I didn't mean to intrude," he said. "I only wanted to hear Louise play."

"No intrusion," Jane said. "You're welcome to join us."

Alice nodded her agreement. Louise hoped he would say yes as well.

He shook his head, however. "Not this Sunday, thank you, but I'd love a rain check if that'd be all right."

"You've got it," Jane said. "Name the day and I'll cook something special." She and Alice said good-bye and headed toward the inn.

"Louise." Roman touched her hands. "Again, it was lovely. Thank you, and I'll see you at our next dance lesson."

"I'm looking forward to it," she said.

As she watched him walk toward his car, she found that she was, indeed, looking forward with enthusiasm to seeing Roman Delwaard again.

Chapter Thirteen

The next day was Independence Day. The sisters had decorated the outside of Grace Chapel Inn with red, white and blue bunting. Behind red geraniums Jane placed an orderly line of American flags. For breakfast that morning, Jane had also used a red, white and blue tablecloth to cover the dining room table for their guests and arranged small wooden statuettes of Uncle Sam here and there.

Besides the normal breakfast fare, on the sideboard she also provided blueberries and strawberries with whipped cream.

Janette was taking a plate to serve herself when Jane bustled into the dining room. "It looks wonderful," Janette said. "So festive."

"Thank you. We like to celebrate the holidays."

"Speaking of which, what do you usually do here in Acorn Hill for the Fourth of July?"

"Well, my mother used to fix holiday breakfast picnics in our garden, and I thought I might have one this year, Unfortunately, last night's shower made the grass too wet for that family treat. They have a parade around noon in Potterston, and fireworks at dusk."

"What about Acorn Hill?"

Jane thought for a moment. "I don't believe anything special is happening this year. To tell you the truth, I've been too busy to think about it much. So has our mayor. Sometimes he'll cook up an event in advance, but nothing this year that I know of."

"Okay, thanks."

Glenna soon joined Janette, and the girls enjoyed their breakfast. The Duceys and Westriches appeared as well, looking tired as usual. "How's it going with the noise?" Jane whispered to Janette when she got the chance.

"Much better," Janette whispered back. "I don't know what they're doing, but it seems to have made a difference."

Jane made sure all the chafing dishes were warm and that there was plenty of food for everyone. Just as she was about to disappear into the kitchen, Roxanna Ducey touched her arm. "We have to leave this afternoon, so I wanted to let you know how much we enjoyed our stay here at the inn."

"Thank you," Jane said. "I hope you got some well-needed rest."

Roxanna sighed. "Not particularly, but we solved the problem of why our kids had so much trouble going to sleep."

"What was it?"

"They needed more exercise, for one thing, and once we figured that out, it helped. But the main reason seemed to be that every night we would give them each a cookie after dinner. One night Loretta and I forgot to give them their dessert, and we noticed that they went to sleep much faster. So we tried it the next night, then the next."

"So that was the secret—one cookie?"

"It was just enough sugar, I suppose." Roxanna shrugged. "Now that we know, we're cutting out all processed sugar and giving them a piece of fruit after lunch. That way they can run it off during the rest of the afternoon."

"I'm glad you figured that out." Jane checked the coffee pot one last time. "Are you heading home today, or do you have somewhere else to travel?"

"We're going to Washington, DC, next," she said. "I have to admit that I wasn't looking forward to it with Randy and Mikey acting up so much, but now I have hope."

"If you're going to the major sights, I'm sure there will be lots of places they can run and play. I hope you have a safe trip."

"Thank you," Roxanna said. "I'm looking forward to some relaxation."

Back in the kitchen, Alice and Louise lingered over their breakfast. "Despite the fact that our Fourth of July picnic was rained out, we must keep up a patriotic spirit," Jane said.

"You're right," Alice agreed. "I feel like we should do something, but I don't particularly feel energetic enough to attend the parade."

"Or the fireworks tonight," Louise added.

"Why don't we invite some folks for dinner and a patriotic sing-along?" Jane asked. "I was planning to cook grilled chicken, red onion and mint kebabs. I've stored away enough chicken for extra guests. Up to twelve, I think."

"What a fun idea," Alice said. "Whom should we invite?"

"Vera and Fred Humbert," Jane said.

"Oh yes. I'd like to hear if Vera's had any luck getting Fred to agree to a vacation," Alice said.

"How about Craig Tracy? Rev. Thompson? Oh, and Henry and Patsy Ley?" Louise suggested.

"Wonderful. They love to sing," Alice said.

"Aunt Ethel and Lloyd, of course," Jane said, then paused. "Louise, would you like to invite Roman? I did promise him a meal. He might like to meet some other people from Acorn Hill."

"I think that would be a wonderful idea," Louise said.

Jane blinked. "You do? I figured you'd kick up a fuss."

Louise shook her head. "Not at all. You were right. Roman's a fine man."

Jane smiled at her sisters. "Well then, what are we waiting for? Let's get on the phone and start inviting. Louise, line up some patriotic music for us to sing around the piano, and we'll bill it as a good old-fashioned sing-along."

Jane gathered the items she would need for the kebabs: chicken breasts, olive oil, garlic, oregano, salt, pepper, lemon juice, mint and onion. Then she lined up all the metal skewers she owned, since there would be twelve people at the table. Many of the women would be full with just one kebab, but some of the men might want more than one.

She heard the phone ring but didn't answer it because she hadn't washed her hands after touching the raw chicken. Soon Alice entered the kitchen. "That was Vera. When she heard what a lovely dinner you were preparing on short notice for so many people, she asked if she and Fred could bring homemade strawberry ice cream for dessert."

"Tell her yes and thank you. I hadn't even planned dessert yet."

"Will do." Alice headed back toward the telephone in the reception area to relay the news to Vera.

While Jane finished the marinade, she thought about decorations. The dining room already looked festive. Should she decorate the parlor, where the piano was? If they were going to have a sing-along, that's probably where they would spend most of their time after dinner.

In the end, she moved the piano shawl from the baby grand and replaced it with some of the leftover red, white and blue bunting. Then she placed a vase in the middle of the bunting, planning to add appropriate flowers from the garden before dinner. "There," she said, standing back to admire her handiwork. "The parlor is ready."

Jane called Craig Tracy, who said that he would love to attend. Alice and Louise phoned the others because Jane was busy in the kitchen. They were delighted to report that everyone else was eager to participate in the impromptu dinner and sing-along.

Jane thought that Louise's eyes seemed to shine, and she teasingly asked her if it was because of Roman Delwaard. Normally unflappable, Louise seemed to blush slightly, then smiled at Jane. "I suppose I am happy about his acceptance. I want you and Alice to get to know him."

At their age, bringing home a beau to meet one's father seemed archaic. Jane mused to herself that bringing someone home to meet one's sisters, however, was about the next closest thing.

The Duceys and Westriches said good-bye to the sisters, with the men offering special thanks for Jane's cuisine. They packed up their cars and left for Washington, DC.

Janette and Glenna had already headed to Potterston for the day, vowing that they would take a day off from their writing to observe the parade and stay for the fireworks much later. All three sisters bustled around the house to make sure they were ready to receive their company. Fortunately, everything seemed to be in order, and Jane whipped up pitcher after pitcher of fresh, cold lemonade for the evening meal, adding the juice of a lime to each.

Everyone seemed to arrive at the same time. Jane had been hoping to be present when Roman made an appearance. She wanted to see Louise's reaction. She was certain her oldest sister was smitten with the football coach, and the idea pleased her. Louise deserved a little romance in her life. In Jane's eyes she was often far too serious with her piano teaching and organ playing. It would do her good to let her hair down occasionally, and if Saturday's date had been any indication, Roman Delwaard was an excellent match for Louise.

"Th-thank you for having us." Pastor Henry Ley shook Jane's hand as he entered the living room. His stutter meant that he seldom gave sermons, though he was Grace Chapel's associate pastor; but he helped the church in other ways, such as contributing to the church board and counseling troubled members of the congregation. A short, thin man with white hair and glasses, he wore his customary white shirt with tan pants. His wife Patsy greeted Jane with a girlish giggle. "We're so excited to be here. It'll be so much more fun than watching a patriotic show on TV."

"Patsy and I think that p-people don't sing enough anymore," Pastor Ley said. "We love coming to your home to visit."

"We're delighted you could come," Jane said. "It should be a fun night."

Fred and Vera Humbert showed up with homemade strawberry ice cream, which Jane put in the freezer until it was time for dessert. Alice and Louise had set the table earlier, and Jane ushered everyone to the dining room so that she could bring in the kebabs.

Everyone oohed and ahhed over the skewers. Jane had alternated cubes of chicken, mint leaves and slices of onion, seasoning them all with olive oil and lemon juice. Alongside the kebabs she served a Greek salad, which she hoped Nia Komonos and her mother might be proud of.

"This looks delicious," Ethel said, examining the tomatoes, cucumbers, red bell peppers, onion, feta cheese and kalamata olives in their olive oil and red-wine vinegar dressing. "I may regret it tomorrow, but I'm dining well tonight!"

Everyone laughed. "Dive in, everybody," Jane said, taking her place at the table.

It was an informal dinner, and Jane was happy to see

that everyone seemed to be laughing and talking easily. She was also pleased that everyone who had not known Roman Delwaard before introductions some thirty minutes before now treated him as an old friend.

Jane found herself seated next to Vera. At one point she leaned over and whispered so that Fred wouldn't hear. "Any progress on getting a vacation?"

Vera sighed. "Not yet. I picked up some travel brochures, though. I'm having trouble deciding on a location. You've traveled a lot. Do you think you could help me?"

"I'd be glad to."

"Thanks, Jane." Vera sighed again. "I never knew Fred Humbert would be so dedicated to his job or so set in his ways."

After dinner, the men volunteered to clear away the dishes, and Jane brought out bowls of the Humberts' ice cream, which everyone pronounced delicious and the perfect dessert for a wonderful holiday meal. Jane served coffee and tea for anyone who wanted them, and not long after, someone took up the cry for them to adjourn to the parlor for singing.

"I've b-been looking forward to this," Pastor Ley said. "Singing is the only time when I d-don't stutter." He laughed at his own comment.

"I'm not much of a songbird," Pastor Thompson said, "but I like to warble along. How about you, Roman?"

He smiled cheerfully. "I'm completely tone deaf. Louise has already granted me permission to be her page turner at the piano."

They trooped to the parlor and settled in for some old-fashioned singing of patriotic songs: "Yankee Doodle," "This Land Is Your Land," "You're a Grand Old Flag" and "When Johnny Comes Marching Home Again."

Lloyd, who was a Korean War veteran, suggested they sing military hymns, so they launched into "Anchors Aweigh," the "Marine Hymn" and "Off We Go into the Wild Blue Yonder."

After much singing and laughter, everyone paused to catch his breath. "How about 'Semper Paratus'?" Roman asked. "It's the Coast Guard's song."

"Were you in the Coast Guard?" Louise asked.

Roman nodded.

Jane noticed that Louise beamed as though she had learned something marvelous about Roman Delwaard.

"Unfortunately, I can't sing," he said.

"I think I know it," Pastor Ley said, and in his beautiful tenor voice, he broke into the song.

Louise followed along as best she could, but Jane observed that her eyes were not on the keyboard but on Roman Delwaard's face. This, she decided, was a new attitude for Louise Howard Smith, and she very much approved.

They closed with "America the Beautiful," "My Country 'Tis of Thee" and "The Star-Spangled Banner." The party broke up after that with everyone saying what a lovely time the sisters had provided. Roman and Louise lingered on the front porch before he left. Jane went to the kitchen to clean up and had just hit the start button on the dishwasher when Louise entered.

"I'm sorry, Jane. I wanted to help you. Cleaning up after twelve people is a lot of work."

"That's all right," Jane said. "Alice helped me for a bit, then I told her to lie down. She looked tired. Cleaning up gives me time to think."

Louise sat at the kitchen table. "That's what I need."

"Roman?" Jane grinned, towel drying a glass pan.

Louise nodded. "I like being in his company, Jane. I really do."

"Is that a problem?" Jane sat beside her at the table.

"No, but it seems like it should be."

"Why would you say that? I watched you two tonight and you seemed genuinely happy together. You're allowed some romance and a personal life, you know."

"It's not as though I was unhappy before I met him," Louise said. "I have you and Alice and Cynthia, of course. Speaking of Cynthia, what will she say?"

"I think she would be happy to know that her mother has found a new friend, don't you?" Jane asked gently.

"I suppose." Louise sighed.

Jane tapped her lightly on the shoulder. "You're worrying too much. Save that for the dance floor. How are the lessons coming, by the way?"

"Beautifully," Louise said. "Roman is a natural. I don't know if it's because he's an athlete or if he's just one of those people who take to dancing immediately, but we're doing well. We're meeting again tomorrow. The competition is in a few weeks."

"I'm pulling for you two to win." Jane winked. "Both on the dance floor *and* off."

Tuesday, Jane cleaned the rooms the Duceys and Westriches had recently vacated. Louise had piano lessons to teach all day, and Alice was working at the hospital. As Jane tidied up, she decided that she would contact some of the census people the next day and ascertain which needs they would accept help with.

Craig advised her that he would be busy getting ready for a wedding, so Wednesday she headed out on her own. She drove to where she and Craig had first begun. She knocked on the door of Bonnie Ethedridge's trailer home, and Bonnie soon answered with her three older children and the baby close at hand. Maybe it was Jane's imagination, but Bonnie seemed to eye her suspiciously. "What are you doing here, Jane?" Her voice was polite, but the tone less friendly than last time.

"I came to make sure you and your family don't need any help."

Bonnie shifted the baby to her other hip. "I told you we were doing fine, and we are," she said, pursing her lips together. "However, if you'd like some help from us, I'd be glad to oblige. We don't have much to give, but I can run errands or my kids can entertain at that old folks' residence. Old people seem to like to see kids."

"I'll keep it in mind. Thanks."

Jane was about to ask Bonnie if she had done something to offend her when Bonnie said, "Excuse me, but I've got something on the stove. Bye."

That was peculiar. Maybe I'm just imagining things. Jane next drove to Bernice's trailer. The elderly woman answered on the first knock, ushering Jane into her home. "Come in, Jane. I'm so glad to see you."

At least I'm welcome here.

The button collection on the wall gleamed from the bit

of light that peeked through the partially open Venetian blinds. Jane explained her purpose for coming, and Bernice smiled. "You know I do fairly well on my own."

"Yes, but we'd like to help. How about getting some Books on Tape that you could listen to? Or someone to get your groceries on a regular basis."

"Bonnie does that," Bernice said. "I hate to hurt her feelings."

Jane frowned. Maybe that was why Bonnie had been so curt. Perhaps she had heard that Jane wanted to relieve her of her errands for Bernice and had taken offense. "I only thought that Bonnie has her hands full with four children," she said gently. "You might want someone to shop for you on a more regular basis, anyway."

"That might not be a bad idea." Bernice fumbled and patted Jane's knee. "I know your heart's in the right place, dear. As for the Books on Tape, yes, I'd love that. I do miss reading."

Score one. At least I have something to show for my questioning.

Jane stayed a little longer, then told Bernice that she had other people to see. She promised to be in touch as soon as possible, then headed for the Gilpins' home.

Inge Starr answered the door, and when she saw Jane, her smile fell. "What are you doing here?"

Jane sighed. "Have I done something wrong? Please be

honest with me, because that's the second time I've gotten that response today."

"It must be because of that newspaper article," Inge said. "We didn't know you were going to act like some sort of government agent when you came here before."

"What article? Oh, you must be talking about the interview I did with the *Acorn Nutshell*, right?"

Inge folded her arms and nodded. Jane felt a sense of dread wash over her. "I haven't read it yet. What does it say?"

"I guess you can read it for yourself." Inge nodded toward the kitchen in the house and allowed Jane entry. At Inge's gesture, Jane sat at the table and read the front-page article. "'Local Seeks to Do Good,'" she read, groaning inwardly at the headline. She read the article with trepidation, wondering who in the world Carlene had interviewed, because it didn't sound like her.

"Why, this makes me sound like some sort of goody two-shoes," Jane said. "I want to help people, but I sound like someone carrying around baskets of food and provisions for the destitute."

"Isn't that how you see yourself?" Inge said.

"No! Not at all. I want to give people a hand, not pat them on the head. Everyone I've spoken with is a thriving, active human being. I want to help them reach their potential, but not—"

"Keep them at the poverty level at which Miss Moss seems to feel we live?" Inge finished.

Jane nodded. "Exactly. Oh my goodness. No wonder Bonnie was so cold to me. Bernice either hadn't been read the paper or is entirely too forgiving. Inge, I am so sorry."

Inge sat in a chair next to Jane's. "That's okay, Jane. I hoped you weren't really like that. But I'm curious about what you had planned for us."

"I knew that you and your parents don't drive, so I thought maybe someone could drive you into town occasionally." Jane peered at Inge. "Was that wrong of me? I wanted to help, but maybe I've overstepped my boundary."

Inge pursed her lips. "It's true that we don't drive, and it's caused a hardship on us. Our neighbors are often busy, and we hate to impose."

"It wouldn't be an imposition if someone *wanted* to help," Jane pointed out. "Does that make sense?"

Inge nodded. She ducked her head, but not before Jane noticed the tears in her eyes. "What's wrong, Inge?"

"You're being so k-kind," Inge said, sniffling. "Especially about something that's so s-stupid."

"What's stupid?" Jane asked.

Inge raised her head. "We don't drive because we were all involved in a bad auto accident over twenty years ago. I was just a girl. My father was driving the car. We suffered some bumps and bruises, and I broke a finger, but mostly we were just shaken up. Since then, my father has never driven. Nor my mother. They didn't want me to learn how to drive either, when the time came, and truthfully, I didn't want to."

"But you ride in cars, yes?" Jane asked. "You just don't drive?"

Inge nodded. "That's why it's so silly. I don't even really remember the fear anymore, and I don't think my parents do either. We're all so set in our ways, though, that we don't know how to get out of the rut."

"Would you like to learn how? Do you think your parents would like that?"

Inge thought for a moment, then nodded.

"You can take driving lessons. I think sometimes the best way to face fear is head-on. As for your parents, they're so talented at what they do—gardening and your father's model trains—that I feel certain they could help other people, whether or not any of you drives."

Inge wiped her eyes and smiled. "I'd like to help other people. My parents too. What can they do?"

Jane smiled. "There's a residence for retired people on the other side of town that needs some attention—the building *and* the residents. Would your mother be interested in planting some flowers around the place to spruce it up? Tend some plants inside? Maybe teach the residents how to grow or care for living things?"

"She'd like that," Inge said. "I'd like to help her. What about my father?"

"Well," Jane said, thinking fast. "Perhaps he could set up some of his model trains for the residents. I think they and their visitors would like to have something to watch." Jane paused. "Do you think your parents would like that?"

"Yes." Inge laughed. "Yes, I do. Let me go get them."

She left to call her parents in from the backyard, and Jane leaned back in her chair. At least she'd learned what had caused Bonnie Ethedridge's chill. Jane couldn't be angry at Carlene; she was only highlighting the human-interest angle of the story. Somehow, however, Jane had come across as too much of a do-gooder, something by the world's definition she decidedly was not. Most of the folks in Acorn Hill knew her well enough to read between the lines, but she hoped that none of the other new friends she'd made would give her the cold shoulder. She didn't want to jeopardize Lloyd's plan before it had even a chance to be implemented.

Chapter Fourteen

Friday morning Jane headed for Town Hall. Lloyd had called together the various church committees that would meet to work on the needs identified by the census. Ellen Moore met Jane at Grace Chapel, and they walked to town together.

"I read the interview with you in the *Acorn Nutshell*," Ellen said, smiling.

Jane groaned. "I hope I never hear another word about that. I'm so sorry, Ellen, I didn't intend to make it sound like I was doing everything myself. I wanted Helping Hands to get credit. Your ministry has already done a lot of good and pledged a lot of help."

"I understand, Jane," Ellen said, laughing. "We all know you and your heart. Besides, what difference does it make who gets *credit*, as you call it, as long as we're able to help people?"

"I had a word with Carlene—not chastising, of course, because she meant well. When she realized how the article sounded, she apologized and said she'd run another article and leave me out of it entirely."

"Maybe we'll have more information to add after our meeting today."

At Town Hall, Bella had set up folding chairs in a circle and placed a pitcher of water and glasses on a nearby table. Justine Gilmore represented the Methodist Church, and Alta Talton represented the Presbyterians. Justine was the single mom of an eight-year-old, and Alta was a bright-eyed, petite woman in her early eighties. They greeted Jane and Ellen with open arms before everyone sat down to start the meeting.

"Should we wait for Lloyd?" Jane asked.

Alta shook her head. "Bella said that he would probably be late and we should start without him."

"We've gathered all the needs that Lloyd has mentioned and made a master list," Justine said. "We thought that needed items, for example, could be donated and collected through our various committees, then inventoried and distributed."

"That sounds wonderful," Ellen said. "What have you ladies come up with, itemwise?"

Alta consulted her list. "A drive to collect oscillating fans for those without air-conditioning, for starters. We also found a need for canned goods."

"The community food pantry can help there too," Jane put in.

Alta nodded. "That's what we thought. But we'll need a way to keep it up."

"The Good Apple Bakery volunteered to donate day-old bread and leftover pastries," Ellen said.

"Excellent!" Justine scribbled in her notebook. "What about service-oriented projects?"

"Home improvements for those who need repairs but can't afford them—our church's youth groups should be good at that," Alta said. "A food delivery service for the elderly and shut-ins. Lloyd said we might be able to make that a regular project."

Jane took her own notes, writing furiously as Alta and Justine talked. "It sounds wonderful, ladies. How about specific needs?"

"We each made a list," Justine said, passing two pieces of paper to Jane. "We gathered these from the other census takers. Lloyd said you have a list of your own."

"I do," Jane said, looking over the others' pages. There were only a few specific needs listed, which made sense. The other census takers besides Jane and Craig had worked the inner portion of Acorn Hill. Needs seemed to be greater farther from town.

There was much work to be done.

After her meeting, Jane headed back to Grace Chapel Inn. She was supposed to give Alice's high school girls a basic cooking lesson. First, however, she drove to Three Seasons. There she found Elena Nole at her usual station, the reception area, filing. The short blonde hummed as she studied the contents of a manila folder, but she stopped when she saw Jane.

Jane sighed and held up her hands. "Now before you say a word, I had nothing to do with that article. I certainly meant no disrespect to you or your residents."

Elena broke into a smile. "Honey, I knew that. Frankly, I just like to see my sweet people get some attention."

Jane sighed inwardly with relief, then smiled. "Do you have time for a coffee break, Elena? I have a couple ideas about how to help the residents here."

Elena was out from behind the receiving area as fast as her plump legs could carry her. "I'm all ears, Jane. Let's sit in the lounge."

Alice sat in the kitchen, worried Jane would not return from her meeting in time to teach the girls some cooking basics as she had promised. The girls were due to arrive at two o'clock, which was now only five minutes away.

The back door opened and then shut with a bang. "Whew!" Jane said, rushing into the kitchen. "Am I late?"

Alice sighed with relief. "You're just in time. The girls should be here any minute."

"Fortunately, I'm ready to begin. It sounds like some of them are already doing some heavy cooking for their families."

Alice nodded. "It's difficult when their mothers work and they have brothers and sisters who depend on them. They should be enjoying their teenage years instead."

"I agree," Jane said. "But we also want to make sure that they're eating properly and feeding their families well."

She reached into the refrigerator and pulled out a plate of cookies. "For the sake of good nutrition, I made these whole-wheat cookies with carob bits. I don't think they'll notice any difference from the store-bought kind, except that these are actually pretty good for you."

"I know firsthand that they're delicious," Alice said. "Good thinking."

Jane pulled some sheets of paper out of a drawer. "I also printed off these recipes of healthy meals and snacks, with nutritious accompaniments on the back. This cookie recipe, for example, has the suggestion of skim milk to go with it."

"That's great." Alice cocked her head. "I think I hear them at the front door."

Jane tied an apron around her waist. "Send them in. I'm ready."

The girls spilled into the house when Alice opened the front door. She had advised them to wear old clothes in case things got messy. Each girl wore a T-shirt and cutoff shorts, looking more like the girls Alice had first met. With the exception of Esmeralda, however, all the girls seemed happier and smiled more readily. Especially Julie.

"Right this way," Alice said, leading them to the kitchen.

"Hi, girls," Jane said. She seemed to be completely at ease with the teenagers. When introductions were finished, she beckoned them toward the table. "Have a seat and let's get down to some other business before we start cooking."

The girls sat, squabbling only briefly over chairs. When they were quiet, Jane said. "How many of you cook on a regular basis?"

All four of them raised their hands.

"That's great. I have no beginners here. You ladies are already experienced."

They looked at each other with pride.

"Tell me some of the meals you prepare," Jane said, pointing at Isidra. "Let's start with you and go around the table. Name one of your favorite, easiest meals."

"Tacos," Isidra said.

"Canned soup," Julie said, ducking her head when the others laughed.

"Crackers and cheese," Sabrina said.

"Nachos," Esmeralda said. She tipped her chair back and grinned.

"*Oooh!*" Jane said in mock horror. "Nutritionwise, you all fail."

A chorus of dismay was the response.

"What?"

"What's wrong with tacos?"

"The cheese on crackers is protein, right?"

Jane held up her hands. "I agree that cheese has protein and tacos are okay on occasion. We're going to talk a little bit about nutrition, however, and taking the time to make healthy meals for yourselves and your family on a regular basis."

Esmeralda groaned. "This isn't going to be one of those four food-groups lectures, is it?"

Jane smiled. "I won't insult you with a breakdown of the Food and Drug Administration's latest recommendations. I think you all know what the standards are over the years: fruit, vegetables and lean proteins. Keep the sugar to a minimum, ditto the fats. Any questions about that?"

The girls looked at one another, then shook their heads.

"Good," Jane said. "Let's move on."

She passed out the recipe sheets and discussed some of the menus.

"Baked pork chops?" Sabrina wailed. "I can't do this."

"Sure you can," Jane said. "And to prove it, I've got some chops here for you to practice on." She pulled a pan from the refrigerator, explaining how to make the easy marinade for the pork that was listed in the recipe. While she talked, she pulled out a baking sheet and showed them how to line it with aluminum foil. "That makes cleanup easier later. Just wad up the foil and toss it in the trash. The baking sheet stays clean."

Sabrina, Isidra and Julie liked the idea of less cleanup.

"What if your family doesn't like pork?" Esmeralda said.

Alice sighed. Leave it to the girl to try to throw a damper on things.

"You can do the same thing with chicken," Jane said. "Now, here's another thing, girls . . ."

As Jane continued her discussion, Esmeralda seemed to lose interest. She moved from her place at the table over to Isidra's, trying to engage her in conversation. When Isidra would have none of it, Esmeralda moved back to her area, sighing.

At last the girls put their individual pieces of pork on the baking sheet and popped it into the oven to bake. Jane called them over to the counter, where she took some time to show them how to prepare fresh green beans. Suddenly, Esmeralda called, "The pork's on fire!"

Everyone whirled around. Sure enough, smoke was finding its way out of the oven, and its odor suggested that the cause was something other than overcooked pork. Jane turned off the oven and opened the kitchen windows wider. After she had waited an appropriate amount of time, she opened the oven door. Smoke billowed out, and the detector in the kitchen beeped mercilessly until Alice, standing on a chair, reached up to stop the dreadful noise. Calmly Jane used tongs to remove a charred, smoking clump of material, which she placed in the sink and covered with water.

When the smoke had cleared, she wiped her forehead and peered into the oven. "The fire's out, but I'm afraid our chops are ruined."

The girls expressed their dismay. Alice and Jane, however, focused their attention on Esmeralda. "What, exactly, happened?" Jane asked the girl.

Esmeralda shrugged. "They just caught on fire?"

Jane continued to look at her.

"All right," Esmeralda said, sighing. "I put a pot holder in the oven."

"But why?" Alice asked.

"So it would be handy when we were ready to take the meat out." She smirked, daring Alice to pursue an excuse beyond the lame one she offered.

Alice felt that she had reached the end of her patience with Esmeralda. Perhaps it was time to tell Lilia that she had failed with the girl and that Esmeralda needed another outlet for the rest of the summer. She had done little but disrupt the other girls and spoil their learning and fun. "Esmeralda, I'd like to speak with you privately," she said.

Esmeralda scowled. "I don't see why."

"Go with her, Esmeralda," Isidra said, frowning. "You need to hear what she has to say."

"Yeah," Sabrina said. Julie nodded.

Alice pushed through the swinging door to the dining room. To her surprise, Esmeralda followed. She did, however, hold her head up defiantly. "Yeah?" she asked.

"Sit down," Alice said, gesturing at a chair. Esmeralda sat.

Alice quickly prayed for the right words, as she always did when she had an unpleasant confrontation. Something told her to get right to the point. "Why are you making things difficult for the other girls? I thought they were your friends."

"They are." Esmeralda scowled. "You're not."

Alice shook her head. "This isn't about me, it's about

you girls. You don't have to like me to participate in the group."

Esmeralda blinked. Clearly this was a tactic she hadn't expected. "I *don't* like you," she reiterated, as though trying to goad Alice into anger.

"Duly noted," Alice said calmly. "Why do you want to sabotage the other girls' fun though?"

Esmeralda didn't say anything. Alice started to ask her again, but the girl blurted out, "The others like you. They don't like me anymore."

Instantly Alice felt sorry for the girl. She saw Alice as competition for her friends' attention. "I'm not here to replace you," she said gently. "I never could. I'm not one of their—or your—contemporaries."

"Yeah, but they don't like me," she said stubbornly.

Alice prayed for further wisdom. "If they're not as friendly toward you, perhaps it's because of the way you're treating them. Or your attitude toward our time together."

"I don't feel part of the group," Esmeralda mumbled.

Alice put her hand on the girl's shoulder. "But you are. You're part of this team. I think the girls are just waiting for you to act like a true member and work with them, not against them."

Esmeralda sighed. "Are we finished?"

"Will you at least think about what I've said?"

"Sure, sure. Can I go?"

Alice nodded. Esmeralda banged through the swinging door back into the kitchen, and Alice took a moment to deal with her discouragement. Only time would tell if she had gotten through to the teenage girl.

That evening, Louise was off for a dance lesson with Roman after dinner. Alice helped Jane with the dishes, washing the pans that were too big for the dishwasher. "You're awfully quiet tonight," Jane said. "Are you still thinking about the cooking lesson?"

Alice nodded. She relayed the gist of what she'd said to Esmeralda. "Do you think I did the right thing by talking to her?"

"I'm sure of it," Jane said. "You were dead on too. From the girls' conversation in the kitchen, I gathered that Esmeralda is bitter because her family situation is unhappy. I think she envies others with more stable backgrounds . . . like us."

"I can't help but feel sorry for her," Alice said. "Her mother is single and busy with work. Her brother is older and probably doesn't have time for her. She has to care for her younger sisters. No wonder she feels abandoned by her friends."

The phone rang and Jane picked up the extension.

"Grace Chapel Inn. Oh, hello, Cynthia. No, your mom's not here. She's at a dance lesson."

Jane paused for a long while. "Actually, she's the teacher. It's a competition the Potterston Dance Club is having, and she's teaching an inexperienced man the steps."

Another pause. "His name is Roman Delwaard, and he's the football coach at Franklin High." They chatted awhile before Jane said, "Yes, I'll tell her you called, dear."

She hung up the phone and turned back to Alice. "Where were we? Oh yes, Esmeralda. You feel sorry for her and that she feels abandoned by her friends, even though she's pushed them away."

Alice nodded. "That's right."

"Well, you know that old saying about always hurting the ones you love," Jane said. "It seems to me that she's pushing the last of her friends away from her even though she desperately wants their approval. Teenagers often use mixed-up logic."

Alice nodded. "Kids don't have a corner on that at all. Some adults act like that too." She sighed. "I just wish I knew how to reach her."

"Keep including her as one of the team, as you said. My guess is that she'll come around," Jane said, handing Alice the last item to be dried. "What's your next activity?"

"We're going white-water rafting at Sabrina's request."

"How fun," Jane said. "Are you looking forward to it?"

Alice weighed her answer. "I feel a bit nervous, but I remind myself that I was anxious about the rock climbing as well. Conquering that challenge turned out to be quite exhilarating. I'm glad I did it, and I'm sure I'll feel the same way about the rafting. When it's over, that is."

Jane laughed and popped Alice playfully with a dish towel. "You'll do fine."

$\backsim$

"Whew. I think I need to catch my breath," Louise said. She and Roman had just finished a fox-trot, and she was slightly winded. "I'm not as fit as I used to be."

"You've still got quite a spring in your step," Roman said.

"Thank you," she said with a flourishing curtsy. When she rose, she found him smiling at her. She blushed under his gaze but returned the smile. "Have you thought about what dance you'd like for us to perform for the actual competition? We also need one in reserve in case of a tie."

"You're the teacher," he said, crossing his arms. "Which one do you think we're better at performing?"

Louise thought for a moment. "I think the waltz is still our strong suit, but you've picked up the fox-trot quickly too."

Roman's expression went serious. "May I ask you a personal question?"

She nodded.

"What would you say to teaching me the Lindy Hop? That used to be your favorite dance, didn't you say?"

Louise smiled. "Yes. Would it surprise you to know that I still think fondly about that dance?"

"Why should it surprise me?"

"I'm sixty-five years old, Roman. I'm not as limber as I was when I danced regularly."

He studied her for a moment. "Do you *feel* old, Louise?"

The question surprised her. Did she? "I don't feel old when I'm around you," she said honestly.

He caught her gaze and held it. "Would you teach me the Lindy Hop, then? I want dancing to be fun for you."

His thoughtfulness touched her, and she knew immediately that he had nothing but her best intentions at heart. Roman didn't want to take Eliot's place; he only wanted to fill an emptiness in her heart that he instinctively knew needed to be filled. Throughout their brief relationship he had sought her happiness—the concert, the flowers, dinner. Now he only wanted to give dancing back to her, to allow her to reclaim the joy she had once known.

"Are you sure you want to learn that dance?" she asked.

The swing music and rapid movements made it more suited for younger people.

He nodded, eyes twinkling. "I'm sure."

Louise smiled. "Then let's start with the basics. We start in a closed position..."

When she got home, Louise was still smiling from the lesson. Alice and Jane were in the living room, relaxing and chatting. She had just settled in to recount her evening with Roman when the phone rang.

"Who could that be?" she asked, checking her watch. It wasn't past bedtime, but it wasn't early enough for friends or potential guests to call either.

"I'll see," Jane headed for the extension by the stairs.

"I hope it's not an emergency," Alice said to Louise. She shivered. "I never like calls at night."

"Nor I," Louise agreed.

Jane returned. "Louise, it's Cynthia."

"Cynthia!" Louise arose from the sofa. "Is she all right?"

"She's fine," Jane said, then bit her lip. "I was so interested in hearing about Roman that I forgot to tell you she called earlier while you were out."

Louise sighed with relief. "I'm glad it's nothing urgent."

She left the living room and headed for the phone in

the reception area. She lifted the receiver, eager to chat with her daughter. "Hello, Cynthia. How are you?"

"I'm fine, Mother. How are you?"

"I'm fine."

A long pause ensued. "Jane said you were teaching a man to dance."

"Yes."

"That the Potterston Dance Club is having a competition?"

"That's right."

Cynthia laughed. "My goodness, I'd say we have some catching up to do."

Louise laughed lightly. "Perhaps we do, dear."

"Jane said he's the football coach."

"That's right. I've been teaching him to dance for the competition, so we've had a chance to get to know one another. He's a very nice man, and we have a lot in common."

"Such as?"

Louise switched the receiver to her other hand. "Cynthia, would you like to come for a visit? Maybe it'd be easier for us to talk in person."

"How did you know that was what I was going to ask? I was hoping to visit *and* find some quiet time to work on a special literary project. May I come tomorrow?"

"Of course, dear."

"If the inn is booked, maybe I can share your room or stay with someone else."

"We have two vacancies, so you can have your pick of the available rooms."

"Thank you, Mother. I'll see you tomorrow."

"Good night, dear."

Louise hung up the phone and went back to the living room. Jane and Alice looked at her anxiously. "Is everything all right?"

Louise felt a rush of emotion, as she always did when she thought about her only daughter. "Cynthia is coming to visit tomorrow."

"That's good news," Alice said. "We haven't seen her for a while."

Louise sat on the edge of the sofa. "She knows about Roman. Do you think she'll be upset?"

"I'm sure everything will be fine," Jane said. "She's probably very pleased that you're broadening your social life."

Louise fingered the strand of pearls at her neck. "I hope so."

Chapter Fifteen

O n Saturday Cynthia arrived just before lunchtime. Louise had not been expecting her until much later as she knew the drive was at least six and a half hours.

Louise was helping Jane and Alice set the table when Cynthia rounded the door jamb into the kitchen. "Hello, everybody."

"Cynthia!" They all beamed, and Louise gave her a hug. Then Alice and Jane embraced their niece, delighted, as always, to see her.

"We were just about to eat lunch," Jane said. "Are you hungry?"

"Famished." Cynthia sat down. "Whew! It feels good to be out of the car. I left my luggage in the front hallway until you ladies tell me which room I may have tonight."

"How would you like the Garden Room?" Louise asked.

"The Garden Room would be lovely." Cynthia smiled at her mother and aunts. "So how are the owners of my favorite bed-and-breakfast? Jane and Alice, I want to hear what you're doing this summer."

Jane told her about the census, and Alice told her about her high school girls. Cynthia propped her chin in her hand and listened to it all. "You are the most fascinating aunties a woman could have. I don't know how you find time for everything that you do. You could put women my age to shame."

"We do like to keep busy," Jane said while she worked at the counter. "Lunch today, however, is nothing special—just artichoke-and-tuna paninis." She set a plate of sandwiches on the table.

"*Just?*" Cynthia laughed, eyeing the plate. "This looks delicious, Aunt Jane. I would have come all the way from Boston just to try one." She took one from the top of the stack.

"When do you have to go back?" Louise asked.

"I have Monday off so that I can work on this special project here. My boss was happy to let me find a quiet place to work if it meant I would finish sooner." She glanced around the table. "I won't interfere with anyone's plans, will I?"

"Not mine," Alice said.

"Nor mine," Jane added.

"Mother?"

Louise smiled. "I have a dance lesson tomorrow afternoon."

Cynthia smiled back. "With your fledgling dance student?"

"Yes, dear. I hope you don't have plans for me. I can't

break the…appointment. The dance competition is getting closer and closer. We need the practice."

"Do you think you have a chance to win?" Cynthia asked.

Louise explained that only Roman was eligible for an award, then added that she thought he had a lot of natural talent and that they might have a chance. While she talked, Cynthia continued to smile but said nothing.

"What's the special project you're working on for the publishing company?" Alice asked.

"I'm doing a final read of a new author's manuscript," Cynthia said. "She had to make a lot of changes, and I'm reading for continuity. It's a wonderful story and, as always, I love working with children's books."

"Do you ever want to move into working with adult books?" Jane asked.

"Not really. I've had offers, but I really like where I am now. Speaking of which, I need to pop by Nine Lives Bookstore and talk to Viola. We've got another great children's book coming out soon, and I want to make sure that she plans to stock it." She took a bite of her sandwich. "Is this ciabatta bread, Aunt Jane? It's very good."

"It is. I'm glad you like it."

"Would you like to walk to Nine Lives, Cynthia?" Louise asked after lunch. "That would give us a chance to catch up."

Cynthia nodded. "I'd like that. Let me help to clear the

table, then I'll put my luggage upstairs, and I'll be ready to go."

While Cynthia settled in the Garden Room, Louise waited downstairs in the parlor. She found herself playing *Rhapsody in Blue*, smiling as she did so.

"I haven't heard that in a long time," Cynthia said, standing in the doorway.

Louise stopped in the middle of a measure. "Goodness. I didn't hear you."

"Go ahead, Mother." Cynthia took a seat in one of the Eastlake chairs. "I'd like to hear you finish."

Louise smiled. "Very well." She picked up where she had left off, and soon she forgot that Cynthia was in the room. Absorbed in the music, she forgot about everything but the sheer joy of playing. She had also forgotten how deceptive *Rhapsody in Blue* could be—lively and invigorating, but complicated and demanding.

When she finished, she let her hands linger on the keyboard for a moment. She always needed a moment to return from the performance dream world to reality. She blinked and was back in the parlor. Cynthia rose and applauded.

"That was beautiful, Mother. I haven't heard you play so well in years."

Louise smiled. "Thank you. Are you ready to go to Nine Lives?"

"I am."

Cynthia and Louise walked toward town. They talked of inconsequential things until a suitable pause presented itself. Louise smiled. "Do you want to talk about my new friend, Roman Delwaard?"

"I'd love to." She stopped beneath a sheltering maple. "Tell me about him."

Louise told her how they had met and everything she knew about Roman. When she was finished, she fell silent.

"It sounds like you're happy," Cynthia finally said, after a few moments.

"I am. Roman is not like your father, of course, but—"

"Nor would I want him to be," Cynthia said quickly. "And I don't believe you see him that way, do you?"

"Of course not. But he is just so kind and interesting. I enjoy his company."

"Mother." Cynthia took her mother's hands. "I'm glad you do. I'm delighted to see you happy. Everything you've told me about Roman Delwaard makes him sound like a wonderful man and a good friend. Hearing you play *Rhapsody in Blue*, I wondered why you seemed so different. I made the connection when you told me about the concert the two of you attended."

"What connection?" Louise asked.

"Roman has brought joy into your life. He's taken the time

to get to know you, and he surprised you with the concert tickets. I know that he cares about you, Mother. I really do."

Louise slumped her shoulders with relief. "I'm so glad. I was afraid you would be upset and think that I wanted Roman to take your father's place."

"I know you don't. I also know that you're entitled to some male companionship. Being sixty-five doesn't mean you should be cut off from the world."

Louise laughed. "I certainly hope not. Please don't tell me that's what your generation thinks."

"*Nooo*, but sometimes we're a bit selfish and think only about what's best for us and not our parents." She took Louise's hand and squeezed it. "If I've ever been guilty of that, please forgive me."

"There's nothing to forgive," Louise said, smiling. "It might be rather boring, but would you like to go to the dance lesson tomorrow afternoon?"

"To meet Roman?"

Louise nodded. "If you have the time."

"I'll make the time." Cynthia smiled. "I'd love to."

Jane tidied up the kitchen after lunch. The phone rang, and it was Craig on the other end, his voice enthusiastic. "Hi, Jane. I've closed the shop for the day. Are you ready to go?"

"As soon as I run upstairs to change clothes, I will be. It won't take but a minute."

"Great. I've got all the supplies, and I'll be right there."

Jane went to her room, changed into her grubbiest pants and work shirt, then said good-bye to Alice.

"I think what you're doing is lovely," Alice said. "I'd like to join you, but I need to get some more information about our white-water rafting trip."

"There should be plenty of future opportunities to help," Jane said, then winked. "I'll be pressing you into service then."

She left Alice and went to wait on the front porch. Craig arrived in no time, and she hopped into his pickup, feeling like a kid going on a field trip.

Craig grinned at her as he put the truck into gear. "I'm as excited about this as you seem to be. I never thought I'd be so worked up about a painting project."

"It's only a start. Three Seasons needs more than just a coat of fresh paint, but maybe it will brighten things up a bit. The committee is lining up some people to come out and interact with the residents."

"And Bonnie Ethedridge volunteered her kids, don't forget."

Jane nodded. "I think she was right. Elderly people *do* like to see children. It reminds them of being young and cheers them up."

"You're going to talk to Dotty Gilpin about landscaping the outside of Three Seasons, right? I'll be glad to contribute the flowers and plants."

"I'm going to see if I can get Dotty into your store to chat with you about that. I'm sure she'll have some good ideas. We can get some of the youth in town to help with the planting. Then Dotty can oversee things, even as the seasons change."

"Maybe the residents would like to get involved too," Craig said. "By the way, where are we starting to paint today at Three Seasons...the lobby?"

Jane shook her head. "When Elena told the residents we were going to start painting, they decided to draw a name from a hat. The winner will get their room painted first."

"Who won?"

"The Stonehouses. Remember that sweet couple with the Victorian furnishings and clothing to match?"

Craig nodded.

"I'm glad they won. Their room looked most in need, in my opinion. The wallpaper was peeling, the baseboards were horribly scuffed..."

Craig pretended to frown. "Are you sure this is a two-man job? Maybe we need to call in the cavalry."

Jane laughed. "I'm sure we can do it. Maybe not all this afternoon, but we can get started."

"Right."

When they reached Three Seasons, Elena was waiting for them at the door. All the residents were in the lobby. When they saw Jane and Craig, they applauded.

"Thank you," Jane said, approaching the group. "But I'm not sure what for."

"You're bringing us more than just paint," Irina Stonehouse said.

One of the unmarried women nodded. "You're showing us that you care. So many young people don't think about us older folks anymore. Always too busy, always too impatient."

Jane smiled. "It may not take us too many days to paint all the rooms, and we hope to spend more time here getting to know each one of you."

"And we hope to bring other friends as well," Craig said.

Irina smiled. "Eh?" Irwin, her husband, said, cupping his ear. "What did he say?"

Irina pressed closer to her husband, speaking directly into his ear. "He said that they're bringing other friends."

"Oh good." Irwin nodded, his eyes shining. "I can't hear well, but I like to have other people around. Friends are good."

Jane looked at all the bright faces. She turned to Craig,

who was smiling as well. "Yes indeed," she said. "Friends are definitely good."

$\backsim$

Volunteers among the residents had helped the cause by removing the wallpaper from the room, so Jane and Craig started their work by prepping the walls and trim. The Stonehouses had decided they didn't want wallpaper this time, just fresh paint. After the scraping and sanding was done, Irina studied the bare walls with Jane. "I think it's time for a more contemporary look," Irina said. "Don't you?"

Jane smiled. "I think you should choose whatever makes you happiest. Personally, I like a more contemporary look, but that's just me."

Irina pressed her hands together. "We're all so excited about the changes to our little community. This will give us all something to look forward to. Irwin and I were discussing the other day that we needed a change." She leaned toward Jane and whispered, "I might even try to find some more modern clothes. The ones I wear make me look too much like a grandma."

"I think that would be lovely, Irina. If you need any help, I know a wonderful woman named Nellie who runs her own clothing store in Acorn Hill. She'd be glad to advise you, and I'd be delighted to introduce you to her."

"Thank you, dear." Irina winked. "I may take you up on that."

Jane sat down with the Stonehouses and a color chart, pointing out various combinations. It didn't take them long to select a sea-foam green with an off-white color for the trim. "I always did like the beach," Irina said. "I love the name *sea foam*."

Craig called Fred Humbert, who sent someone from the hardware store over with the proper paint. While Jane and Craig were stirring the first paint can, Sylvia Songer arrived.

"Sylvia!" Jane set her wooden stirrer in the can and rocked back on her heels. "What are you doing here?"

The seamstress grinned. "I heard about what you were doing, and I came to volunteer my services. I can certainly make new draperies, if anyone wants them."

Irina smiled. "Oh, how lovely! I like them so much better than blinds."

Jane introduced Irina and Irwin to Sylvia, then vice versa. Sylvia studied the Stonehouses' room and the paint colors they'd selected. "I think a white sheer with a bit of ruffle would be nice. If that's not too feminine for you," she said to Irwin.

"Eh?" He cupped his hand around his ear. "Who's feminine?"

"The drapes, dear," Irina said loudly, leaning toward her husband. "She wants to make us white ruffled drapes."

"Oh! Fine, fine," he said, smiling at Irina. "Whatever you want. What makes you happy makes me happy."

He took her hand and squeezed it. She squeezed back, happy. Jane glanced at Sylvia, and they both nodded. It was so nice to see a couple so much in love, even after more than sixty years of marriage.

"Let me take some measurements, and I'll start the work as soon as I can," Sylvia said. She pulled out a tape measure and marked the windows, checking twice before she wrote down the numbers on a piece of paper. She then quickly sketched out her idea and showed it to Irina.

"That would be lovely, dear," Irina said. "Exactly what I like."

"Great." Sylvia tucked the paper into her pants pocket. "I can't say how long it will take me, but I'll start on it today. Meanwhile, I'd better get back to the store."

"Thanks for coming," Jane said, touching her friend's hand. It was just like Sylvia to volunteer her time and talent to help someone else. Perhaps the attitude would be as infectious as Jane had hoped.

The next morning Louise was seated at the organ for the Sunday service. Was it only last week that Roman had visited Grace Chapel? She smiled at the memory. He was not present today, having returned to his own church in Potterston, but it was nice to see Cynthia sitting in the pew with Jane and Alice. Cynthia was always delighted to greet friends, of which she had made quite a few even though she had never lived in Acorn Hill. Louise, of course, was extraordinarily proud of her successful, poised daughter and more than happy to see her at any time.

Thank goodness Cynthia seemed eager to meet Roman and didn't have any objections. If Louise was at all nervous about Cynthia's presence this afternoon at the dance lesson, it was because she worried that her dancing ability wouldn't be up to Cynthia's expectations. It *had* been many years since she had seen her parents dance. Louise had been sprier then. She certainly didn't want to appear awkward to her daughter.

As they drove to the rec center in Potterston, Cynthia spoke fondly to Louise about Acorn Hill and its citizens, remarking how good it was to see everyone again and that Rev. Thompson's sermon had been inspiring. "Fred Humbert looked a little tired," she said.

"I know he's been working hard at the store," Louise

said. "Summer is one of his busy seasons. With the nice weather, people are tackling all their home repair and gardening projects."

"How's Vera doing?" Cynthia asked. "She looked a little tired too. I would think she'd be well rested, since she doesn't have to teach during the summer."

"I think she's worried about Fred. I only hope her concern for him doesn't affect her own well-being."

When they arrived at the rec center, Roman was already waiting in the studio. He smiled at Louise, then Cynthia. "Dear, this is Roman Delwaard. Roman, this is my daughter, Cynthia. She surprised me Friday night by announcing that she was driving down from Boston. I hope you don't mind, but I invited her to watch our dance lesson."

"Not at all." He beamed at Cynthia. "It's a pleasure to meet you. I've heard so much about you, and I know your mother must be delighted that you're in town for a visit. Louise, we can cancel our lesson if you'd rather spend time with Cynthia."

"No, no," Cynthia said. "You two go ahead. And it's a pleasure to meet you too, Mr. Delwaard. My mother has said many nice things about you too."

"Please call me Roman. Do you dance as well as your mother?"

"Not a step." Cynthia shook her head. "I'm afraid it's not an inherited trait. That's one of the reasons I wanted to come today. I used to watch dance movies with Mother when I was growing up—Ginger Rogers, Fred Astaire, Eleanor Powell—all the great dancers. Oddly enough I never had enough interest in learning how to be a hoofer myself, but I have a great appreciation for it."

"I hope you'll go easy on Roman and me." Louise laughed. "We have fun, but we're no professionals."

Cynthia took the CD player from her mother's hands. "Let's see what you've got. Tell me what track to play, and I'll start it up for you."

Louise's palms felt damp. Why on earth should she feel nervous about Cynthia's watching them dance? "What shall it be, Roman?"

"Let's go with a waltz, since that will be our first choice."

"Very well. Cynthia, the waltz is the first track."

Cynthia hit play, and Roman and Louise began to dance. How different it was now from their first lessons, when she had had to count. Now they danced together smoothly, with her following his lead, moving naturally in time to the music as though they were nineteenth-century characters in a movie.

When the song was over, they stopped, somewhat

breathless and pleased with the dance. Remembering that Cynthia was present, they turned to her. "Your mother, of course, was wonderful, practically a second Ginger Rogers," Roman said. "What did you think of this old duffer? Think Fred Astaire's reputation is safe?"

Cynthia smiled broadly. "I think you were both wonderful. Truly. If you don't win the competition, Roman, I'll be quite surprised."

"Louise thinks we've done well with the waltz," Roman said, "but we have to have a second dance prepared. In the event of a tie, they ask the couples to perform something different."

"What have you selected?"

"The fox-trot," Roman said. "Louise thinks we're doing well with that too."

"Oh, really?" Cynthia folded her arms, affecting a mock stern expression. "Let me be the judge of that."

"Second track, Cynthia." Louise smiled at Roman.

He returned the smile. "Let's show her how two old foxes trot, shall we, Louise?"

When the session was over and everyone had said good-bye, Louise and Cynthia drove back to Acorn Hill, laughing and recounting the lesson. "I had a great time, Mother,"

Cynthia said. "Thank you for inviting me. I loved watching you dance."

"If you're interested in it, you should consider taking lessons yourself."

Cynthia smiled. "Maybe someday. For now I'm content to watch others."

Even though she was fairly confident of the answer, Louise waited a moment before asking, "Did you like Roman?"

"Very much. He's a good friend for you to have, Mother. If the relationship develops into something more serious—"

"Who said anything about that?" Louise laughed lightly.

"You can't deny that you two are fond of each other."

"That's true. But we're just friends...good friends, as you say."

Cynthia smiled. "Isn't that how most special relationships begin?"

Louise went silent, concentrating on driving. Cynthia was still young and idealistic, romantic even. It was ridiculous to think of there being anything stronger than friendship between two people in their mid- to late sixties.

Wasn't it?

Chapter Sixteen

Monday morning, the girls met Alice in the living room at Grace Chapel Inn before they embarked on their white-water rafting trip. Jane was preparing a picnic lunch for them to take along, and Alice had selected the route to the park area. She thought it would be good for them to eat together before their adventure. The brochure she had received said that there were picnic tables and vending machines for drinks.

The girls were dressed in shorts and long-sleeved shirts, their hair pulled back into ponytails or braids. Alice herself wore a pair of long khaki shorts and a cotton shirt, and all wore low-cut sneakers or running shoes.

"You look great, Miss Howard," Isidra said.

Julie nodded. "Yeah. Like you're a regular Paula Bunyan or something."

"Thank you." Alice laughed. "You girls look like you're ready for adventure yourselves."

"I am," Sabrina said. She flipped back one of the two short braids she sported. "I've been looking forward to this for a long time."

"Have any of you girls gone rafting before?" Alice asked.

They all shook their heads, including Esmeralda, who looked glum. Alice noticed that Isidra, formerly Esmeralda's best buddy, teamed up with Julie more frequently. Ever since she had conquered her fear of rock climbing, Julie had broken out of her shell bit by bit. The makeover session especially seemed to boost her confidence. She smiled and laughed more, talked more freely, and seemed to focus more on interacting with the others rather than on drawing into herself.

Esmeralda, on the other hand, spoke less frequently and seemed more self-absorbed. As the other girls paid less attention to her, she seemed increasingly caustic and unhappy. Alice wished that she could get it across to Esmeralda that her unpleasantness was driving away the very friends who could help her. She feared, however, that Esmeralda would have to learn it on her own. Alice only hoped that the lesson was not too hard on Esmeralda. In the meantime, Alice would be as kind to her as possible, turning the other cheek when necessary, and pray that the girl would come around. She would pray, too, that Esmeralda would see how much the other girls and Alice herself could truly care for her.

Sabrina and Isidra chatted about their clothes, which apparently they'd purchased just for the trip. Julie approached Alice. "Are you scared to go rafting, Miss Howard?" she whispered.

"I am," Alice whispered back. "How about you?"

"Not as much as I was about the rock climbing. I'm scared of heights, but water doesn't bother me too much."

Alice didn't point out that while the belays would have protected them in the event of a fall, there was no safety net for rafting other than their life jackets. She had made certain that all the girls could swim, however, and that they would receive safety instructions before they actually put in at the river.

Casting her own fears aside, Alice glanced at Esmeralda, who sat slumped at one end of the sofa, idly petting Wendell, the gray tabby the sisters had inherited at their father's death. Wendell seemed to enjoy the attention, but Esmeralda looked as though she could use a little of her own. She glanced enviously at Sabrina and Isidra, who were laughing.

Alice nodded at Esmeralda. "Do you think she's afraid of our rafting trip?"

Julie shrugged. "I don't know. She doesn't seem afraid of much except being nice." She flushed. "That wasn't a very nice thing for *me* to say, was it?"

Alice shook her head. "Esmeralda seems to be lonely," she said. "Maybe the trip will help cheer her up."

"I hope so." Julie sighed. "Nothing else seems to."

Jane entered the living room, a large picnic basket on

her arm. "Here you go, ladies. I've made an assortment of sandwiches—peanut butter and jelly, turkey and ham. There's also a relish tray of carrots, celery sticks and olives. For dessert, you have sugar cookies with sprinkles."

Sabrina rubbed her stomach appreciatively. "*Mmm*. Can we eat now?"

Isidra laughed. "You're such an athlete. You're always hungry."

"And *as* an athlete, I've got to keep up my strength." Sabrina put her hands on her hips.

Julie laughed too. "I'm no athlete, but it does sound good. I think I can wait until we get to the picnic grounds though. It'll be so much more fun to eat by the river than indoors."

"Now there's a young lady with common sense," Jane said. "Have a wonderful time. Alice, I'm counting on you to take lots of pictures. Do you have that disposable water-proof camera I got you?"

Alice patted her shirt pocket. "I do indeed, and I intend to take lots of photos to commemorate this event."

Esmeralda raised her head. "Can I take some, Miss Howard?" Her voice dropped to a mumble. "It doesn't look like I'll have anything else to do."

"Yes, Esmeralda." Alice handed her the camera. "In fact, why don't you be the photographer for the trip. We'll need you to paddle, of course, no getting out of that—this is a team sport. But we need someone to chronicle our event."

"Sure," Isidra said, smiling at Esmeralda. "Lilia would like to see some pictures of what we've been doing."

Esmeralda's face brightened momentarily. "Yeah," she said. "They'd be nice to show her."

They thanked Jane again for the picnic basket, then piled into Alice's blue Toyota. She headed the car toward the park, which lay some twenty miles to the west. The Tuskoga River flowed through it, and the area was a popular attraction for white-water rafters. Alice had already made arrangements with Granite Outfitters, a skilled group that would conduct a short training and safety lesson, then send a guide with them in their inflatable raft. The contact person had suggested that since none of their group had previously rafted, they should choose a novice course. He assured Alice that they would still experience plenty of thrills.

When she informed the girls that they would be rafting at the novice level, they all booed.

"Come on, Miss Howard, don't you trust us?"

"We're in good shape. We can handle something more challenging."

Esmeralda, seemingly back in Isidra's good graces, seemed emboldened enough to speak out as well. "Do you think we're babies or something? If *you're* scared, maybe you should just stay on the bank and watch."

Alice gripped the steering wheel. "I have to participate in every event with you girls. Yes, I am a little scared, Esmeralda, but facing our fears can help us to grow stronger, don't you think?"

Shamed by looks from the other girls, Esmeralda didn't respond. Instead, after a pause, she addressed her companions. "When we get to the park, let me take your picture. We'll compare it to how we look after the ride is over."

When they reached the river, they found a large building where presumably they could check in for their excursion. Esmeralda snapped several photos as the girls mugged for the camera, and Alice was pleased by the teens' spirit.

"Let's check in first, then have our picnic," Alice said. She led them to the designated window and a twentysomething blond man with an athletic build greeted her.

"I'm Alice Howard, and these four girls and I have a reservation for a rafting trip."

The man checked the appointment book and pointed to it with his finger. "Yep, right here. I'm Randall Coates, and I'll be your instructor and guide on the trip. You're a little early, however. We're not scheduled to begin for another hour."

"That's fine." Alice held up the picnic basket. "We brought a lunch."

"Great! If there's anything left, save it for me." He smiled. "Meet me back here in one hour."

Alice thanked him, then led the way to a shaded picnic table on the bank of the river. She could already see several groups beginning their rafting excursions, but apparently the girls walking behind her could only discuss their guide.

"Did you see his dreamy eyes?" Sabrina sighed.

"I think he winked at me," Isidra said.

Julie shook her head. "No way. He was looking at Miss Howard the entire time."

"I'm glad he's going to be our guide," Esmeralda said. "If the rafting trip is boring, at least he'll be nice to talk to."

"You're going to be busy paddling like the rest of us," Sabrina said. "There won't be any time for flirting."

Esmeralda tossed a thick braid over her shoulder. "You never know. Besides, I bet this trip won't be any more exciting than one of those little boat rides at a kiddies' amusement park."

"Girls, please help me to set out the lunch," said Alice.

They opened the basket and put the sandwiches on paper plates. The girls reached for the food, chattering, but Alice cleared her throat to gain their attention. She folded her hands. "I think we should pray first," she said softly.

The girls pulled their hands back from the food and set them in their laps, duly chastised. Alice closed her eyes and spoke from her heart. "Thank You, Lord, for the fellowship we have enjoyed so far this summer and for the fun we will have today. Please keep us safe during this adventure. Thank You for the food set before us that Jane kindly prepared for us. May we all be as kind in our concern for others, especially our friends. Amen."

"Amen," the girls said quietly. After a moment of post-prayer reverence, they resumed their teenage-girl chatter. Alice was delighted to notice, however, that none of it included any further discussion of Randall Coates.

After they finished eating, they threw away their trash and put the aluminum cans in a recycling bin by the rafting building. They packed up what was left over from their lunch and went to check in for their prerafting lesson. A young woman worked behind the counter this time, and she told Alice that she could hold the picnic basket for them in a cool place until they were finished with their rafting trip.

Just as Alice handed it across the counter, Randall Coates appeared from a back room. He grinned at Alice and the girls. "Are you ready to go?"

"Yes!" they yelled in unison. Alice smiled gamely.

Randall took them outdoors to a quiet area away from

the picnic tables and the traffic at the building. Alice could see the river sparkling behind Randall, and she felt a tiny surge of trepidation. Then she chided herself for an overactive imagination. She had ridden in boats before, even canoes. This was no different and would, in fact, be a great team-building exercise for her and the girls.

While Esmeralda snapped a couple of candid group shots, including one of their guide, Randall explained that he was a student at Penn State who worked with Granite Outfitters during the summer. "I've loved white-water rafting since I was just a kid," he said, "and I want you all to love it too. It can be a challenge—nothing but you, your fellow rafters, your raft and your paddle against the water." He eyed each one of the girls—and Alice—with a serious expression. "That's also a good lesson in life. Rely on those around you, the boat and paddle you've been given to navigate life, and, most importantly, the courage within to face whatever is thrown your way."

The girls nodded soberly, soaking in every word. Bemused, Alice wondered if they had listened to what he said or whether they were distracted by his handsome face and bright smile.

"Now." He smiled broader. "Courage is wonderful, but we also rely on something else—a life jacket." He handed one to each of the girls and to Alice, and he showed them how to wear it. He waited until they had buckled the straps, then went around to each person to check for security. He tugged a strap here and loosened another one there until he was satisfied. "You may think you know how to wear one, but when your life might depend upon it, you had better make doubly sure. Safety is my first job as your guide. The next thing you need are these."

He reached into a canvas sack and pulled out helmets. The girls groaned.

"Gross!"

"Ugly!"

He grinned. "Ugly they may be, but they can save your life. If you were to fall out of the raft, you could hit your head on a rock and be knocked unconscious. You might drown."

The girls accepted the helmets. He showed them how to put them on and again checked to make sure that the equipment was secure.

Next he discussed the basics of the boat—how to get in and out, where they would all sit, and how they should paddle. "It may sound ridiculous, but if you're paddling one way and your buddy is paddling another, you could be working against each other and against control of the boat. It should go without saying that since I'm your guide, you should always listen to me. I'm the captain of the ship, and you're my crew. This is a class-one course we'll be paddling today, and we won't see much, if any, white water. But there's always the potential for danger, and I'm responsible for the safety of everyone aboard. Got it?"

They nodded soberly.

He handed them each a sturdy plastic paddle and lined them up as though they were already in the boat. Then he showed them how to stroke the paddle through the air as though they were actually paddling.

He gave them a few more instructions, then decreed it was time to put in.

"Put in what?" Esmeralda asked.

"That means getting our raft into the river. 'Take out' is when the trip concludes."

"Sounds like fast food." Sabrina giggled.

Soon they were at the river and waiting for their raft. "Does everyone put in here, even people going on more difficult courses?" Alice asked Randall.

"No, ma'am. The others usually have to drive elsewhere. This is just where the novice courses begin."

Alice's trepidation grew as they got into the boat, but once inside with a paddle in hand she felt more confident. The large inflatable rubber craft seemed secure enough. Esmeralda snapped pictures.

Randall took his place in the boat, and Esmeralda snapped another picture of him. He posed like a stern captain, hands on hip and mouth in an obliging scowl. When she finished, he laughed. "Are we ready to go?"

"Yes!" they chorused.

As they started their journey down the river, Alice began to relax. The river was, indeed, easy. Randall told them when and where to paddle. Sometimes he would say "right forward" or "left back" or perhaps "stop paddling." As he had commanded them to do on shore, so they obeyed on the water.

The water lapped against the raft as it eased its way downstream, and occasionally it lifted the boat and passengers slightly up, then set them back down. When it did, the girls shrieked with delight. Only riffles and small waves presented themselves in the rapidly moving water, and obstructions such as rocks were easy to see and avoid with Randall's guidance. Alice relaxed even more.

The voyage was tranquil and filled with beautiful things to see. Eventually, Randall called out that they were near the end of their journey. Then he shouted, "We've got a challenge up ahead. I see a hump, which is where water is forced up over a submerged rock. We don't want to scrape the bottom of our boat, so let's steer around it."

The passengers obeyed his commands, steering clear. Just as they rounded the hump, however, Randall, said, "We need to stay out of the hole, the area just beyond the rock."

At that moment, Esmeralda rose slightly to take a photo of the area. In her excitement, Isidra rose too. "Can you see the rock that's causing the hump?"

Esmeralda twisted around for a better shot, and her elbow clipped her half-risen friend. With a scream, Isidra went over the side.

Randall heard the scream and saw Isidra in the water. "Stop paddling!" he commanded.

Everyone could see the top of Isidra's head bobbing in the river. He cupped his hands around his mouth. "Point your feet downstream and try to float on your back."

Alice watched, worried. "She's not in the right position," she said. She could see the girl struggling, but she wasn't gaining any forward motion. Without thinking, instinct kicking in, Alice slid over the side of the boat.

She vaguely heard the girls scream and Randall shouting something, but she focused on Isidra. Fortunately, she was only a little downstream from the girl, and Alice swam hard against the current to reach her. Alice felt a rush of relief when she grabbed Isidra's hands, but the girl struggled frantically, her head partially submerged.

Alice realized Isidra must have caught her foot on something that was holding her underwater. Holding onto the girl's hand, Alice dived and followed the girl's legs. Isidra's left foot was trapped between two large tree roots. Alice quickly lifted one, and Isidra broke free.

Isidra shot up, her head now above the surface. Alice bobbed up beside her, and they both gasped for air. Alice took Isidra's arm. Following Randall's earlier instruction, she let the current carry them both downstream feetfirst toward the boat.

Randall had managed to stop the boat in a calm area. By the time they reached it, Isidra was swimming on her own, but she and Alice both needed help from the girls and Randall to get back into the boat.

"Are you . . . all right?" Alice asked Isidra.

The girl nodded, her breathing slowing to a more normal level. "My foot…was caught," she said to the others. "Alice…saved me."

Randall's face looked pale. "You scared me, Alice. I thought you'd fallen overboard too. I'm glad you realized what happened to Isidra."

"My nurse's instinct told me to move quickly. When I got to her, I knew she was caught. Sure enough, her foot was trapped between a couple tree roots."

"Let's rest here a minute and catch our breaths," Randall said.

The girls, who had been quiet, all began to fuss over Isidra, who assured them that she was all right. Randall talked to Alice, who noticed out of the corner of her eye that Esmeralda sat to one side, alone.

The last leg of the journey was quiet, with no more

mishaps or major challenges. When they took out, a van was present to drive them back to their starting point. Alice was glad she had brought a change of dry clothes for herself, and that she had a blanket in the trunk of her car to keep Isidra warm. Even though all the other girls were somewhat wet from their ride, at their age, they considered it a reminder of their adventurous voyage.

Physically and emotionally tired, Alice drove them all back to Potterston and delivered them to their homes. Esmeralda, who had remained quiet during the trip, asked to be dropped off last. When she was alone with Alice in the car, the girl swiveled in the front seat to face Alice and burst into tears.

"Why, Esmeralda," Alice said, leaning across the gear shift to embrace her. "What's wrong?"

"I knocked Isidra…my best friend…into the water." With a continued halting voice, she explained how she had knocked Isidra overboard while trying to take a picture.

"It was an accident," Alice assured her. "It sounds as though Isidra shouldn't have been standing either. She's partly to blame."

Esmeralda sniffled loudly. "You saved her life." She stared at Alice with awe. "How did you do that? I couldn't do anything. When I saw Isidra in the water…" Her voice choked with emotion.

Alice embraced her tightly. "I know how much you care

for her. She feels the same way about you. Fear causes people to react in different ways. If I jumped in, it's because I've been a nurse for so long. I'm accustomed to the idea of people needing help. I've had a variety of first-aid and training classes over the years too."

"You…you're a hero," Esmeralda said.

Alice shook her head. "I only did what I've been trained to do."

"Do you think Isidra can forgive me for knocking her into the water? Then for not doing anything?" Esmeralda asked softly. "I don't think she knows it was all my fault."

Alice nodded. "Of course she can forgive you. She's your best friend."

"What about the other girls?"

"We're a team, remember?" Alice smiled. "Members stick together. Maybe you should talk to them the next time we get together."

Esmeralda drew a deep breath. "That's a good idea. Thank you, Miss Howard." She paused. "Can you forgive me for the mean way I've treated you since we started these activities? I don't know why I did. I was wrong, and I'm sorry."

Alice smiled. "Apology accepted. Thank you, Esmeralda. All I've ever wanted—all your friends have ever wanted—is for you to be part of the group."

"From now on, I will be." Esmeralda smiled. "I promise."

Chapter Seventeen

*T*he next morning, Tuesday, Jane was fixing a late breakfast of pancakes and bacon for the sisters. Cynthia had left for home, and it seemed quiet in the house without her. Glenna and Janette had eaten earlier and were slaving over their research papers.

Alice had recounted the rafting incident when she returned home the day before, but Jane and Louise were still in shock. Carlene had already called that morning to get an interview with Alice over the phone. Carlene had to rush to include it in the next day's edition of the *Acorn Nutshell*.

"I'm ready for things to return to normal," Alice said, taking a piece of bacon from the plate Jane set on the table.

"I'm so proud of you for rescuing Isidra," Jane said, setting a platter of pancakes alongside the bacon. "Mostly I'm happy that you're both all right."

"Amen to that." Louise lifted two pancakes onto her plate.

"*Yoo-hoo!*" Ethel appeared in the kitchen, having come through the back door followed by Lloyd Tynan. "I'm not interrupting anything, am I? Lloyd wanted to talk to Jane, and I told him you ladies would probably be finished with breakfast by now."

"We're not, Auntie. Hello, Lloyd." Alice greeted the mayor, who stood beside the sisters' aunt.

"I can come back," Lloyd said, eyeing the breakfast table.

"Oh, have a seat," Jane said. "There's plenty for all."

"If you're sure…" Lloyd said, pulling up a chair. Ethel sat beside him, and Jane rose to fetch two more plates and eating utensils.

"This looks delicious as usual, Jane." Ethel smiled.

Lloyd expressed the same opinion and smiled broadly. "Jane, I have good news for you. The town council voted yesterday to add a request in Acorn Hill's quarterly reports for voluntary contributions. The proceeds will go specifically toward helping with the needs you and Craig and the others identified during the census."

"That's wonderful!" Jane set cups of coffee in front of Lloyd and Ethel. Her guests attended to, she sat back down. "When will it start?"

"It may take several months to get through red tape and have the paperwork cleared, printed and distributed, but it certainly should be ready in time for winter. I'm sure folks will need extra care during the cold months."

"I'm grateful for all your hard work, Lloyd," Jane said.

Lloyd waved his empty fork in the air, chewing, then swallowing a mouthful of pancake. "It's a win-win situation for everyone. By the way, I heard about the redecorating job you and some of the others are doing over at Three Seasons. It looks great, from what I hear."

"We're happy to help," Jane said. "The committee of churches has some of their youth lined up to visit and chat with the residents on a regular basis. They're taking board games and plan to play charades—things that will keep the residents' minds engaged. Elena said that would go a long way toward their good health, both mental and physical."

"You're doing a good job chairing that committee," Lloyd said. "I've talked to members from the various churches, and they're all very pleased. I also got a phone call from Thomas Gilpin. I believe you know him. It seems he heard that Three Seasons could use some livening up. He works with model trains, and he volunteered to set up a track for the residents. With the owners' and residents' permission, of course."

Jane smiled. "I'm sure they'll be delighted."

Jane walked to Town Hall that afternoon and was pleased to find Thomas Gilpin walking near Nine Lives. They greeted each other, and he explained with obvious pleasure that a neighbor had driven him to town so that he could buy some hardware at Fred's and just enjoy a change of pace. He also filled her in on his ideas for installing a train set at Three Seasons.

"I think that what you are doing will provide a lot of happiness for the residents." Jane patted his arm.

Thomas agreed. "I've got another surprise for you, Miss Census Lady."

"What's that?"

"Dotty, Inge and I are all going to take driver-education lessons. We figured it's about time we conquered our fears and got back on the horse, so to speak. It's been too many years."

"I'm proud of all of you," Jane said. "It takes a lot of courage to face a fear, particularly an old one."

"If it wasn't for your prodding, we wouldn't have. We realized we're ready though. Dotty's looking forward to gardening at Three Seasons. Inge heard about that elderly woman—Bernice, is it?"

Jane nodded.

"Anyway, Inge wants to help her, but she needs a driver's license to get to her place on a regular basis."

Jane could barely suppress a smile. She could see Inge, so tender with her own parents, visiting Bernice. Even though

Jane would never have thought of it, Inge had seen the need and made her own decision to help. Perhaps being a Good Samaritan was contagious. A lot of citizens in Acorn Hill were certainly doing their best to help their neighbors.

Friday afternoon, Alice and Louise drove together to the Potterston Rec Center. Louise had a dance practice with Roman, and Alice was meeting her girls for a pickup basketball game. She was grateful they didn't expect her to play. She was there only to watch.

"When is the dance competition?" Alice asked Louise as she drove.

"Two weeks from Saturday."

"You don't mind if Jane and I come, do you? I heard the dance club is selling tickets to raise money for charity."

"Not at all." Louise smiled. "I hope you get your money's worth."

"I'm sure we will. Cynthia told us how good you and Roman are. Jane and I can't wait to see for ourselves. You're not nervous, are you?"

"A little bit," Louise said. "We've been doing well in practice, but I'd like to see Roman win. He's worked hard."

At the rec center, Louise went in search of Roman. Alice found the girls already at play on the basketball court. They stopped abruptly when they saw her.

"Hey, Miss H," Sabrina said. "Glad you could join us."

"Yeah." Panting from exertion, Esmeralda threw one arm around Isidra's shoulders for support. "Good to see you."

Alice smiled fondly at them all, then said, "How are you, Isidra? No ill effects from your diving exhibition?"

Isidra and her friends burst out laughing.

"Nah, I'm fine. We wanted you to play basketball with us—"

"I never said I'd play," Alice interrupted.

Julie shuffled her feet impatiently. "Anyway, we have something to say to you. You first, Esmeralda."

She stepped forward. "Miss Howard, I wanted to formally apologize to you in front of my friends. You've helped us have fun and learn and grow the last few weeks, and I've done nothing but bad-mouth everything you did. I'm sorry about that."

"Apology accepted. Again," Alice said.

"And we apologized to Esmeralda for ignoring her the past few meetings," Julie said. "We were angry at her because she seemed to want to ruin our fun, but we shouldn't have excluded her. That was wrong."

Sabrina and Isidra nodded.

"Esmeralda apologized to me," Isidra said. "She claims she accidentally knocked me out of the boat the other day. She said you told her the same thing that I did, and you were right. I shouldn't have stood up. She was just trying to get a photo."

"And I did." Esmeralda reached into the back pocket of her shorts for a plastic packet. "There are other shots, but I brought these. Here's the photo I took just before Isidra fell in the water." She frowned slightly. "I kept shooting pictures after you jumped in to save her. Here's you at her side, then the two of you swimming back toward the boat." She bit her lip. "Or maybe you don't want to see those."

"I do," Alice said, "but not for the reasons you might think. I'm proud of you for taking these, Esmeralda. It takes a strong person to take photos under pressure. Many photographers have done so and won awards or exposed situations that others needed to know about. Did you enjoy using the camera?"

Esmeralda nodded.

"Maybe you should consider photography as a hobby," Alice said. "Who knows? It might lead to something bigger, like a stint at the Franklin High newspaper or even submissions to Miss Moss at the *Acorn Nutshell*."

Esmeralda smiled, tucking the pictures back into her pocket. "I'm glad to hear you say that, Miss Howard. I got a ride and gave copies of these photos to Miss Moss. It was too late to run them in Wednesday's issue, but she promised to put them to good use."

Alice managed to smile for Esmeralda's sake, but she wished the girl had kept the photos to herself. Alice had heard far too much talk in the last few days about her rescue of Isidra. Everywhere she went, people stopped to congratulate her and also to beg her to recount her adventures. Never comfortable in the limelight, Alice only wanted the hoopla to die down.

"Come on, Miss H," Sabrina said, tossing her the ball. Alice managed to catch it without dropping it. "Show us what you can do. Let's play some ball."

Alice looked down at her clothes. "But I'm wearing tennis shoes."

"They'll be fine for basketball," Esmeralda pointed out. "They may not be high tops, but they're fine for the court. Come on. We're a team, remember?" She winked at Alice.

Alice couldn't help smiling. "Very well. But don't expect much."

When Alice and Louise returned home, both thoroughly exhausted from their respective activities, they found Jane in the kitchen already working on supper.

Alice sniffed the air appreciatively. "What's on the menu tonight?"

"Fresh tomatoes filled with chicken salad," Jane said. "It's not very inspiring, but it seemed like a good night for it. It's been so warm today. Oh, by the way. Alice, you had a phone call from the Potterston TV station. They want you to call back before their deadline tonight."

Alice took the number and headed for the phone in the entryway. What could a TV station want with her? She dialed the number, and a harried-sounding woman answered the phone. "Felice Miston."

"This is Alice Howard. I'm returning a call, but I'm not certain to whom."

"Oh, Alice Howard!" Felice's voice noticeably lightened. "Thank you for calling us back. I was afraid you wouldn't be able to, and I was hoping to get an answer before the weekend."

"An answer about what?" Alice asked, confused.

"I'm sorry. I've been in such a rush today. I'm the producer for *Good Day, Potterston*. You're familiar with our program?"

Alice didn't watch much television, but she was vaguely

aware of an early morning show that originated in Potterston and spotlighted local citizens. "Yes."

"We heard about your rescue of the teenage girl in the Tuskoga River, and we'd like to interview you, live, on our program Wednesday morning."

Alice flushed even though no one could see her. "Anyone would have done the same. I wasn't the only person in the boat. I was just first to respond, that's all."

"You're being modest. Tell me about your relationship with the girl."

Alice explained her work with the four teenagers, and Felice stopped her midsentence. "That's wonderful. You've been working with teenagers and you saved one's life?"

Alice gripped the receiver tighter, trying to get a grip on her emotions as well. "As I said, anyone would have done it."

Felice paused. "Miss Howard, there are several kinds of people that I deal with. Those who want to use the media for their own glory, those who distrust the media and those who are what I call genuine people—those who shun the spotlight at any cost. Obviously you're not the first type. Are you the second or the third?"

Alice considered the question. "Perhaps a little of both," she finally admitted. "I don't want to be the focus of special attention. That's for certain. The girls are the important story here, not I."

Alice could hear Felice tapping a pen against a desk. "I see your point completely, and I appreciate your honesty. I also appreciate your modesty."

Alice let out a relieved breath. "I care about these girls, and I don't want to be elevated for what I did. I've seen a lot of changes in them already, and I don't want to jeopardize that."

"We'd still love for you to come on our show. Our viewers would love to hear about what you've done and what the girls are doing too. How about if you *and* the girls come on the show? That way we could talk to all of you. That would give us a chance to hear their story."

"About the rafting rescue?" Alice asked, still somewhat suspicious.

"Our host would talk about that, of course, but our viewers would also like to get a glimpse into these girls' hearts. What it's like to be a teenager in these times . . . How being in a program like this helps them . . . That sort of thing."

"Very well. I'll provide you with phone numbers. If you call the girls and they and their parents agree, I'll appear on the show with them."

"Wonderful! I'll get back to you Monday with all the details. Thank you, Miss Howard."

Alice hung up the receiver. She hoped she had done the right thing.

Wednesday morning, with all the girls able to attend, Alice drove to Potterston at five o'clock. She was beset by yawns she couldn't seem to stifle. She hoped she could keep her eyes open long enough for the interview, which was scheduled for the time slot between six-thirty and seven. Louise and Jane promised to watch on the small TV in the kitchen.

When Alice got to the station, a young woman in a stylish hairdo and tailored pink suit met her at the front door. "I'm Felice Miston. We spoke on the phone," she said in her straightforward manner. "Let's get you back for a bit of makeup before your segment."

Somewhat bewildered, Alice followed as Felice led the way down darkened halls. It was too early for the rest of the station and the majority of its workers to be in action.

When Felice opened the door to the room marked Makeup, Alice was shocked to find Sabrina, Isidra, Esmeralda and Julie already sitting in chairs.

"Hi, Miss Howard."

"What's up, Miss H?"

Felice gestured to an empty chair, smiling. "Have a seat, Alice. Our makeup lady will be right with you. As you can see, she's already finished with the girls."

Alice looked closer. The girls all wore dresses, apparel she had never been certain they possessed. From the looks of it, the dresses were all brand new. The girls' hair and makeup had also been prepared for them, and they all looked beautiful.

Yet more than their outward appearance signified their beauty. Their eyes shone, and their smiles and conversation with each other said that these girls were happy to be among friends. Each one tried to talk about her makeup and clothing experience, vying for Alice's attention.

"So my mom said I *had* to have a new dress for this interview—"

"We found this skirt at one store, and the blouse at another. And then—"

"Look how a little mascara makes my eyes stand out! It's just like we learned at our makeover lesson. I—"

Alice held up her hands. "You all look lovely."

"So do you, Miss Howard," Esmeralda said. "I like that blue dress."

"Jane helped me pick it out. She said not to wear any bold prints, or black or white."

The makeup artist smiled at the teenage banter, but cautioned, "I have to hurry. Apparently they've moved your segment up. Someone else canceled."

Before Alice knew it, the woman had applied a minimum of makeup and was done. A moment later Felice bustled into the room. "We're ready for you." As she led the girls and Alice down the hallway, she gave rapid-fire instructions about the cameras and how to act naturally. "I'm sorry you won't have time to have a formal introduction to Don Burns, our host," she said, "but I'm sure you've already heard we've bumped up your segment."

Alice nodded. Everything was moving so fast, she didn't have time to be nervous.

"We're in a commercial break right now," Felice said, ushering Alice and the girls onto the program's set. It looked like someone's living room, complete with an easy chair, which Don Burns sat in, and a sofa and loveseat alongside. The set backdrop looked like cardboard up close but gave the appearance of a living room wall from a distance.

"Don Burns," the man said, leaning over to shake Alice's hand as Felice arranged the girls on the sofa and loveseat. A technician rushed to connect tiny microphones to the guests, pinning them on their collars or lapels.

Don smiled at his guests. "Just be yourselves," he said. "This will be fun."

Alice noticed that Felice had left the seat beside her on the sofa empty. Shouldn't one of the girls be sitting next to her? She turned to alert Don to the mistake, but one of the technicians was signaling them from beside a camera. "Don, we're back in five, four, three—" He mouthed the final two words, then pointed his hand at Don.

The red light went on above the camera. "Hi, we're back.

I'm Don Burns, and you're watching *Good Day, Potterston*. With me now is Alice Howard from Acorn Hill." He turned to her. "Good morning, Alice."

Alice concentrated on Don, rather than the camera, as Felice had instructed. "Good morning, Don."

"Alice has been working with these four girls to the left, teenagers in a summer program. Girls, will you introduce yourselves?"

They went down the line, smoothly giving their names and smiling pleasantly. Alice was proud of them for their poise.

"As I said," Don continued. "Alice has been working with these girls during the summer. We're going to get to that in a minute, but first, we have a surprise. Alice, we didn't tell you the whole reason we wanted you here, because my producer said she thought you might not agree to come. But today we want to honor you with Potterston's Good Citizen award."

"But I don't live in Potterston," she said.

Don smiled. "No, but the girls do. And the Potterston Good Citizen Patrol, of which this show is a proud sponsor, gives the award to anyone they feel is worthy. Wilma Banks, come on out."

A well-dressed woman about Alice's age walked briskly onto the set, holding a plaque. She sat in the empty space on the couch between Alice and Esmeralda and held up the plaque next to Alice.

"Alice, I'm Wilma Banks, president of the Potterston Good Citizen Patrol. On behalf of our organization, we want to present you with this plaque as a token of our appreciation for being a good citizen."

"We understand you saved this young lady's life," Don said, beckoning toward Isidra.

Alice felt her face flush. "Yes, but—"

"Beyond that," Wilma interrupted gently. "We want to thank you for helping these girls have an active, safe and enjoyable summer. For the viewers, Alice works part-time at Potterston Hospital and also helps her sisters run a bed-and-breakfast in Acorn Hill. Though she leads a busy life, she graciously volunteered to fill a need by helping these girls. Thank you, Alice."

Don and the teenagers applauded. Wilma left, and Don motioned for the girls to scoot in closer to Alice. She held the plaque a bit awkwardly, not sure where to look. "Congratulations, Alice," their host said. "Tell us about how you came to work with these girls."

Alice explained how Lilia had initially contacted her to fill in for her while she was on maternity leave. As Alice glanced at their smiling faces, she realized that she never would have been as happy with the dull, relaxing summer she had originally planned. Who wouldn't want to spend time with these four beautiful teenagers?

"Girls, can you tell us about some of the things you've done this summer?" Don asked.

Sabrina talked about the makeover and the rock climbing. When she was finished, Julie added, "I was scared to death, but Miss Howard encouraged me to do it."

"I was scared too," Alice admitted.

Don laughed.

"Maybe she was," Julie continued, "but we made it together."

Alice nodded. "I think we both learned something that day about facing our fears."

"Speaking of fears, who wants to tell us about the white-water rafting trip?" Don asked.

Esmeralda raised her hand. "I will," she said. She told about their excitement that day and how everything had been going smoothly. Then she related how she had accidentally knocked Isidra overboard.

Isidra shook her head. "It wasn't her fault. I shouldn't have been standing."

"You must have been frightened," Don said. "Tell us what happened."

"I went underwater and was pulled into what our guide called a hole. It sucked me under a little, which wasn't a big deal, I figured I could swim free. But when I tried to swim up, I realized my foot was caught on something. If I'd been thinking, I would have just crouched down and tried to free myself. I panicked, though, and wasted energy struggling. The next thing I knew, Miss Howard was beside me, getting my foot free."

"Wow!" Don said. "So Alice, what were you thinking? You'd never been rafting before, but you jumped in?"

"I knew she was in a dangerous situation, and I wanted to help," Alice said. "I was fortunate to be able to move the tree roots that had her foot pinned. Then we made it back to the raft."

"We have some photos of the event. Esmeralda, you had a camera, right?"

She nodded. "Miss Howard loaned it to me."

"Take a look at these. There they are on the monitor."

Alice looked at the photos, side by side on the studio monitor.

"Look at you in action," Don said to her. "That's amazing."

Alice paused. "I think the fact that the photos were taken at all is more amazing. Esmeralda did a good job. I think all the girls are amazing, and I hope they're happy with themselves. We've had a lot of fun together, and we've also learned a lot about each other."

"And about being a team," Esmeralda said, smiling at Alice.

The other girls nodded.

"Alice, all I can say is that if more people would volunteer their time to help others, our community would be a better place. That's why the Good Citizen Patrol gives the award— not only to honor the recipient, but also to encourage others to help out."

"It does make a difference in a community," Alice agreed, thinking of Jane's census work and Louise's help with the dance club. She wanted to talk about that, but Don was already wrapping up the segment, thanking her and the girls for being a part of the program.

Backstage, the girls exclaimed over Alice's plaque, which read "Potterston Good Citizen Patrol honors Alice Howard" and bore the month and year.

"That's really cool, Miss H," Sabrina said. "We knew about the award, but we were sworn to secrecy."

"All of you?" Alice asked, amazed.

They nodded, smiling.

Alice smiled back. "All I have to say is that you girls deserve this award too. You're all good citizens in my book. You've learned a lot about yourselves and helping others. When the summer's over, I want you to carry these memories into the school year and throughout the rest of your lives. Will you?"

They all solemnly nodded that they would, their faces beaming with delight. Alice choked up, and she hugged them all, one by one.

Chapter Eighteen

A week and a half went by, and suddenly it was the night of the dance competition. Louise rode with Jane and Alice to the Potterston Rec Center, agreeing to meet Roman there so that he wouldn't have to drive out of his way to pick her up in Acorn Hill. He and Louise had decided that win or lose, they would celebrate by going to Guido's afterward.

The studio was packed. Spectators filled the portable bleachers. Jane and Alice wished Louise good luck, then went to join the other onlookers. Louise headed for a back room where all the dancers were supposed to meet. All of them were dressed elegantly, and many appeared nervous. She found Roman right away, looking extraordinarily dapper in a dark suit and red tie. He took her hands and smiled. "You look beautiful," he said.

Louise blushed, unaccustomed to such compliments. If she was honest with herself, she had dressed for him, not the competition. She wore a flowing blue skirt that flared below the knees, a matching blue-ruffled blouse and the pearls, of course.

"Are you nervous?" he asked.

"More than you, I think." She laughed lightly. "You look calm and collected. And quite dashing in that suit, I must say."

"Thank you." He bowed. "It's now officially my good-luck waltzing suit."

Dressed elegantly as well, Ben and Gail Cohen called for everyone's attention. "We're ready to begin," Rabbi Cohen said. He smiled at the dancers. "You all look wonderful tonight. I have everyone's music, and all we need to do is draw for the competition order. We'll let the ladies pick. If you'll come forward . . ."

Louise drew a number from a basket Gail held. Rabbi Cohen took it and called out loud for everyone's benefit, "Number three."

When she returned to Roman's side, he said, "That's good. There are ten couples, so we're neither too early nor too late."

"One more thing," Rabbi Cohen said loudly over excited chatter. "We're asking you all to wait here backstage until it's your turn to compete. We're not trying to be mean. We simply don't have enough seats around the dance floor to accommodate everyone." He shrugged, grinning. "Who knew? Anyway, good luck to you all. In my eyes, you're all winners."

He and Gail took the first competitors to the dance floor in the main room. Louise heard the music begin to play. "So now we wait," she said.

"Do you want to limber up?" he asked. "We could practice here in a corner."

"If you do."

"I'm okay," he said. He held her hand. "Louise, it'll be fine. Remember, it's just for fun."

She relaxed. "You're right."

It wasn't long before Gail tapped Roman on the shoulder and told him and Louise they were next. She told them to wait at the door until they heard Rabbi Cohen call their names.

"And now we present Louise Howard Smith and Roman Delwaard."

Louise and Roman looked at each other and smiled, then glided out to the dance floor as they had practiced. She fleetingly wondered where Alice and Jane were sitting. Then she heard the beginning note of their song.

They waltzed across the floor, moving as one. Roman's athletic abilities stood him in good stead, and she thought again what a quick learner he had been. They smiled at each other, and she relished this special occasion. She forgot all about the competition.

Too soon, however, the dance was over. Louise was

jolted back to reality as the audience applauded. She and Roman curtsied and bowed respectively, then they were back in the waiting room while the next nervous couple took their place on the dance floor.

Louise smiled at Roman. "That was wonderful," she said simply.

"You were a great teacher," he said. "I couldn't have done it without you."

"And I wouldn't have enjoyed it with anyone else."

Suddenly he leaned over and kissed her on the lips. It was nothing more than a quick touch, but it surprised her all the same. Somehow it seemed right. She smiled at him, and he smiled back.

They moved to the refreshment area and got two glasses of punch, then moved to a quiet area with two chairs. "How do you think we did?" he asked.

"I think we did very well. Don't you?"

"From my limited dancing experience, yes. There's no telling how we'll stack up against the other contestants though," he said.

They discussed some of their steps, analyzing this and that. Suddenly Gail was calling all the dancers together. "They're ready to announce the winners. Please make your way to the ballroom."

Roman and Louise held hands as they followed the other

dancers. They all lined up behind Rabbi Cohen, who turned to smile at them all. Then he addressed the audience. "I am so proud of all these dancers. It was difficult to tell the experienced from the amateurs, wasn't it? They were all great."

The audience applauded.

"So it's no great surprise to me that we have a three-way tie," Rabbi Cohen said. "That means that we'll have the three couples each dance one more time, a dance different from their first one. There will be no third and second place, only one couple as the winner. Dancers, if you're one of these three couples, please step forward when I call your name. Audience, please hold your applause until I've called all the finalists' names."

He named a young couple, who smiled and stepped forward. Roman squeezed Louise's hand. Rabbi Cohen called another couple's names. Then he said, "Louise Howard Smith and Roman Delwaard."

Louise and Roman stepped forward, smiling. The audience applauded for all three couples.

Rabbi Cohen told the finalists to go back to the waiting room and tell Gail what their second dance would be. Louise was surprised when she heard Roman tell Gail, "We'll be dancing the Lindy Hop."

"But I thought you wanted to do the fox-trot," Louise said. "It's our better second dance."

Roman touched her elbows gently. "I'll admit that I decided to go through with this competition to settle a bet with my daughter. Then I just wanted to have fun. Which I have. Finally, I just want you to have fun."

"I have too, but—"

He put his finger over her lips. "Then don't argue with me. This is your favorite dance. I don't care if you think we're too old. Let's show that crowd what we can do."

She smiled. "All right, Roman. I'm with you."

He nodded. "Good."

This time they were the final couple to dance. Louise felt no nervousness at all, even though it had been years since she had danced the Lindy Hop in public. Wouldn't Jane have something to tease her about for a long while?

When the music "Sing, Sing, Sing" began to play, Louise felt at least twenty years younger. So did her feet. She and Roman didn't attempt the trickier movements, but they had fun nonetheless. When the song was over, they were considerably wearier than after the waltz. But again the audience applauded enthusiastically—more so than the first time, Louise thought—and the dancers gathered near Rabbi Cohen to wait for him to announce the winners.

"How'd we do?" Roman whispered to her.

Louise shook her head. "It doesn't matter. I had a great time."

He smiled at her. "Me too."

After consulting with the judges, Rabbi Cohen returned to the group. Again he thanked all the dancers. "Dancing is about joy," he said. "My wife Gail and I learned that years ago."

Louise thought about the baby they'd lost, and she smiled sadly.

"To live is to know joy," Rabbi Cohen continued. "But to dance is to experience it."

He read the piece of paper, then smiled at the audience. "The winning couple is…"

He announced the names, the youngest couple of all ten. Louise and Roman smiled at each other, applauding as Rabbi Cohen handed the happy woman—the novice dancer—the plaque.

When the crowds thinned out, Louise and Roman found Alice and Jane. "You two were *wonderful!*" Jane said. "Louie, I'm, I'm…speechless."

"You were marvelous," Alice said. "I'm sorry you didn't win, but you two looked like you were experiencing that joy Rabbi Cohen talked about."

Louise and Roman smiled at each other. "We were," Louise said.

They chatted for a couple minutes before Roman said, "If you'll excuse us now, we have a date at Guido's. I'll see that your sister gets home safely."

"We'll wait up," Jane whispered to Louise, winking.

Settled into a booth at the Italian restaurant, Louise and Roman recounted the evening over sampler platters. They didn't talk about what they could have or should have done; they spoke only of the good points of their dancing—the dips and sways in the waltz, the bounciness of their steps in the Lindy Hop.

Roman took Louise's hand and, suddenly serious, said, "Louise, I have some bad news."

"Oh?" She straightened.

Roman sighed. "This is going to be hard. I wanted to wait until after the dance competition so that I wouldn't upset a good thing by mentioning it earlier."

"Is everything all right, Roman?" Louise's stomach dropped. She hoped nothing was seriously wrong.

"Yes . . . and no. Remember that college friend of mine, the one who lives in Colorado?"

Louise nodded.

"He became ill, and he asked me to take over his job. I love coaching at Franklin High, but I feel that I should help out my friend, at least until he has a chance to regain his health. The job would put me closer to my children and grandchildren, it'd be a step up in the coaching world, and my assistant at Franklin is willing to fill in for me. It'll be good for everybody." He paused, and his smile looked bittersweet. "Except us."

Louise smiled back at him, though it felt forced. "It's a good situation for you, Roman. I'm delighted that you can be closer to your children *and* have a chance to help your friend."

"I wish I could offer you some kind of future." He took her hand. "There are always e-mails and phone calls."

Louise squeezed his hand. "Yes, there are, but I think we both know our dancing days are over."

"One never can be sure."

"What a wonderful summer I've had, Roman."

"I hoped you'd feel that way. My decision has been awfully difficult, and I've valued our relationship so much."

"Me too," she said softly, feeling a lump in her throat.

After their drive to the inn, he walked her up the steps to the door. "Thank you for a lovely time, Roman," she said. "I'd ask you in for coffee, but I have to get up early tomorrow."

"And the organ awaits." He smiled. "I'll be thinking of you tomorrow morning when I'm listening to the organist at my church."

"You're welcome back at Grace Chapel any time," she said. "I'd love to see you."

"I may take you up on that before I leave town," he said softly. He leaned closer, then kissed her as he had done at the rec center. "Thank you for all you've done, Louise. It was more than just the dance lessons. I'd ask to take you on another date, but I don't think that'd be fair to either of us."

She nodded. She felt the same way. "Take care, Roman," she whispered.

He smiled, then headed back to his Cadillac parked at the curb. Louise slipped inside the house, not surprised to find Jane and Alice waiting up for her in the living room, books in their hands. With a sigh, Louise kicked off her shoes and sat down wearily on the sofa. The night had been physically and emotionally exhausting.

"Did you have a good time?" Jane asked.

"The dance was fun. So was Guido's." She paused and sighed. "Roman told me that he's leaving town. He's moving to Colorado."

"Oh, Louise," Alice said.

Jane's face fell. "I'm so sorry, Louise. Is he taking a new job?"

Louise nodded. "He wants to be closer to his family as well. I understand completely."

"That's too bad," Jane said. "You two seemed to have a nice thing going."

Louise brightened. "We did, didn't we? The best part is that I know romance can be a part of my life."

"That's true," Alice said.

"I'll always be grateful to Roman for that," Louise said, then yawned. "I'm exhausted. I don't know if I can make it up the stairs."

"It's been a busy summer for all of us, hasn't it?" Alice asked.

Jane looked thoughtful for a moment. "It's been a summer of service for us, in a way, service that brought us its own reward in the form of happiness."

"Doing things for others is often like that," Louise said. "I thought I was going to help Roman learn to dance, but he helped me even more."

"I thought I was just going to help Lilia Joly, but the girls brought me a lot of happiness too," Alice said.

"Same for me and the people I met through the census work," Jane mused. She tucked her feet under herself. "It's sort of like the breezes that blow during the summer months. They always have a certain feel to them, don't you think? They rustle some of the tree leaves, and that movement causes more leaves to rustle. Or the breeze ripples standing water, which causes more water to move. When you stop and look, you can see that the breeze, even though slight, can make a lot of things change. Sort of like helping people. One person really can make a difference."

Louise thought about her words. "That's very true, Jane. We should never forget that."

Jane snapped her fingers. "I almost forgot. Did you see Vera at the dance tonight, Louise?"

She shook her head. "Why?"

Jane grinned. "She and Fred are leaving on a Caribbean cruise in two weeks. They're both as happy as can be."

"What?" Louise said, sitting up straight. "How did she convince Fred to take some time off?"

"She didn't have to," Alice said. "Fred had been planning it all along, keeping it a secret from her. It's his anniversary present to her."

Louise smiled. "Imagine that. Vera will return thoroughly rested, which will renew her enthusiasm for getting back to the classroom."

Jane laughed. "Which, theoretically, means that they'll learn more."

Alice nodded sagely. "You were right, Jane. One person really *can* make a difference."

About the Author

The late Jane Orcutt is the best-selling author of thirteen novels, including *All the Tea in China*. She has been nominated for the RITA award twice. A proud wife and mother of two sons, she lived in Fort Worth, Texas.

Tales from Grace Chapel Inn

Once you visit the charming village of Acorn Hill, you'll never want to leave. Here, the three Howard sisters reunite after their father's death and turn the family home into a bed and breakfast. They rekindle old memories, rediscover the bonds of sisterhood, revel in the blessings of friendship and meet many fascinating guests along the way.